As I cycled fast down my own road, I felt as if I were borne on a stream of the purest, most powerful emotion. It almost seemed to lift the bicycle off the ground. Everything seemed entrancing, permeated by the atmosphere of joy – the prospect of a hearty supper that my landlady would have waiting for me, of a hot bath that I needed, and of the blessed sheets of my own bed. Myrtle, Myrtle. The sting of cold air on my forehead, the strange brilliance of the street-lamps, the bare trees waving in the shadows.

I put away my bicycle and slammed the garage door. I was thinking of Myrtle, and I looked up at the sky. There were stars, sparkling. I was feeling happy, and I had left Myrtle looking sad. Why, oh why? I am an honest man: one of my genuine troubles with Myrtle was that I could never tell whether she was looking unhappy because I would not marry her or because she was feeling cold.

Works by the same author

William Cooper

SCENES FROM
PROVINCIAL
LIFE

Methuen

A Methuen Paperback

SCENES FROM PROVINCIAL LIFE

ISBN 0 413 53090 6

First published in Great Britain 1950
by Jonathan Cape
Reissued 1969 by Macmillan London Ltd

This edition published 1983
by Methuen London Ltd
11 New Fetter Lane, London EC4P 4EE

Phototypeset by Tradespools Ltd, Frome, Somerset
Printed in Great Britain by
Richard Clay (The Chaucer Press) Ltd, Bungay, Suffolk

This Book
is Dedicated to
Peggy

CONTENTS

PART ONE

PART TWO

PART THREE

PART FOUR

INTRODUCTION

Scenes from Provincial Life came out in 1950, apparently the first novel of a writer who in fact proved to have published fiction before under his own name, H. S. Hoff. It won good reviews and then increasingly it began to exert an influence on a number of writers rather younger than its author, who was born in 1910. 'Seminal is not a word I am fond of,' wrote one of them, John Braine, 'Nevertheless I am forced to use it. This book was for me – and I suspect many others – a seminal influence.' Now, looked at from today's standpoint, it seems to belong to the fifties as exactly as a certain kind of tweed sports-jacket. In saying that, I have no intention of belittling or limiting it, of suggesting that it counted then but not now or that its only importance was as an influence; anyone who reads it for the first time in this new edition will find it in all things fresh, alive and very perfectly done. But this other importance of the novel has grown rather clearer; *Scenes from Provincial Life* has a lot to do with a stylistic turn that happened about the time the book came out, and perhaps even *because* the book came out, a turn which affected the fortunes of the postwar English novel and made them rather different from those of contemporary American or French fiction. It was a modest revolution (like all the revolutions of the 1950s in England), but it was quietly considerable and significant. The novel's qualities are not perhaps what one would ordinarily expect in a radical book. It is a fairly simple (but artfully simple) lyrical novel set in the English provinces, self-conscious about the ordinariness of the life it deals with and the particular limitations and innocence of the main characters, caught in their twenties and their teens and in that sharp state of emotional intensity that belongs to the hunt for partners. The book doesn't even have the 1950s as its subject – it is set, of course, on the other 1930s side of that considerable cultural divide that was formed by the war. And the writers you might be led to think of as you read it are possibly H. G. Wells or, going further back and in a rather different direction, Turgenev. All this hardly sounds like a testament to modernity; and those critics who have seen the modern novel as marching resolutely forward from the ground cleared by Joyce and Proust, to greater technical complexity, greater crises of fictiveness, greater manifestations of modernist style, have been ready to cry *retreat!* at the book and its influence. But if it is true that a good part of the literary styles and temper of the 1950s was set by this book, and then by this *sort* of book, there may be good grounds for supposing that what it stands for was a movement towards fictional expansion and survival.

To show that, one needs to look at the particular value and interest of the novel itself; but a little more needs saying first about the fact that the novel did obviously count as the representative of a particular force at work in postwar fiction. For the progress of the novel has usually depended on an oscillation between two parts of its powers and its nature. Novels tend to lie, as Iris Murdoch once observed, somewhere between the 'journalistic' and the 'crystalline'; which is to say that they can participate in the contingent and particular realities of the world as they are known and shared *as* realities, or they can explore art as a specialised knowledge, being concerned with the mode of existence of words, languages, structures, fictions. *Scenes from Provincial Life* is not of course an artless novel, but it is the novel in its empirical form. It could and did stand for an important swing away from the stylistic backlog of modernism, or what William Cooper calls the 'Art Novel': a swing towards an art of reason, an art of lived-out and recognisable values and predicaments, an art, even, of the social places we associate with ordinariness – the provinces, the lower middle classes, the world of growing up and getting on.

Virginia Woolf once suggested that modernism had set the writer free, led him from the kingdom of necessity to the kingdom of light, by allowing him to dispense with traditional plot and character, traditional detailing and chronology, the need to tell a story or report material reality. But such freedom, as we can see from the deep sense of predicament that marks the great works of modernism, was of course itself conditioned. In any case, the revolt against the Victorian 'reality' and the Victorian conception of the artist produced a new convention, and a new socially specialised locale for art in the cosmopolitan and avant garde intelligentsia. By the postwar period the root-conditions of modernism were more or less exhausted in English society, and the cultural dominance of Bloomsbury was certainly coming to an end; it was hard for the new generation of English writers to take up the modernist mode for the exploration of their culture. Cooper later placed himself in the context of an explicit revolt against the 'Thirties' novel in its mannerist and experimental guise, and against the French *anti-roman*. Art, he said in an essay of 1959, depended not on a series of attacks on the powers and place of the human mind, but an assertion of mind. It needed not a *reductio ad absurdam* of experience, but experience itself as it is given. It needed not the intense specialisation of the artist in his own universe, but the sharing of the extant universe with others. Or that, at least, is what I read him as saying, since it is an argument that influenced me very considerably, just as his novel influenced me: not only in what I wrote, but in my very belief that I could, on the basis simply of intelligently being, become a writer.

So what came out of the novel and its climate – it is a simple truth that criticism has a way of forgetting – is that we do not need to abide by the climate of modernism, since it is not historically inevitable. I would not say, as William Cooper sometimes seems to say, that modernism does not count; and I would certainly deplore an evident slackening of scale that became part of the climate brought about by feelings of this sort. But we should also remember that this sort of statement is a statement on behalf of the humanist powers of art and their connection with life. It is an assertion that we live life above all in the realm of the given; that to find ourselves alienated from society or absurdly placed among things is an intellectual or technical abstraction as much as a recognisable truth, and it can be a limitation on our way of knowing ourselves or our world. It looks now as if we are moving into another phase of ideology and alienation theory, of grand resentment about the given realities and their meanness; and no doubt, if the novel still counts at all, it will seek to show that. But *Scenes from Provincial Life* has no such resentment about the given world, and it believes too in the active powers of the living mind and the consonance between that and the making of art. There is no assumption that the truth about man is that he is alienated, that realities are an enormous deceit, that the artist has no words left that are uncorrupted. Rather it is a book about how dense, substantial and complex life is, taken on its ordinary terms; and about how a writer can take fictional life from such things; and how even if the provinces are not cosmopolis and the place of high and abstract art they still have a culture which can itself lead to art. It is not all a writer today might say, but it is enough.

II

What is this provincial life from which the scenes of the novel are thrown up? It is the life of a largish provincial town left deliberately unnamed ('I will not describe our clock-tower in detail, because I feel that if you were able to identify our town my novel would lose some of its universal air'). If Cooper says that with mild self-irony, he also says it to make his town a representative instance of the familiar social web in which men live, amid composed institutions (pubs and the grammar school, parks and cafés, the market-place and the clock-tower) and equally composed if sometimes strange customs (like the Sunday afternoon visits of Mr Chinnock, 'regular as clockwork', to the landlady's niece). The story is firmly set in its place, or one ought to say its culture; and amid a particular strata of its life, its intelligent if not quite intellectual young people. If they do not quite belong, in the sense that they are somewhat shockingly advanced, if they seem to have yearnings that take them outside and beyond, if their roles don't always quite fit ('What *can* I behave like?' wonders Joe Lunn, the narrator, when told he doesn't behave like a schoolmaster), then that is provincial life too. They are schoolmasters and accountants and commercial artists who are also writers and poets and painters, but although they may be more ambitious in their aims and their feelings than others, this does not separate them dreadfully off from their world. Joe is cautious about the proprieties and the bohemianism of all the group is of the most modest kind; even Myrtle's gramophone-record-playing sessions and her late nights are, by his sense of fitness, going a little too far. But of course the point is that they feel their place as well as their detachment from their place. And because of that, even though the action really concentrates on four figures only, it gives us a full sense of the community that surrounds and feeds them. Throughout the novel they talk of leaving it, to go to America under the fear that Hitler's aggression in Europe will end with a totalitarian state in England: 'Though we were three very different men, we had in common a strong element of the rootless and the unconforming, especially the unconforming. We had not the slightest doubt that were some form of authoritarian regime to come to our country we should sooner or later end up in a concentration camp.' But one senses, of course, that they won't leave, for it is the web of relationships, these meeting-places and events and the things that go with them, that stay real in the novel. The impending disloca-tion is an unreality. The dangers of 1939 count, of course, and they do finally *become* real; but that is beyond the end of the story.

But that isn't to say that the characters are passive, unintelligent or unaware of what is happening. The nar-rator and his friends are all lively-minded people who are seeking to make sense of their passions, their ambitions, their environment. They have a strong sense of their slightly excessive pretensions; that is particularly true of Joe Lunn, and is part of his tone as the recollecting narrator. They enjoy bold emotional manoeuvres but they usually end up with an unwonted feeling of tenderness, responsibility or concern. They are not grand masters or moralists of personal relations, but they do know how to give them their due, to care sufficiently about others while caring sufficiently about themselves. The relationship between Joe and his mistress Myrtle, with Myrtle shifting beyond passion to marital ambitions and Joe wriggling to be free for ends not clear even to him, is conducted with a certain moral toughness on Joe's part but also with a precise moral delicacy. That, indeed, is one element that keeps it alive for so long; another is the human inconsistency by which feeling in any case countermands logical decisions, and which sets up those contrary pulls for permanence and impermanence which are central to the lyrical mood of the novel. Joe is half the ironist about these matters, and half the man of feeling:

> It was a light evening, and I could see from a long way off that she was in a state of abysmal depression. She had begun to look sadder and sadder during· the last days. I suppose I was unfeeling and detached; I thought of it as her 'I'll-never-smile-again' expression. Really, she overdid it. I felt genuinely upset and, such is the weakness of my nature, faintly irritated by remorse. I kissed her warmly on the cheek.

If this sort of alternation of emotion is so very recognisable, it is because Joe is comically independent of the situation and also inevitably drawn, by 'something like instinct', as he says, to the power of the person, the place, and the feeling. The tone is a mixture of lyricism and comedy, which means that we are not asked very explicitly to judge matters of moral quality and characteristic; in any case, Joe can claim the privileges of the narrator to be independent from that sort of judgment. But we do recognise, in what Joe does and feels and the way he tells the story, the presence of a real intelligence which includes, among other virtues, the capacity to know oneself as absurd or ridiculous or obstinate and yet forced to act according to certain decencies. As Joe says, that becomes the more important if one believes one *isn't* a good man. All the characters show this kind of inconsistency, and it is very much what makes for the ebb and flow of life and feeling out of which the book is made. But my point is that it is the sense of living in a society and in the context of the values of a culture that has an existence in place and time that makes this so much alive.

We can see, of course, what this culture is; its roots are basically domestic and practical, and it thrives through a kind of middle-class and unromantic good sense. It supposes that people are relatively comprehensible and relatively rational, and you can know sufficient about them to share feelings and values and make relationships. But then there are elements of the unknowable and the strange, which are personal and are as much there in oneself as in others. So relationships have a kind of mysterious rhythm to them; and one acts in the middle of them with a certain intelligent degree of comprehension of one's lovers and friends, and another element of incomprehension, a sense of the 'unknowable' that is 'something like instinct'. One catches in Cooper's style a certain conventionalised quality about the conversations, something tangental in them as each character follows out his own expression of the self's needs; but of course this is not the Pinter-esque convention that really nobody can communicate with anyone else, that they live in totally subjective systems of reality. It is really only in a fictional world that is both public and private that you can have a genuine sense of the moralities of actions and relationships; and that Cooper gives us, the moral life of the ordinary world. For though Joe is an artist, and expresses his obstinacy sometimes as a matter of artistic need, it is out of that ordinary stuff that he makes his choices and finds his feelings. His strains, and those of the other characters, come from life and not from art; and art comes later, as the act of recollection, the turning of experiences offered and created as thoroughly authentic into 'material', 'delightful and disastrous, warm, painful

7

and farcical. I reach for a clean new notebook. I pick up my pen.'

The book is made of this sort of illuminated and worked life. It is indeed *scenes* from provincial life – moments of meeting and parting, episodes of friendly conversation, love-making, love-talking – but a sequence of scenes distilled into an emotional whole. The action consists basically of a succession of episodes in the lives of the four central characters, caught up with many surrounding ones, and it covers the spring and summer of 1939. A good deal is kept out of the telling to make the distillation exact. Before the action begins, the two essential relationships – the affair between Joe, the schoolmaster narrator, and Myrtle, the commercial artist; and that between his friend Tom and *his* boyfriend and protégé Steve – have already begun. After it ends, in the coda of the last chapter, comes the roll-call of marriages and the record of war-experiences. The threats of Hitler and marriage hang over the basic sequence – that phase of human life before marriage which does work out as a pattern of scenes and crises, imperfect understandings and regrets, strong feelings and cautious fears – and help us to see that the phase of life must by the very nature of love and history come to an end. The ebb and flow of feelings comes to contain – as Joe says of Myrtle's feelings – 'too much ebb and not enough flow', and it moves, through its small world of constant meetings and a few basic locales, gradually toward final dissolution:

The end. And I knew with certainty she was there at last. I did not know the reason. I supposed that something I had said or done during the last few days must have been the last straw. I do not even know now what it was, and if I did I should not believe in it as she did. To most of us the movements of the soul are so mysterious that we seize upon events to make them explicable.

The theme *could* have led to a tragic mood of betrayed hope in passion that affects many nineteenth-century novels, but of course that is not the tone. For the novel is very much a comic novel, a comedy of authenticity; Joe's late and not entirely final discovery about Myrtle – '.... I can only say that to the very depths of my soul I was fed up with her' – has that touch of truth that fiction only catches in rare moments. This is the authenticity of its culture *and* of its modernness, and it is what helps us to feel that the book is a book of its time.

Many critics lately seem to have suggested that what characterises this kind of fiction is its sociological realism; I have been trying to suggest that if this means anything it means a much fuller use of the languages and tones of its culture than that phrase usually suggests. For the novel is much more than a report; it is a lyrical and comic evocation that is very carefully made and worked. We can see this in the position and character of the narrator, Joe, himself; and the kind of comedies and ironies he plays over his story. He stands in a position beyond it, a position more advanced in time and in a bigger world. And so he can see the elements of innocence and absurdity in the story he tells: 'We were completely serious about it [the state of the world], and we became even more serious even as our actions became more absurd.' The provinces and the past intertwine as a recollected place and let him, too, be a little ridiculous; but his absurdity, and that of Tom, with his dubious insights into human conduct, Myrtle, with her red setter and her gun, and Steve, with his contradictory responses to the role of protégé, is part of the common fortune. For Joe as narrator does finally belong to this world, and so he is neither emotionally nor technically patronising. His own lack of feeling, his absoute refusal to marry Myrtle – these things which are the spring of most of the events – are his own foible and also his human right, part of his intelligent ridiculousness. The irony is therefore not complex and the tone is comically generous, the tone of a human openness that condemns very little, observes a great deal, and carries a wide range of feelings. Joe is the lyricist of the novel and the man who also sees life-history as a stuff to write about; his independent obstinacy is a convincing part of his total psychology as man who also happens by nature to be a writer. The art he makes, the book he writes, is as much a product of this sort of life and place as the experience he feels. Life is a sequence of scenes and felt moments, something that derives from what exists in the given world to experience, to know, and feel; and novels are the products of one's own life-history, the product of all one's delights and disasters ('I think of all the novels I can make out of them – ah, novels, novels, Art, Art, pounds sterling!'). Joe's are not the modernist ironies of artistic distance, but they are those of character which somehow become those of an artistic position. So Joe not only makes a world as a writer must (as when he chooses not to emphasise politics for reasons of literary necessity: 'For some reason or other political sentiment does not seem to be a suitable subject for literary art'), and he does not only judge that world as a writer must; he also finds one in life. You can be an artist because you have intelligently seen, known and can shape the experiences of the ordinary world.

III

It was no new discovery, of course. The book's newness lay in the particular kind of ordinary life, the particular culture, it found; and in the way it brought that alive as a vision, a pattern of motives, meanings and significance, a way of living in the present. This has a lot to do with the way many writers in the 1950s did find means of bringing a sense of cultural observation and moral analysis of their changing society into relation with a new, an idiosyncratic, and very often a comic viewpoint upon it. If, over that period, the viewpoints and judgments of a provincially 'irreverent' (to use a favourite reviewer's word of the period) fictional attitude became vigorous enough to consti-tute a rich literary perspective, then clearly a great deal of credit is due to William Cooper. One has, perhaps, to remember how little this particular class and viewpoint has been presented in the fiction of the previous two decades to feel how important this opening out was; but it would not have been important had there not been writers who could manage the task with the kind of perfect lucidity William

Cooper brought to it. But I must also stress that *Scenes from Provincial Life* is in fact much more accomplished than many of its successors. It brings its language (usually) and its perspective (always) so thoroughly alive that it has a survival-value profoundly in excess of any sociological interest in it that might also hold us. If, too, it helped to keep alive the social and moral tradition of the English novel vigorous, in a phase where the direction of the form itself seemed uncertain, that was good fortune; its real and final interest is the pleasure we can still take in it, here, as it stands.

MALCOLM BRADBURY

PART ONE

CHAPTER I

TEA IN A CAFÉ

The school at which I was science-master was desirably situated, right in the centre of the town. By walking only a few yards the masters and boys could find themselves in a café or a public-house.

I used to frequent a café in the market-place. It was on the first floor, and underneath was a shop where coffee was roasted. A delicious aroma drifted through the maze of market-stalls, mingling with the smell of celery, apples and chrysanthemums: you could pick it up in the middle of the place and follow it to the source, where, in the shop-window, a magnificent roasting-machine turned with a flash of red enamel and chromium plate – persistently reminding you that coffee smelt nicer than it tasted.

Two or three times a week I had tea in the café with a friend of mine named Tom. He was a chartered accountant, and the offices of his firm were in a building between the school and the market-place. By specializing in income-tax claims, Tom made a comfortable living: it could have been luxurious, had he accepted the invitation of certain townspeople to visit their business premises after hours and falsify their returns. Tom had other things to do in his spare time.

We had been friends for several years. Both Tom and I had literary ambitions. During my six years spent teaching in the town I had published three novels. Tom had published one. I secretly thought I was three times as good a writer as Tom. At this time, February 1939, I was aged twenty-eight and Tom twenty-seven.

For reasons of delicacy I will not disclose Tom's surname. Other things about him it will be impossible to conceal. With the best will in the world you could not help noticing immediately that Tom was red-haired and Jewish – it fairly knocked you down. He had rich, thick, carroty curls and a remarkable nose. He was nearly a stone heavier than me; and he gave the impression that he would be a good deal heavier than that, were he not always engaged in bustling physical activity. He had a rounded head, with greenish eyes and a rather pouting mouth. He was intelligent and high-spirited, and I was very devoted to him. It was not apparent that he had a formidable personality.

Sometimes what a man thinks he is can be just as interesting as what he really is. In Tom's case it was just as interesting and decidedly more wonderful; it had an endearing romantic grandeur. Tom saw himself as a great understander of human nature, a great writer, a great connoisseur of the good things in life, and a great lover. He did not see himself as a great chartered accountant. Nor did he see himself as a great clown – in that respect not differing substantially from the rest of us.

Tom possessed a formidable capacity for psychological bustling. In an easy agreeable way he bustled other people into doing things they did not want to do. He was always trying to bustle me, especially for instance over our country cottage. Tom and I shared the tenancy of a cottage ten miles outside the town, and the arrangement was that we should spend alternate week-ends there. Now I had two very strong reasons for wanting to stick to the arrangement: one was my legal right, and the other was because I was visited there by a young woman, a very pretty young woman called Myrtle.

My desire to preserve my legal right was therefore unusually strong. Tom, made in a different mould, did not see it that way. In a style more heroic, more passionate, more expansive, more wonderful than mine, he systematically tried to bustle me out of my turn.

There was some basis for Tom's picture of himself. He was courageous and he had a great fund of emotion: he had a shrewd down-to-earth insight into human nature and tireless curiosity about people. He was the ideal listener to one's life-story – the only trouble was that in order to encourage the next person to tell his life-story Tom was liable to repeat under the seal of secrecy one's own.

I usually arrived in the café first. It was superior, and chosen by me because there were no cruets and bottles of tomato ketchup on the tables at tea-time. Tom thought this showed I was finicky. 'You wouldn't notice the cruet if you were interested in the human heart,' he said, with great authority.

As the café was superior Tom could never resist ordering his tea and cream cakes with a superior manner. He waved his hand, which was small and comely, in an aristocratic gesture. The waitress appreciated it.

Perhaps I might go so far as to disclose that Tom's name was definitely not Waley-Cohen or Sebag-Montefiore – alas! very far from it. He would dearly have loved to be an aristocrat. He might have carried it off with his hands, but his face was against him. There was nothing coarse about his features, but unfortunately there was nothing even faintly aristocratic. His red hair gave him no help at all, and he was sensitive about it. When he first read *A la Recherche du Temps Perdu*, and discovered that Swann's hair was red, he was overjoyed.

For Tom it was then but the smallest step to identify himself completely with Swann – red hair, aristocratic birth, peculiar sexual temperament and all. 'Ah,' he would say, sighing: 'How I know the torments of jealousy!' And his voice, though low, carried such tremendous emotional weight that I listened with my deepest sympathy.

As Tom came into the café I thought he had an unusually preoccupied expression, but it disappeared as he sat down. When he had concluded the artistic performance of ordering his tea, he said:

'Any news of the book?'

'Not a word.'

Tom was referring to the manuscript of my latest novel. Most young novelists decide somewhere in the early stages of their careers that they have written something a class better than anything they have written before. I had reached this point with my fourth book. My publisher had naturally, but not promptly, turned it down. It seemed to me in my inexperience that my publisher asked one of two things from me: either to write my previous novel all over again just as it was, or to write it again with a stronger story, sharper characterization, deeper revelations of truth and much, much funnier jokes.

For the benefit of anyone who does not already know, I can say that the recognized thing to do, when a young novelist has written the first novel that he thinks good and it is turned down by his publisher, is to send the manuscript to a writer of distinguished reputation. This is what I did. An earlier novel had produced an unsolicited letter of praise from Miss X.Y.: she had consented to read the manuscript of my latest. Her secretary had acknowledged receiving it three weeks ago.

'Not a word?'

'I suppose she's busy,' I said, for some reason or other trying to excuse her. I think I felt I had to excuse my ally.

Tom raised his eyebrows.

'How's Myrtle?' he asked tactfully.

'All right.' As might be expected I was continually haunted by the possibility of Myrtle's not being all right.

I said diffidently: 'We had a very enjoyable Sunday together.'

Tom's eyes appeared to bulge a little with disapproval.

'Why don't you let her come out on Saturday night? You know perfectly well she wants to.'

I felt badgered, and tried to sound confident. 'Propriety, my dear Tom. I don't want to risk village gossip and so on.'

It was natural for Tom not to let pass an opportunity for getting the better of me.

'How completely unrealistic of you.' He shrugged his shoulders in the manner of a great understander of human nature. 'You introverts.'

Tom and I had recently been studying the works of Jung. We were agreed that by Jungian definitions he was an extravert and I an introvert. Consequently he saw fit to use the word 'introvert' as a term of abuse.

I knew perfectly well that it was unrealistic. The real point was that I had said 'propriety' because I was too ashamed to say 'caution'. I did not let Myrtle live with me in the cottage for the same reason that I did not call regularly upon her family – in fact I never went near them. Caution.

I did not reply to Tom.

'It would not do for me,' he said. He smiled reminiscently, like a great lover. 'I like my Saturday nights.'

'So you may!' I said, and laughed aloud. 'You don't live in the shadow of a girl wanting you to marry her!'

Tom replied amiably: 'My dear man, I live in the shadow of something else.'

I saw the truth of this remark. The reason Tom did not live in the shadow of a girl wanting him to marry her was that when it was his week-end to occupy the cottage he took out a boy.

I nodded sagely.

'Ah,' said Tom, with a sigh. 'The shadows one has lived under! It makes one feel very, very old.'

One of Tom's women loves had been absurd enough to tell him that she thought he was an 'old soul'. Tom had taken it very seriously, and for months afterwards had gone about feeling older in soul than anyone we knew. It was only quite gradually that his oldness of soul had worn off, and it still cropped up on occasion.

I did not take him up because he had previously proved conclusively that I was a young soul.

I poured out some tea, while Tom began eating a chocolate éclair. We were sitting beside the window, looking out on to the tops of the market-stalls. The ridges of those at right angles to the last rays of sun gleamed with a golden light. In the air hung faint blue fumes from the coffee-roaster below. There seemed to be a lot of people wandering about, carrying baskets and bunches of bright yellow daffodils.

'You probably ought to have Myrtle out on Saturday nights, anyway,' Tom said.

'Why?'

'You know where she spends them when you won't have her.'

'Yes.' I did know. Often it was with a young man named Haxby.

'Well, if you know ...' Tom's voice trailed off doubtfully. I could see that he was thinking again 'You introverts'.

I considered the matter. Tom was not the only person who

thought my behaviour towards Myrtle was strange. To me it seemed perfectly understandable. I loved Myrtle but I did not want to marry her – because I did not want to marry anybody. That was the point, and I was puzzled that everybody else found it so difficult to comprehend. Having had to put up with so much opprobrium, I was rather on the defensive about it. Many a man before me had not wanted to be married, I argued. It might be called abnormal, but nobody could pretend it was unusual. My argument made not the slightest impression. Nor did other people's arguments make any impression on me. I did not want to be married, and that is all there is to it.

And yet I have to admit there was something more – such is the contradictory nature of the heart. I hated the idea of Myrtle marrying anyone else.

'Now,' said Tom, 'I want to talk to you seriously.'

Our main conversation was to be about his week-end in Oxford. The friend of ours with whom Tom had been staying was Dean of the small college at which I had been educated. His name was Robert, and he was a few years older than us. He was clever, gifted and wise; and he had a great personal influence on us. We had appointed him arbiter on all our actions, and anything he cared to say we really accepted as the word of God. We spent most of the time talking about the state of the world.

I listened. Tom and I talked a good deal about politics – so did we all, Myrtle and her friends, the masters in the staff-room, even the boys. Unfortunately it is very difficult to write about politics in a novel. For some reason or other political sentiment does not seem to be a suitable subject for literary art. If you doubt it you have only to read a few pages of any novel by a high-minded Marxist.

However I am writing a novel about events in the year 1939, and the political state of the world cannot very well be left out. The only thing I can think of is to put it in now and get it over.

Robert, Tom and I could be called radicals: we were made for a period thirty years earlier, when we could happily have voted liberal. The essence was that we thought life for us would be insupportable in a totalitarian state. We did not argue very much: it went without saying. It may have been because we thought of ourselves as artists: it may not – we might have been just the same if we had not been artists. Though we were three very different men, we had in common a strong element of the rootless and the unconforming, especially the unconforming. We had not the slightest doubt that were some form of authoritarian regime to come to our country we should sooner or later end up in a concentration camp.

So much for our political sentiments, if that is what they should be called. They led us to be deeply pessimistic about the state of the world. We were completely serious about it, and we became more serious even as our actions became more absurd.

When Tom said he was going to tell me what conclusions Robert had drawn, my spirits sank. Our spirits had been low ever since we came to the conclusion that the government of our country was not disposed to challenge National Socialism, though never so low as on the night the Prime Minister returned from Munich. I always recalled buying an evening newspaper: Tom was with me and we spread it out between us to read it together. And a great wave of despair overwhelmed us, the deeper and the blacker because in some inexplicable way we felt caught up in responsibility. We had still not recovered from it in the spring of 1939. Our sense of shame had induced a mood in which we became certain that the same thing would happen again. And the second time would be the last.

'The old boy says that if there isn't a war by August we shall be refugees by October.'

I stared at Tom, thinking 'March, April, May...'

'We ought to be thinking about moving,' said Tom, 'while there's a reasonable amount of time at our disposal.'

The idea had made fleeting appearances in our talk during the last few months. Tom's big, greenish eyes bulged unblinkingly.

'He's beginning to bestir himself.'

I felt there was nothing for me to say. I glanced through the window. The sun had disappeared from the market-place and naphthalene flares were flickering out brightly from the stalls.

Tom went on: 'He's decided America's the best place. He proposes I should go first.'

This proposal was obvious because Tom was Jewish while Robert and I were not. I thought it was hard luck on Tom; because his attitude would have been just the same if he were not Jewish, and because of the three of us he probably had the greatest share of physical courage – certainly he was the most rash.

Tom began to outline his plans. We thought we were men of more than average intelligence and gifts and we were not particularly alarmed at the prospect of having to make our way in another country – certainly we were not alarmed at all so long as the project remained in the air.

My spirits rose a little. I could not help seeing our gesture in a romantic light. We were proposing to leave our country for the sake of Freedom. I have to confess that I sometimes saw us as Pilgrim Fathers, though admittedly of a rather different type from the originals. And in moments of honesty I realized that there was a distinct attraction in the idea of leaving everything, and – more detestable still and never to be admitted to Tom – even in the idea of leaving everybody.

I thoughtfully inscribed a pattern on the tablecloth with the haft of my knife.

'I advise you to start considering what you're going to do about Myrtle,' said Tom.

I blushed. 'What do you mean?' I said, as if I had not the slightest idea what he was talking about.

'You presumably aren't thinking of taking her with you to America, are you?'

'I hadn't thought about it,' I said.

'Really!' said Tom, with a mixture of incredulity and indignation. It was clearly, 'You introverts' again.

'There's no hurry, is there?' I said amiably. 'I shall finish the year out at the school.' I was thinking of the delight with which I should hand in my notice in July.

'I should have thought it was hardly fair to Myrtle,' said Tom. 'You do intend to tell her, of course, don't you?'

'Of course,' I said, with the mental reservation that it was to be in gentler terms. 'Actually we've discussed it already. She. knows that it's a possibility.' I knew that Myrtle, though I truly had discussed it with her, did not think for a moment that it would ever happen.

'If it were me,' said Tom, 'I should probably begin breaking it off now.'

Immediately my memory took me back to a previous occasion. I had been in love with a married woman whose husband earned £5000 a year against my £350. 'If it were me,' Tom had counselled, 'I should break up the marriage.' Happily it was not Tom.

Tom said: 'You don't consider her feelings as I should. It could be done understandingly and subtly.'

I thought there was a contradiction somewhere, as there was in most of Tom's counsels, but I could not put my finger on it before he went on.

'I think I should lead her to feel that it was' – he waved his hand elegantly – 'best for both of us.'

'In that case you don't know Myrtle!'

Tom shrugged his shoulders.

We abandoned the topic, and went on planning how to earn a living in America. I was troubled all the same. Tom was capable of infecting me with doubts. I was in a vulnerable position, because I knew I was behaving like a cad. I intended to go to America. I did not want to marry Myrtle.

But was it essential that Myrtle should be left behind? I wondered. I did not want to make up my mind. Tom was probably right on psychological grounds. The point that Tom, with his penchant for violent ridiculous upsets, did not see but which occurred to me only too readily was this: outside psychological grounds, breaking it off with Myrtle had for me a very obvious drawback. I drew the generalization that one's friends find nothing easier than advising a course of action which involves ceasing to go to bed with one's young woman.

I did not tell Tom what I intended to do.

CHAPTER II

A DAY IN THE COUNTRY

After Sunday lunch at the Dog and Duck, Myrtle and I strolled back over the fields to my cottage. It was a regular thing – I saw to that.

On Sunday mornings she came out on her bicycle, looking fresh and elegant and lively. Sometimes she found me washing-up my breakfast pots in the scullery, where I had been keeping an eye open for the flash of her handlebars coming up the lane; sometimes she found me having a bath under the pump, which provoked a blushing, sidelong glance and the remark: 'Darling, I don't know how you can stand that cold water'; and sometimes she found me just ready for a bit of high-toned conversation about reviews in the Sunday newspapers.

'Darling, I've brought you this.'

It might be anything that had caught her fancy, a tin of liver *pâté*, or a book of poems by T. S. Eliot. This time it was a bunch of freesias. I should have received a tin of liver *pâté* much more warmly, a book of poems by T. S. Eliot much less.

Then we set out for the Dog and Duck. The cottage was two miles from the nearest public-house; but over the fields, choosing gaps in the hedges and jumping narrow brooks, we could get to the Dog and Duck in twenty minutes. Neither of us had any inclination to exhaust ourselves in the labour of cooking lunch.

The stroll back was singularly pleasurable. It did not take too long. Also it gave our lunches time to digest, and brought to our notice the beauties of nature.

As we had been his regular customers for over a year, the

24

pub-keeper shared his lunch with us; and his wife, to please either him or us, cooked it superbly. Myrtle and I drank two or three pints of beer apiece while waiting for it: Myrtle would have drunk more, but I thought it would not be good for her. Then we sat down to slices of roast beef, red and succulent in the middle and faintly charred at the edges; apple pie with fresh cream liquid enough to pour all over it; and cheese, the unequalled, solid, homely cheese of the county.

We walked very slowly at first, for we both took a pleasure in digestion. We patted our stomachs and sighed at the prospect of the first hill. The country rolled gently, and there was a second hill to climb before we came in sight of the cottage. If I happened to belch, Myrtle gave me a ladylike look of reproach and I begged her pardon. I took her by the hand.

At the top of the first hill we looked around. It was a heavenly afternoon. The sun was shining. It was only the end of February and we could feel its warmth. The rime on the naked hedgerows had melted, and drops of water glittered like the purest glass on twigs and thorns. The sky was covered in a single haze of milky whiteness; and the tussocks of grass, wilted and brown and borne down with water, caught heavily at our feet.

'How I long for the spring,' said Myrtle in a far-away tone. Her voice was lightly modulated and given to melancholy.

It was on the tip of my tongue to say: 'Yes, and when it's spring you'll be pining for summer.' It was true: she had a passion for hot weather. But had I said it she would have looked hurt. Instead of speaking, I glanced at her. What I saw was entirely pleasing. The sooner we reached the cottage the better.

Myrtle was modestly tall and very slender. She was wearing grey slacks and a cerise woollen sweater. Her breasts and buttocks were quite small, though her hips were not narrow. She was light-boned, smooth and soft. There was nothing energetic or muscular about her. She walked with a languid, easy grace – I walked with a vigorous, over-long stride and perpetually had the impression that she was trailing along behind me.

Myrtle felt me looking at her, and turned her face to me. It was oval and bright with colour. She had round hazel eyes, a long nose, and a wide mouth with full red lips: her hair was dark, her cheeks glowed. She smiled. Then she turned her head away again. I had no idea what she was thinking. I was thinking of one thing only, but Myrtle might easily have been thinking about El Greco – equally she might have been thinking about the same thing as me.

Whatever she was thinking about, whatever she was doing, Myrtle preserved a demeanour that was meek and innocent – especially meek. Sometimes I could have shaken her for it, but on the whole I was fascinated by it.

With a demeanour that was meek and innocent, Myrtle had two characteristic facial expressions. The first was of resigned reproachful sadness; the other was quite different, and only to be described as of sly smirking lubricity. As her face was both mobile and relaxed, she could slip like a flash from one expression to the other, naturally, spontaneously and without the slightest awareness of what she was doing.

We walked down the first hill, and this seemed to me an opportunity for moving a little faster. I was not as relaxed as Myrtle. However, she comfortably took her time, making a detour to cross the brook by a plank. Two horses, their coats shaggy with moisture, raised their heads to look at us. The brook was high with spring water, and the weeds waved in it sinuously. I put my hand on Myrtle's waist.

As we climbed the opposite hill Myrtle called to the horses, but they sided with me and paid no attention.

At the top of the hill we always paused and sat on a gate for a few minutes. It was a sort of ritual, and to me it seemed a thoroughly silly sort of ritual. Below us we could see the cottage. No sooner had I settled on the top bar than I was ready to leap off again. But Myrtle always took her time, and as she went by atmosphere I could never tell how long it was going to be. It was at such moments that I sensed the great gulf between our temperaments: Myrtle went by atmosphere and I went by plan.

My plan was lucid and short. There, shining in its cream-coloured wash, small, intimate, isolated from every-thing, was the cottage. I felt as if my skin were tightening. No doubt I had a hot fixed look on my face.

Suddenly Myrtle slid down from the gate and quietly made off beside the hedgerow.

'What on earth?' I began, jumping down.

She stooped, and I saw that she was picking some celandines she had spied on the brink of a ditch. She held them up, glistening in the sunshine.

'What are you going to do with those?'

Myrtle's face promptly took on a distant unconcerned look, as if she were going to start whistling. I laughed aloud at her, and grasped her to me.

'Darling!' I cried. I kissed her cheeks: they had a soft bloomy feel.

I slipped my hands down from her waist. She struggled away from me.

'We're in the middle of a field, darling,' she said.

It was my turn now. I am too direct to look lubricious. I took her firmly by the hand. 'Come on, then,' I said. And down the hill we went, in the plainest of plain sailing.

Whatever she was doing, Myrtle preserved a demeanour that was meek and innocent. She preserved it to perfection as I finally turned back the sheets for her. Yet, meek and innocent though her demeanour was, virginal and ladylike, anything else you may be pleased to call a nice girl, it was more than Myrtle could do, not to take a furtive sideways glance at me. I caught her.

I have said that Myrtle had two characteristic facial expressions. As a result of her furtive glance she managed to wear both of them, resigned, reproachful, sad, sly, smirking and lubricious, all at once.

Some time later we were just finishing a short rest. Idle thoughts floated vaguely through my mind. A spider was spinning down slowly from the corner of the room. Nameless odours stirred under my nose. A crow's wings flapped past the window. I was sweating profusely, because

Myrtle insisted on having a lot of bedclothes. It occurred to me that there is a great division of human bodies, into those which feel the cold and those which do not. Myrtle and I belonged one to each class. How many marriages, I meditated, had been ruined by such incompatibility? Marriage – my thoughts floated hastily on to some other topic.

Myrtle was wide awake. I thought she was probably thinking how a cup of tea would refresh her. Suddenly I heard the sound of a car coming up the lane. We never expected to hear any traffic go by the cottage. It was approaching at a moderate speed, and I thought I recognized the sound of the engine. I jumped out of bed and ran to the window.

I was just too late to see it pass, so I flung down the sash and put my head out. Again I was just too late.

'Who was it?' said Myrtle.

'It sounded like Tom's car.'

'What was he doing here?'

I shrugged my shoulders. I had my idea. There was a pause.

'Don't you think you ought to come away from the window, darling?'

'Why?'

'You've got nothing on.'

'All the better . . .' Out of respect for her delicacy I closed the window with a bang that drowned the end of my remark.

She was smiling at me. I went over and stood beside her. She looked appealing, resting on one elbow, with her dark hair sweeping over her smooth naked shoulder. I looked down on the top of her head.

Suddenly she blew.

'Wonderful Albert,' she said.

I may say that my name is not Albert. It is Joe. Joe Lunn.

Myrtle looked up at me in sly inquiry.

I suppose I grinned.

After a while she paused.

'Men *are* lucky,' she said, in a deep thoughtful tone. I said nothing: I thought it was no time for philosophical observations. I stared at the wall opposite.

Finally she stopped.

'Well?' I looked down just in time to catch her subsiding with a shocked expression on her face.

'Now,' I said, 'you'll have to wait again for your tea.'

'Ah . . .' Myrtle gave a heavy, complacent sigh. Her eyes were closed.

In due course we had our tea. Myrtle felt the cold too much to get out of bed, so I made it. She sat up and put on a little woollen jacket: it was pretty shell pink to match the colour of her cheeks. Her eyes seemed to have changed from hazel to golden. We held an interesting conversation about literature.

I felt a slight check on me when I held literary conversations with Myrtle, because her taste was greatly superior to mine. I wrote novels, and when she brought to light the fact that I had no use for long dramas in blank verse, I felt coarse and caddish, as if lust had led me to violate a creature of sensibilities more delicate than I could comprehend. Secretly I thought she was invariably taken in by the spurious and the pretentious, but this I put down to her youth. She was only twenty-two.

It grew dusky outside while we finished our tea. As we settled down again, the firelight began to glow on the ceiling. A wind was rising in the branches of the elm trees across the road, furiously rattling the bare twigs against each other. 'If only we could stay here,' was what we were both thinking from time to time; and at first sight it was not obvious what prevented us. Certainly it was not obvious to Myrtle at all. It was with difficulty that in the end I persuaded her to get up.

'Come along, darling,' I said. I was thinking how necessary it was for us to get back to the town, she to her parents' home, I to my lodgings. Atmosphere did not indicate to Myrtle that this was the case.

'It's so cold outside, I shall die,' she said, hopelessly.

I bent down and kissed her: she put her arms round my

neck. I could not resist it.

At last we were dressed and ready to go. I drank the remainder of the milk.

'I know you need it, darling,' Myrtle said in a subtle tone that I could not quite place.

A final glance round the living-room, at the dying fire and the empty flower-vases, and we went out into the darkness. There was a moment of nostalgia, as I turned the key in the door. We felt impelled to say something foolishly sentimental, like 'Goodbye, little home'.

On the journey back our spirits rose again. We pedalled cheerfully against the wind, our lamps flashing a wavering patch on the road ahead. We had good bicycles, with dynamos to light the lamps. Myrtle said she was tired, and sometimes I tried to tow her, but it was too difficult an operation mechanically.

The lights of the town came into view, looking particularly bright in the cold, wintry air. In the distance lighted trams passed each other slowly. The roads on the outskirts were lined with trees, and there were big houses far back from the road: this was the way into the town which did not lead through the slums. Big lamps swayed over the tram-lines: in their light I could see Myrtle's eyes glowing. I put my hand on her shoulder.

At a cross-roads we parted. It was our convention that it would be indiscreet to go to each other's house. With our bicycles leaning against the small of our backs we embraced fervently. At this time on Sunday night there were few people about, especially when the wind was icy.

'When shall I see you again, darling?'

Myrtle shivered, and looked woebegone.

This was always an apprehensive moment for me. It sometimes happened that I already had an evening booked in advance: Myrtle was certain to light upon it. There was nothing wrong about it, but she made it only too plain that she was wounded. I could never think how to explain and reassure. She had all my love: I wanted no one else: she had no cause to feel a moment's jealousy. Yet she was wounded if I disclosed that there was one evening when I was not free. And somehow I wanted that evening to myself, that evening and possibly one or two more. It was the moment when I sensed another great gulf between our temperaments.

On this particular occasion, I had arranged to go out for supper on Tuesday evening – Myrtle and I lived in the social stratum where the midday meal is often called lunch instead of dinner, but where the evening meal cannot properly be called dinner and so goes by the name of supper.

'When shall I see you again, darling?' I waited with my fingers crossed.

'Not tomorrow, of course.' Then in a melancholy tone: 'And I've promised to go to the dressmaker's on Tuesday...' Her voice trailed off, and returned with surprising briskness. 'Wednesday.'

I kissed her. Relief multiplied my fervour by about fifty per cent. Myrtle looked sad. We arranged to telephone each other, and parted.

As I cycled fast down my own road, I felt as if I were borne on a stream of the purest, most powerful emotion. It almost seemed to lift the bicycle off the ground. Everything seemed entrancing, permeated by the atmosphere of joy – the prospect of a hearty supper that my landlady would have waiting for me, of a hot bath that I needed, and of the blessed sheets of my own bed. Myrtle, Myrtle. The sting of cold air on my forehead, the strange brilliance of the street-lamps, the bare trees waving in the shadows.

I put away my bicycle and slammed the garage door. I was thinking of Myrtle, and I looked up at the sky. There were stars, sparkling. I was feeling happy and I had left Myrtle looking sad. Why, oh why? I am an honest man: one of my genuine troubles with Myrtle was that I could never tell whether she was looking unhappy because I would not marry her or because she was feeling cold.

CHAPTER III
A MORNING AT SCHOOL

Next morning I had to get up and go to school. It was going to be a bright day. The balls of my feet felt springy as I ran downstairs, and as I jumped on to my bicycle the saddle felt springy. Hoorah! for Myrtle, I thought; there is nothing makes a man feel so wonderful as a wonderful girl. Flying downhill past the cemetery I skidded violently in the tram-lines and gave myself a fright: a wonderful girl does not fill a man with courage to face death – quite the reverse.

The school was a big grammar school for boys, in the centre of the town. The building was Victorian, dark, ugly, ill-planned, dirty and smelly.

Instead of going to morning prayers I went down to the laboratory. My task in the school was to teach physics, and for the whole of the morning I was due to take the senior sixth form in practical work. I felt more inclined to prepare the apparatus for their experiments than to take part in communal devotions.

Every so often the headmaster sent round a chit, asking all masters to attend morning prayers, but it produced not the slightest effect. One half of the masters claimed more important matters of preparation, and the other just did not go: I fluctuated between the two. The headmaster was zealous and high-minded, but he had not a scrap of natural authority. He ought to have been a local preacher, on a circuit with very small congregations.

This school was the first at which I had ever taught, so I had no other to compare it with. And I found that like many other men I had no objective recollections of my own school, or of half the things I did there – this appears to be nature's way of avoiding embarrassment all round.

I could not help feeling this school was something out of the ordinary. On my very first day there I overheard a small boy, apparently also on his very first day, say to another small boy in the crowded corridor: 'It's like Bedlam, isn't it?' After six years I still could not improve on this innocent description.

The small room used as a laboratory by the sixth form was on the ground floor at the end of the building. I could only get to it by going through the main laboratory, which was empty. Though both rooms were empty neither was quiet. Traffic roared past a few feet from the windows, while upstairs the school was singing its head off with 'Awake, my soul!'

There were four boys aged eighteen or nineteen in the senior sixth form, and they did experiments in pairs. I was at work, with all the cupboard-doors open, when one of them came in. He was mature in appearance, and greeted me in a friendly fashion.

''Ello, Joe,' he said. 'I'n't it a luvly day!'

The local dialect was characterized by a snarling, whining intonation: Fred spoke it in the soppy, drawling, baby-talk of the slum areas.

The school did not have number one social standing in the town, and the pupils all came from the lower middle class and upper proletariat. Fred came from the proletariat. He was strong and stocky, with a sallow, greyish skin. His hair was covered with brilliantine and his hands were always dirty – I thought it was the grease off his head which made his hands pick up the dirt so readily.

Like Fred, most of the older boys called me by my Christian name, outside the lessons if not inside. I had wanted to get on free-and-easy terms with the boys – how else could I find out all about them? – and I had achieved the feat with little trouble, chiefly through letting them say anything they liked.

To an outsider the manners of my pupils must have been surprising. It happened that I was not given to being surprised; which very soon made the manners of my pupils more surprising still. The boys, when they discovered there was nothing they could say that would shock me, relapsed into the happy state they appeared to be in when I was not there.

At one period the upper forms had devoted a few days of their attention to choosing theme-songs for members of the staff. I was told that mine was 'Anything Goes': it seemed to me fair. Unfortunately my free-and-easy attitude was strongly disapproved of by my senior master. He wanted to have me sacked, and frequently expressed his point of view to the headmaster.

It was absolutely necessary, if I wanted to become a novelist – and that was the only thing I wanted do – that I should keep my job. Nevertheless I found it unbearably tedious to pretend to be surprised when I was not, to be shocked when I was not, to be ignorant when I knew all about it, and to be morally censorious when I did not care a damn. To be frank, I found it impossible.

Fred was mooning about, so I told him to get out the travelling-microscope. At this point a boy called Frank came in.

Frank was the eldest and the cleverest of the four. He was captain of the school rugby football team, more because he had an eager, pleasing personality than because he carried a lot of weight. He had wavy hair, high cheek-bones, and a rather long nose that, to his secret sorrow, turned up at the end. Had it not been for his nose he would have been very handsome. He was an old friend of Tom's.

'Have a good week-end?' he said.

'Very.'

He glanced at me briefly. I suspected he had found out from Tom where I had spent it, though the cottage was supposed to be a secret. All the boys showed powerful curiosity and imagination about the private lives of the masters.

'It's time you and Trevor tried to find Newton's rings,' I said. It was a difficult experiment, appropriate as Frank had won a scholarship to Oxford.

It may not have occurred to everybody that most schoolmasters are preoccupied not with pedagogy but with keeping the pupils quiet. There are numerous methods of achieving this, ranging from giving them high-class instruction to knocking them unconscious.

Frank began to search for his experiment in the index of a text-book. Fred interrupted him.

'Fred,' I said, 'you and Benny can do Kater's pendulum.'

This was where my guile came in. The experiment necessitated one of them counting the oscillations of a pendulum and the other watching a clock, so precluding all foolish conversation.

Suddenly there began a distant roar as the school came out of prayers. They thundered down the staircases out of the hall, stamping their feet and raising their voices. It was no longer possible to hear the traffic outside the windows.

The last two boys, Trevor and Benny, came into the laboratory. Benny was big and ugly and heavy, with the comic-pathetic expression of a film-comedian. He generated a superabundance of emotion and physical energy, and he was not clever.

Trevor was quite different, unusually small, fair, pale and delicately formed. He had beautiful silky golden hair that he was always combing. He was languid, petulant, sarcastic, quick-tempered and horrid to anyone who gave him an opening. I was quite fond of him because he was intelligent and inclined to be original. He wanted to be an artist, and he had failed badly in the Oxford scholarship examination. I was worried about his future, and afraid that we might have trouble with him one day.

'What are we going to do, sir?' said Benny, standing too close to me and hopping about from one big foot to the other. Trevor went and combed his hair in front of a glass cupboard-door.

I paused for a moment. A form was assembling in the main laboratory next door and the wooden wall between was resounding like a huge baffle. There was a loud hallooing shout from a master, and the noise subsided. I explained to my pupils what they had to do. Then I sat down in my chair to meditate.

One of the boys asked a question. 'Do as you like,' I said. I addressed the form as a whole. 'It's important that you should all learn to be resourceful.'

Trevor turned his small sharp face and laughed nastily.

'It saves you a lot of trouble.'

I did not speak to any of them.

'Come on, Trev,' said Frank, and ran his fingers through Trevor's hair.

Benny dropped a couple of metre sticks on the floor. On picking them up he discovered he could make a clacking noise by shaking them together. In a few moments this pleasure palled and they were all settling down to work.

I began to think about Myrtle.

The brightness of the day was beginning to be manifest. A pale ray of sunlight cut across the little room and glimmered on the green-painted wall. Trevor was trying out a piece of asbestos soaked in brine over a bunsen flame, and it made spluttering yellow flashes. Sounds of all kinds kept the room echoing. It was another day in which you could feel the air cleared and sharpened by dormant spring. My thoughts drifted into fantasies as they do when I listen to music.

There was another hallooing shout in the room next door. Then silence.

'It's Roley,' said Frank. Roley was the boys' name for my senior master, Roland Bolshaw.

There was a crash against the wall: it was the unmistakable sound of a boy being knocked down.

'The sod!' said Trevor, in a superior accent.

'Oo-ya bugger!' said Fred, in the language of the town.

We listened, but nothing else happened.

Frank went on polishing a lens with his handkerchief.

'You haven't got anything to do,' he said. 'Haven't you brought a novel to read?'

I shook my head. He had reminded me of the fact that I did not read much nowadays. I was faced with an inescapable truth: you cannot have a mistress and read. Sometimes my illiteracy made me ashamed: at other times

I thought, 'Bah! Who wants to *read*?'

From his pile of text-books Trevor produced a copy of *Eyeless in Gaza*. I had read it once and found it too unpleasant to read again.

'If I go to my locker I shall have to stop and talk to Bolshaw on the way,' I said thoughtfully.

Immediately Benny was standing beside me. 'Let me go and fetch you something, sir!'

I refused, and that committed me to going through Bolshaw's room.

The headmaster of the school was regarded by staff and pupils alike as ineffective. The result of this diagnosis, right or wrong, was that there was little discipline among the boys, and a high degree of eccentricity, laziness and insubordination among the staff. The manners of the staff were no less surprising than those of the boys. By my simple standards of common sense, about one-third of them not only qualified for dismissal from this school but would never hold a job in any other. To say they habitually cut lessons, or spent lunch-time in a public-house, or held hilarious sessions of beating, was putting it mildly.

There were of course a number of masters, another third, who were ordinary decent men. The sort of men we all remember as the schoolmasters of our youth – a little less clever, shrewd, ambitious and successful than ourselves, but firm, honest and hardworking. Unfortunately these were not the men who made much impression at the time upon any of the boys I had a chance of observing.

My senior master fell into a third category. He was immediately recognizable as a schoolmaster, while at the same time he was impressive. I think he was most impressive because in the staff-room, the class-room, or any other gathering, he had the power of confidently assuming he was the most important person there.

Bolshaw was built on a big scale. He had a large heavy body, with thinnish arms and legs, and a slight stoop. He was fair-haired and blue-eyed, but that is not to say he was an example of nordic beauty. He was in his fifties, and his hair was thinning everywhere except on his upper lip, where it grew in a tough, straggling, fair moustache. He had to blow the whiskers of his moustache away from his mouth in order to speak. His eyes were sharp and clever, and he wore steel-framed spectacles. And he had one of the loudest booming voices I have ever heard.

It was the way his head came up out of his collar, and the way his moustache fell back from his greenish, ill-fitting, false teeth, that gave him the vigorous tusky look of a sea-lion. I could imagine such a head emerging from the surface of icy waters to blow and boom at other sea-lions.

By temperament Bolshaw looked solid and conventional. He was arrogant, lazy, more or less goodnatured, states-man-like, and given to confident disapproval of others. Bolshaw disapproved of me, with enormous confidence: he disapproved of the headmaster with equal confidence. The headmaster was conventional but possessed not a scrap of natural authority. I was solid enough but wilfully showed no signs of decorum.

On the whole, Bolshaw and I did not dislike each other. Had we not been members of the same profession I doubt if we should have quarrelled at all. Bolshaw merely wanted me to behave like a schoolmaster. He wanted me to conform. You may ask, who was he to demand conformity? The answer is, Bolshaw.

Bolshaw had natural authority and he exerted it. He entered the class-room in a solemn, dignified, lordly manner. He was, I repeat, a solid and conventional schoolmaster. On the other hand I am forced to record that he never taught the boys anything.

I bore Bolshaw very little ill-will. I was always interested in his devices for avoiding work, and enthralled by the tone of high moral confidence in which he referred to them. Also I appreciated his sense of humour: he made harsh, booming jokes. It was a pity he was trying to have me sacked.

As I passed through Bolshaw's room I tried to evade him, though nothing pleased him more, when he was supposed to be teaching a form, than to gossip with me. On this occasion I failed. He had adopted the schoolmaster's legal standby for keeping the pupils occupied – a test. He looked up at me as I passed, with his steel spectacles gleaming and his yellow moustache revealing a tusky grin.

I glanced at his list of questions on the blackboard, and then at the form, which was composed of louts. Bolshaw strolled across my path.

'I always think,' he began – it was one of his favourite beginnings, especially for a statement of egregious arrogance – in a loud confident undertone that carried to the other end of the laboratory, 'that I'm the only person who knows the answers to my own questions.'

There was a pause.

'Have you heard this morning's news?' Bolshaw said.

I was a little surprised. At first I thought he must mean Hitler's latest move, but as we disagreed over politics we did not pretend to discuss such things. Bolshaw approved of Hitler in so much as he approved the principle of the Führer's function while feeling that he could fulfil it better himself.

'Simms is away again.'

I looked at him with interest. Simms was the senior master of all the science departments; physics, chemistry, mathematics and biology: as such he was paid more money. Bolshaw, though he spoke as if he were headmaster of the school, was only senior physics master. Simms was a kindly, sensitive, unaggressive old man who suffered from asthma. Bolshaw was waiting for him to retire.

'I told the headmaster only last week,' said Bolshaw, 'that Simms is a sick man.'

I smiled to myself at the phrase. If your friend is ill, you say, 'So-and-so's down with asthma.' 'So-and-so's a sick man' is the phrase reserved for someone you hope will be eliminated to the material improvement of your own prospects: it has a lofty, disinterested sound.

Bolshaw was a power-loving man. Getting Simms's job meant a great deal to him. It meant something to me too; since I argued that if he got Simms's it would be difficult to prevent me getting his, Bolshaw's, job – which also carried more pay. This was only the beginning of my argument.

Bolshaw was not only strong: he was wily and circuitous.
And he was in a position to make the running. Up to date I
had held my own, by at least keeping my job – but this, I
reflected, might not be due as much to my own moral
strength and manœuvring power as to the headmaster's
utter supineness.

'My wife and I went out to see him yesterday. I thought
he was a very sick man.' He spoke with the solemn
grandeur of his knowledge. 'I'm afraid he doesn't believe in
his own recovery.'

I said I thought Simms would recover. 'Asthma's really a
defensive complaint. The poor old man's asthma keeps him
out of the hurly-burly for a while. It may be...'

'I always think,' interrupted Bolshaw, raising his voice
by several decibels, 'the most important thing is that a man
should believe in himself. It encourages the others.'

I had heard enough. 'Do you believe in that boy over
there?' I said, pointing to a boy who was blatantly copying
from his text-book.

The form heard what I said, and there was a sudden
stillness. As Bolshaw turned to look, I made for the door.

In a few minutes I returned, and to my surprise Bolshaw
did not attempt to waylay me again. I was suspicious.

I sat down in my own room and said:

'What's Bolshaw been up to?'

Frank said: 'He came in to see if he could catch us
playing the fool. He threatened Benny.'

'What was Benny doing?' Benny was always playing the
fool.

'Nothing, sir!' Benny put on a look of ludicrous innocence.

'Benny wasn't,' said Frank. 'Roley only said he was so as
to criticize you.'

'Nonsense,' said Trevor malevolently. 'Roley enjoys
threatening.' He giggled.

I began to read.

After an hour or so I noticed that the sun was shining
quite brightly. I stood up and stretched my limbs. I
thought how much less cramped I should feel if I were

sauntering over the fields with Myrtle. I threw my book down on the bench and leaned against the wall. Fred and Benny were counting with concentration; Frank was looking down the travelling-microscope; Trevor was filing his nails. A neighbouring church clock began to chime. Something inside me was chafing, and I said aloud:

'Que je m'ennuie!'

There was a pause.

'Why don't you go out?' said Trevor.

'Go and have a cup of coffee,' said Frank. 'We shall be all right.'

''E can telephone somebody,' said Fred suggestively.

I shook my head. 'It means another encounter with Bolshaw.'

'Go through the window,' said Benny. 'Roley won't know you've gone.'

One of the panes of the window at the end of the room could be opened. If I climbed over the bench I could just squeeze through and drop into the street. I had tried it before.

Benny had already climbed on to the bench and was eagerly holding the window for me.

'We'll promise to help you in again,' he said.

I did not trust him not to play tricks that would bring in Bolshaw and reveal my absence. It was tempting fate; but I decided to risk it.

A moment later I was walking outside in the cold sparkling sunshine. It made a pleasant relief to a morning in school.

CHAPTER IV

TWO PROVINCIAL MÉNAGES

Tom's boy was named Steve, and he was aged seventeen. I suggest that anyone who is in the act of picking up a stone to cast at Tom, should change his target and cast at Steve instead. Many a man, were the truth but known, would find himself in as weak a moral position as Tom: on the other hand any man whatsoever might count on being in a stronger moral position than Steve. Steve had practically no moral position at all.

Steve was tall and gauche and precocious. He was pleasant-looking, with a shock of soft dark hair that kept falling over his eyes, and a wide red-lipped mouth. There was nothing particularly effeminate about him. He hunched his shoulders shrinkingly and wore a faintly rueful smile, as indications of his delicate nature: there was not the slightest need for either, since physically he was well-formed and temperamentally as self-centred as anyone I have ever known.

As with Tom, it was Steve's idea of himself that guided his actions. He saw himself as hyper-sensitive and artistic, in need of protection, help and support. Much happiness and satisfaction was created by Tom's seeing him in the same way. It was Tom's role to give Steve protection, help and support. Their relationship was that of patron and protégé.

I liked Steve. He wrote some poems that showed talent. As I felt that writing poems was a very proper occupation for the young I encouraged him. I subscribed to Somerset Maugham's theory, that creating variegated minor works of art is part of juvenile play: it seemed to me that the young might play at much worse things, such as rugby football which left them tired out with nothing to show for their pains.

Most of all I enjoyed Steve's company. Like most peop of weak moral fibre he was thoroughly engaging. It is a sa reflection that everybody admires persons of strong moral fibre but nobody shows any inclination to stay with them for more than five minutes. We all agreed that it was fun to be with Steve for any length of time.

Though the relation between Tom and Steve was that of patron and protégé, I thought their behaviour was more like that of corporal and private. Tom was energetic and bustling: Steve was incorrigibly lazy. Much of their time together was spent in Tom's giving loud commands: 'Now Steve, do that!' and Steve's putting up, as befitted his station, a token show of obedience.

Steve appreciated readily the advisability of a protégé's retaining his patron; but where his token show of obedience required physical action he was usually careless and inept to say the least of it. This promptly led Tom to give him suitable instruction, to which Steve submitted uncomplainingly – far too uncomplainingly, in my opinion, as much of the information Tom saw fit to impart was grossly inaccurate. Fortunately Tom was satisfied by the act of imparting, and Steve neither knew nor cared about inaccuracy.

Tom was very serious about his devotion to Steve. It was Myrtle and I who had conceived the idea of renting a country cottage, and Myrtle who had found it: it did not take Tom long to see that Steve's devotion to him would be increased if he were able to entertain him over the weekends in the country.

Furthermore Steve sighed with relief when Tom bought a car. Steve did not own a bicycle, and when Tom offered to lend him one there was some doubt about whether Steve could ride it without falling off every few yards. In the end Steve got more than he bargained for, because Tom was a wild and impulsive driver – he had excellent eyesight but he did not appear to use it. Steve, like all the rest of us, was terrified. 'It does him good to be thoroughly frightened now and then,' Tom confided to me, with a meaningful smile. Tom's devotion was very great, but it did not entirely eclipse his shrewdness.

When Tom was arranging to entertain Steve for a week-end at the cottage, it was his habit to indicate that he, like Myrtle and unlike me, went by atmosphere. There is a very simple difference between going by atmosphere and going by plan. If you go by atmosphere you spend week-ends at a cottage when you feel like it – which is every week-end. When I insisted on taking my turn Tom denounced me as cold, methodical and machine-like.

There were additional complications. Tom did not mind my being present when he was entertaining Steve; the last thing I wanted was his presence when I was entertaining Myrtle. And more troublesome still was the fact that I was supposed to conceal Steve's visits from Myrtle – looking back on it, I cannot for the life of me see why. Myrtle would certainly not have been shocked or disapproving. Women take such matters much less seriously than men: they sometimes express passing displeasure at the thought of two men being out of commission as far as they are concerned, but that is all there is to it. I did not think: I acted with cold, methodical, machine-like loyalty to Tom. The result was farce.

The existences of Tom and Steve were enlivened by frequent scenes of passion and high emotion. Mostly it was beyond my powers to fathom what they were about. I really thought Tom invented them. He reproached me with not having scenes with Myrtle.

'I must say I find it slightly . . .' he paused, 'surprising.'

'Indeed,' I said, crossly.

Tom gave a distant, knowing smile, as truths about passion crossed his mind that were beyond my comprehension. I could see that he thought scenes were absent from my life with Myrtle because of serious deficiencies in my temperament, if not actually in my powers as a lover.

Anyway, scenes were constantly present between Tom and Steve, and since Steve was too lazy and conceited to initiate anything they must have originated with Tom. There was one in progress, goodness knows why, over Steve's career.

Steve had left school the previous summer and had been articled to Tom's firm of accountants. It was in the office that they first met. By the spring Steve's helpless and sensitive nature had found its fulfilment in Tom's masterful capacity for support. Steve decided he was not cut out to be an accountant. Trouble promptly broke forth.

Steve's parents had very modest resources, and had been forced to borrow money to pay his premium. Tom, partly because he wanted Steve to be kept in his office, and partly out of sheer common sense, told Steve he would have to stay where he was. Steve began to suffer.

'Think of it, Joe,' Steve said to me. 'Five years as an articled clerk!' His pleasant face contorted with an expression of agony. 'It will be like prison.' He paused, as a worse thought struck him. 'Only *duller*.'

I could not help smiling.

Steve's expression of agony deepened. 'You don't understand, Joe. I can't do *arithmetic*.'

I shook my head.

'I never could,' he said. 'Think of becoming an accountant if you can't do arithmetic.' He glanced at me sharply, to enjoy my amusement. Suddenly the agonized look disappeared, his narrow grey eyes sparkled with hard realism, and his tone altered completely. 'I can tell you it's terribly hard work, too.'

When Steve dropped his nonsense and came out with the truth he was at his most engaging.

I thought it was time to bait him a little. I said: 'Tom will teach you arithmetic. He likes teaching.'

'I don't want to learn arithmetic.'

'What do you want to learn, Steve?'

'I want to learn about love, Joe. Everyone does.'

'I should have thought you were doing quite nicely.'

'I'm not, Joe,' Steve said with force. 'I'm not!'

I shrugged my shoulders. 'You'll be a poet some day.'

'I'll never be an accountant. I never wanted to be. It's

my parents' fault.' Steve looked at me. 'They chose accountancy because it's *respectable*.'

'In that case they made a singular choice,' I observed.

Steve grinned with satisfaction.

I surmised that Tom's conversations with Steve on the same theme had a different tone and went on much longer. Tom took Steve seriously, for one thing, and was easily roused to rage, for another. They had passionate quarrels over whether Steve could do arithmetic.

The upsurge of a quarrel led to an atmosphere of emergency in which previous arrangements about who should go to the cottage were swept aside, that is, if it were my turn. Tom rang me up early on Saturday morning, just as I was about to leave my lodgings.

'Are you having Myrtle out tomorrow?'

I said I was.

'In that case I think we'll come out today. Naturally we'll leave before Myrtle arrives tomorrow.' Tom paused diffidently. 'Steve wants us to come.'

I was annoyed. The only thing Steve wanted was physical comfort and unlimited admiration. On the other hand Tom had special claims because it was only a matter of months before he went to America.

A few minutes later Myrtle rang up.

'Darling, can I come out to see you this afternoon?'

Nothing would have pleased me more, but it was too late to stop Tom. I could not let Myrtle come, because I had told her I was going to be alone, writing.

'I was going to come into town to see you, darling,' I said, resourcefully. 'I thought we might go to a cinema.'

'But darling! . . .' Myrtle's voice broke off in surprise – as well it might, since the day was exquisitely sunny, I was in excellent health, and none of the cinemas sported a film that anybody in his right mind could want to see. I decided to banish Tom and Steve from the cottage immediately after lunch.

At lunch Tom displayed irritation that I had not put Myrtle off.

'What time will she be leaving tonight?'

'About ten o'clock.'

We ate our lunch in a state of tension, which increased on my part as Tom showed no signs of hurrying when the time approached for Myrtle to appear. Tom and Steve were quarrelling because Steve had surreptitiously eaten an apple before lunch and would not admit it.

'There were eight in the bowl before lunch and now there are only seven!' Tom was saying furiously. 'Neither Joe nor I ate it.'

Steve looked sulky and tortured. He was still growing quite fast and he was always hungry. Nobody objected to his eating anything, but he did it secretly and denied it afterwards. Food was always disappearing mysteriously when Steve was about.

'Myrtle will be here any moment,' I said, on tenterhooks.

I should like to point out that I thought none of this scene was in the least funny.

Tom looked at me, disgusted with my incapacity for understanding the overwhelming importance of conflict.

A bicycle bell rang joyously in the lane, and in came Myrtle.

Tom swept forward and greeted her effusively. He presented Steve to her. And then he said:

'How nice you're looking, Myrtle.'

She did look nice. She gave Tom a bright-eyed, smirking look. The smell of her scent caught in my nostrils. I could readily have taken a carving-knife to both Tom and Steve.

'Now what Myrtle would like,' said Tom, 'is a nice cup of tea.'

'I'm dying for one,' said Myrtle, in an expiring voice.

'Of course you are, my dear.' He paused. 'I understand these things.'

Myrtle played up to him shamelessly. 'I know, Tom.'

Tom's face wreathed itself in a silky smile.

Tom's stock method of making an impression on anyone was to indicate that he understood them perfectly. In this strain he was setting to work on Myrtle.

'Now Steve,' he said, 'put the kettle on!'

Steve shambled into the scullery, and reappeared in a

moment looking tragic.

'The primus is broken.'

I pushed him out of the way. The primus was not broken: he had never tried. When I returned with the tea Tom and Myrtle were in full flood of the most inane conversation I could imagine.

'I love dogs,' Myrtle was saying, in a soulful tone.

'So do I,' said Tom, copying it ridiculously.

'I wish I had three.'

'One can't have too many.'

'Red setters,' said Myrtle. 'Don't you love red setters?'

'Wonderful,' said Tom.

'And their eyes!' said Myrtle.

'So sad!' said Tom.

'I know.'

'Just like us, Myrtle.' He gave her a long look.

Myrtle sighed.

Steve and I caught each other's eye, and I signalled him to help me hand round the cups. There was no place for us in the conversation.

At last Tom decided to take himself off. He made signs at me behind Myrtle's back. 'Ten o'clock!'

Myrtle and I stood in the doorway and watched his car disappear round the bend in the road. Big white clouds went floating across the sun. The hedgerows were leafless and glistening – I watched a twittering troop of little birds which every so often took it into their heads to move on a few yards. I did not speak to Myrtle.

'What's the matter, darling?' Myrtle said, innocently.

'Nothing.'

'Is anything wrong?'

'Nothing at all.'

She put her arm round me, but I would not speak. Her body leaned softly against mine. She began to caress me: I decided to sulk a bit longer. I tried harder and harder to go on sulking. Suddenly I turned to her. She looked beautiful.

'I love you,' I whispered into her ear, and bit the lobe of it.

'Darling!' She struggled away from me.

We looked into each other's eyes.

'You didn't mean this afternoon as well, did you, darling?' she said, in a shocked reproachful tone.

'You know perfectly well, I did,' I said, and bit her again.

Instantly Myrtle looked away, and I knew that I had made a mistake. I was being found lacking in romance. I held her close to me. 'Poor Myrtle,' I thought; 'and poor me as well'. I went on holding her close to me till I ceased to be found lacking in romance.

Saturday afternoon passed like a dream – in fact much more satisfactorily than any dream I have ever had. Men can say what they like about dreams. Better awake, is my motto.

We were happy, we were harmonious, we were ravenously hungry. The dusk fell and we cooked a meal. By daylight you could see that the cottage was filled with everybody's cast-off pieces of furniture. At night, by the light of candles and the fire, it was transformed. We lingered over our eating: we lingered over each other. And the clock moved round to ten.

Myrtle showed no signs of going. I ceased to linger over her: she did not cease to linger over me. I had promised to get her away by ten, and it was useless to pretend I had not. Myrtle began to look at me reproachfully. I now suspected her of planning to stay the night; and realized that in a simple way she had broken me down to the idea. She put her arms round my neck. We were one: I would have given anything for her to stay the night with me, sleeping peacefully together. Like husband and wife.

Tom's car drove up, and Tom came in. He saw Myrtle. His face was distorted with anger and passion.

'What, Myrtle!' he said. 'Are you still here?'

Myrtle, not unnaturally, looked surprised and hurt. His tone was very different from that in which he had unctuously explored their identity of tastes earlier on.

'We were just going,' I said.

'That's right.' Tom relaxed a little, and smiled at Myrtle. 'And take Joe with you!'

I stood on my dignity. 'I always take her as far as the main road.'

Myrtle and I stepped out into the night, and picked up our bicycles. There was no sign of Steve in the car. Tom must have left him under a hedge.

We cycled down the lane. It was calm and starless.

'What was the matter with Tom?' She sounded miserable.

'I don't know.'

'He seemed strange.'

I did not speak. This was unfortunate as it enabled Myrtle to hear Tom start up his car and drive away in the opposite direction.

'Where's Tom gone?' she asked.

'Goodness knows,' I said.

I felt furious. Suddenly I felt cold as well. I had forgotten to put on a top coat. There was nothing to do but go back for it. I told Myrtle to wait where she was and pedalled hastily away.

I returned to meet Myrtle wheeling her bicycle towards me, with no light showing.

'The dynamo's broken,' she said, with deep pathos.

I think she thought she was going back for the night now that Tom had gone.

'You must take my spare lamp,' I said. 'You must!' We were nearly at the cottage again.

We heard Tom's car coming back.

'Tom's car's coming back,' said Myrtle, in a voice that had reached its peak of astonishment and could go no further.

I waved my lamp wildly to warn Tom.

The car drew up. Only Tom got out. I presumed that Steve must now be under the seat.

Tom rudely persuaded Myrtle to take my lamp, and we set off again.

We did not speak very much until we came to the main road. There we paused and embraced. Myrtle leaned against me passively, and I tried to revive her.

'Darling,' I said.

There was a long silence.

'You want to get rid of me.'

It was too much for me. I wished Tom were in America and I was not far from wishing he were removed from this world altogether. We stood in the middle of the road, our bicycles ledged in the small of our backs, weeping on each other's cheeks.

'Darling, I do love you,' I said, wondering why on earth we were not married to each other.

I held her face between my hands: it was so dark that I could barely see it.

'Please come to me tomorrow afternoon.'

Myrtle did not speak. A tear rolled on to my thumb.

'Promise, promise!'

Myrtle nodded her head.

I resolved that Tom should be got rid of next morning, if it meant dissolving our friendship for ever. When she came in the afternoon everything should be as if this night had never happened.

I took out my handkerchief and dried her face. In a little while we parted. Then I rode slowly through the empty lanes.

You may wonder why I put up with all this nonsense, why I did not break my word to Tom and tell Myrtle what was going on. There were two reasons. The first I am so ashamed of that I can barely bring myself to write it, but I shall have to write it in order to explain some of the later events: it is this – realizing that I was not a good man, I was trying to behave like one; and to me that meant being patient, forbearing and trustworthy to the last degree.

The second reason is this – frankly, I had no sense.

CHAPTER V

A PARTY OF REFUGEES

I advised Tom to emigrate to America as soon as possible. International events gave me a strong explicit foundation for my advice. From time to time we met for tea in the café and counted the growing roll of disasters.

'A fortnight since Hitler took Memel, and the British Government has done *nothing!*' said Tom.

'Nothing,' I echoed.

Alternately we received gloomy letters from Robert, which we read to each other. 'If there isn't a war by September we shall be refugees by November.' I noticed the date had slipped on a month, but did not point it out to Tom. I thought there was every reason why he should move without delay.

As the afternoons lengthened, we were leaving the window before the lights came on in the market-place. Easter was approaching: blue fumes of coffee mingled with the spring dust that circulated in the wind. The twilight glimmered on hosts of flowers, on waxen Dutch tulips in exquisite shades. Some of the shoppers had discarded their top coats. The weeks were passing: we could feel it, with nostalgia for the summer and apprehension for our fate.

Tom had a newspaper spread before him.

'Chamberlain Pledges Defence of Poland,' he read aloud. 'Balderdash! Poppycock!' Excepting the glare of his greenish eyes, his head began to look red all over. 'We shall give Poland away just like the rest. We shall see Chamberlain fly to Berlin in a golden aeroplane, accompanied by Peace in the shape of a dove.'

I smiled faintly and Tom blinked.

'Why is it always a dove?' he asked me. 'The *horse* of peace would be better. Doves are stupid, back-biting creatures, but horses are noble and intelligent.' He thumped his fist on the table. 'I can't stomach doves!'

The atmosphere lightened momentarily. Tom had the power of being able to hearten me. There was a good robust sense of life in him that made one's troubles seem smaller – one's own troubles, that is: it made his seem larger, absurdly larger.

We began to talk about writing. Tom was not working on a new novel, because of the prospect of his being uprooted. He declared that he was too busy, making preparations, to write: I agreed from observation that he was too busy – he was too busy pursuing Steve. I, on the other hand, had been brought to a standstill by Miss X.Y. She had still not written to me.

'I think you ought to write to her,' said Tom, always counselling action.

I shook my head. I already had some experience of reading unpublished manuscripts, and knew how maddening it was to be prodded by an impatient potential novelist.

Tom shrugged his shoulders, and then began to console me.

'She's bound to like it,' he said. 'She liked your first, and this is so very much better.' He spoke with great authority. His tone reminded me of Robert, whom we both copied when we spoke with authority. 'You're one of the most gifted writers of our generation.'

I did not reply. I was making a feeble effort to discount some of Tom's exaggeration – about five per cent of it.

'She may have sent it to her own publisher,' Tom said. 'I would, in her place.'

I believed him. When he was not in the grip of one of his passions, Tom could be most sympathetic. He was capable of unconsidered acts of kindness. He could be momentarily free from envy and jealousy. It was for this that I valued his friendship. It is characteristic of our own egoism, that we value others for their selflessness.

'It's a remarkable novel.'

I did not speak. I found myself contrasting Tom's attitude with Myrtle's. Whenever we met, Tom asked me first of all if I had heard from Miss X.Y. Whenever I met Myrtle she failed to speak of it unless I raised the subject myself. I had given her the manuscript to read, and I strongly suspected that she had not read it all – my fourth novel, a class better than the other three, forty thousand words longer and nowhere near as funny. For Myrtle not to have read it all seemed to me next door to perfidy.

'How,' I asked myself, 'can Myrtle love me and not want to read my books? How can a woman separate the artist from the man?'

The answer came pat. Women not only can: they do. And they have a simple old-fashioned way of selecting the bit they prefer. At the same time I have to admit that if Myrtle had made the other choice I should have accused her of not loving me for myself. Men want it both ways and I am surprised that women do not make a little more pretence of giving it – especially when they want to marry the men in question.

'What are you thinking about?' said Tom.

'Meditating on incompatibility. On the utter incompatibility of two people who want different things and can't accept compromise.'

Tom's mouth curved knowingly. 'Have you made up your mind if you want Myrtle to go with you to America or not?'

I stared at him. I had not, of course. And I did not like the question.

Tom began to smile. He made a smooth gesture with his hands. He said: 'My dear Joe, there's no need . . .'

'If she likes to go under her own steam,' I said, 'I see no reason why she shouldn't.' I paused. 'She can support herself.'

I made the latter remark with emphasis. Tom had been getting at me: this was my way of getting at him. I meant that our party should not include Steve.

Tom said equably: 'It sounds perfectly sensible.'

'I'm a sensible man,' said I.

'Have you told her definitely that you're going?'

'Not in so many words.' I liked this question even less than the earlier one.

Tom shrugged his shoulders. He began to read the newspaper.

I began to think what I was going to do about Myrtle, which brings me to the point where I must complete my description of her.

Myrtle was very feminine, and I have described up to date those of her traits which everyone recognizes as essentially feminine. She was modest, she was submissive, she was sly; she was earthy in its most beautiful sense.

In addition to all this, Myrtle was shrewd, she was persistent, and she was determined. At the time I thought she was too young to know what she wanted. Looking back on it I can only reel at the thought of my own absence of insight and capacity for self-deception. She knew what she wanted all right: it is just possible that she was too young to know exactly how to get it.

Myrtle was a commercial artist, employed by a prosperous advertising agency in the town. In my opinion, based on her salary, she was doing well. This much at least I could see. At a hint of the intellectual Myrtle's eyes opened in wonderment, at a hint of the salacious she blushed; and at a hint of business she was thoroughly on the alert.

Myrtle had been trained at the local School of Art. She had talent of a modest order – that is, it was greater than she pretended. Her drawings were quick, lively, observant without being reflective, pretty and quite perceptibly original. I, with her talent, would have been trying to paint like Dufy or somebody: not so, Myrtle. There was no masculine aspiring about her. Trying to paint like Dufy with her talent I should have been a masculine failure. Myrtle with feminine modesty and innocence took to commercial art.

Myrtle's talent was not of the primary creative order that sometimes alarms the public: it was the secondary talent for giving a piquant twist to what is already accepted. She was made for the world of advertising. And she accepted her station in life as an artist as readily as she accepted her salary. My efforts to encourage her to rise above this station, which would have brought her little but misery, fortunately made no impression upon her whatsoever.

In her business dealings Myrtle showed the same flair. It was one of her gifts to accept quite readily men's weaknesses.

She was tolerant and down-to-earth about them: she fought against them much less than many a man does.

Myrtle's employer was a middle-aged man who had introduced his mistress into a comparatively important position in the firm – to the envy and disapprobation of everyone but Myrtle. Myrtle accepted that such things were likely to happen, made the best of it, and showed good-natured interest in the other girl. In due course Myrtle found, to her genuine surprise, that the boss began to show much greater appreciation of her work.

So you see that Myrtle was by no means a poor, helpless girl who had fallen into the clutches of an unscrupulous, lust-ridden man. I may say that I saw it, plainly, while I sat in the café with Tom reading his doom-struck newspaper. I was behaving like a cad – admitted. But anyone who thinks behaving like a cad was easy is wrong.

As a result of Tom's pressing me I made a definite plan. It was to include Myrtle in our party of refugees without marrying her.

I was convinced that Myrtle could earn a living in America. If only I could convince *her*! If only I could persuade her to *act* on the conviction! Then there was no reason why our relationship should not go on just as it was.

That was how I came to my plan. It was only too easy for Tom to say afterwards that I never intended to carry it out, that if Myrtle had agreed I should have been something between alarmed and appalled. I at least half-believed it. As a love affair declines one can still go on making plans for a future that does not exist. And that is what I was doing. For, alas! make no mistake, our relationship really was declining.

There is a kind of inevitability about the course of growing love: so there is about its decay. It comes from time flowing along. You can shut your eyes and pretend that you are staying still – and all the while you are just being carried along with your eyes shut. You can make plans – but if they do not fit in with the flow of time, you might just as well save yourself the trouble. So with Myrtle and me. Wanting something different and being unable in our hearts to compromise we were being carried along towards final separation. We appeared to be doing things of our own volition: we had our breaks and our reconciliations. Round and round we went, spinning together like planets round the sun. May I remind you that even the solar system is running down?

To begin with I thought I had had a stroke of luck. Myrtle rang me up to tell me that she had been promoted to a better job in the firm. In the evening she came round to my lodgings for us to drink a bottle of beer to her success. 'Now,' I said to myself, 'now is the time!'

My landlady was clearing away the remains of my supper, when Myrtle sauntered into the room with an alluring whiff of cosmetics. The landlady retired promptly. Myrtle stared at me with a meek smirk of triumph. I kissed her. I wanted to know exactly what difference promotion made to her salary.

When questioned on matters of money, Myrtle always became quite unusually vague and elusive. I asked my questions, and somehow found myself listening to an elaborate account of intrigues in the firm, and adventures of Myrtle's employer and his mistress.

When the turn ended I quietly returned to my aim. Myrtle's face was still lit up with the pleasure of entertaining me. Instead of asking my questions all over again crudely, I led up to them by another spell of enthusiastic congratulation.

Something happened. Myrtle looked at me suddenly with a different expression.

Insensitively I forged ahead.

'It really is wonderful!' I said.

After remaining silent, Myrtle spoke in a hollow voice. Into her words she put sadness and reproach.

'It isn't *really*.'

'But it is!' I insisted. 'It proves you'll be able to get a job anywhere.'

Myrtle said nothing. She stood up and walked slowly across to the window. She stared out.

I was disturbed, but determination had got the better of me. I followed her, and stood beside her. I lived in the back room of a small semi-detached house. We were looking through a french window at a narrow strip of garden that sloped down to the garden of another semi-detached house in the next road. It was dusk.

I patted her. 'The more money you earn, my girl, the better.'

'Why?'

'Because you're an artist,' I said encouragingly. 'And Art must pay.' I kissed her cheek. 'We're two artists,' I said.

Myrtle did not speak. Being two artists is one thing; being husband and wife another, quite different. Then suddenly she turned on me and said with force:

'You *know* that I don't care.'

I looked down. Sad words, they were, falling upon my ear. When a woman tells a man she does not care about her career he ought to make for the door. It means one thing – the end of liberty for him.

I did not make for the door. I was overwhelmed by tenderness and I embraced her. It was no use making for the door because I still had to broach the subject of her taking a job in America.

I broached it. And it was a failure.

I suppose I was being singularly insensitive and obtuse, but I do not know what else I was to do. I thought: 'How strange – she doesn't realize that if she sticks to her career she can follow me to America.' And I will not swear that I did not think: 'And in America she might even succeed in marrying me.'

Alas! the flow of time asserted itself. I made matters worse.

'The world's going to be in a chaotic state,' I said. 'We shall all do best if we can fend for ourselves.'

Myrtle showed no sign of following me. The last thing she wanted to do was to think of fending for herself in a chaotic world. She was powerless to stand outside her personal affairs of the moment.

'I'm sure you could get a job in America.'

'Whatever for?'

'If we all decide to go.'

'Oh, that!' Myrtle moved away from me, as if the idea were tedious and repugnant and unreal.

I realized that I had not the courage to tell her that we were definitely going to America. I thought: 'I must tell her. I must!' And I said:

'I'm sure you'd be a great success in America.'

Myrtle tilted her head back to look at me. Her eyes were round and golden and unbearably appealing. I took her into my arms. You can see that I am both obtuse and a failure as a man.

The conversion went on a little further. I could hardly have been more inept, so I will not record it. I was direct, and for anyone as evasive and suggestible as Myrtle, directness was positively painful. My efforts to discover whether Myrtle's firm had American customers led us nowhere. She replied to my questions in an abstracted tone. I was tormenting her, and that was literally all. We were both completely trapped in our own worlds, quite separate, quite cut off.

At last the conversation dwindled into nothing. I thought Myrtle suffered from a low vitality of interest. I suggested that we should to to the cinema.

Immediately Myrtle perked up. Low vitality of interest, laziness, instinctive self-preservation – which was it? I do not know. We went to the cinema.

That was what became of part one in my plan. I moved to part two. Robert was coming to visit his friends in the town. I asked him to lunch at the cottage on Sunday and invited Myrtle. Tom was out of the way: he was supposed to be taking Steve up to London to see *The Seagull*. I hoped that when Robert saw Myrtle without any distraction, he would deem her worthy to join our party of refugees.

I was anxious. Up to the present Robert had deemed Myrtle distinctly unworthy. On having her presented to him he had commented that his remarks appeared to bounce off her forehead. I was willing to admit that Myrtle had an un-cogitating, unreflective air; but Robert's comment seemed to me both unkind and untrue. Being Robert's comment, it had to be accepted all the same. I was hurt. Myrtle and I may have been quite separate, quite cut off, and all the rest of it: but when Robert said his remarks bounced off her forehead, she was my mistress, my love, my choice and part of me.

I had difficulty in persuading Myrtle to come to the cottage at all while Robert was there.

'You won't want me,' she said. I think she would rather I assumed she was jealous of my friendship for Robert than that she was frightened of him.

Myrtle was abashed by the idea of Robert's being an Oxford don, which she associated, wrongly, not with intellectual but with social superiority. In the society of people she considered her social superiors, Myrtle was thoroughly ill at ease: she was only really completely free with her social inferiors. Robert saw her at her worst.

'Of course I want you, darling,' I said. And encouragingly: 'Robert will want to see you.'

Myrtle stared at me in disbelief. And I thought fate had been hard on me in sending a woman who could not meet my friends.

Nevertheless Myrtle arrived at the cottage bright and smiling on Sunday morning.

'I passed Robert. He's walking.' She glanced at me slyly. 'I told him I couldn't stop because you were waiting for me.'

I felt more cheerful. Robert came. We walked over to the Dog and Duck and had a most enjoyable lunch. Robert and I talked about literature. Myrtle was impressed. She drank an unduly large quantity of beer. Robert was impressed.

We walked home in good spirits, to find Tom in the cottage. He had driven back from London that morning. Robert greeted him affectionately, and so did Myrtle. I did not.

'I have a letter I wanted you and Joe to see.' Tom pulled the document out of his pocket and passed it round.

The letter was from one of the American professional associations of chartered accountants. Tom had been writing about jobs. I did not look at Myrtle. I had warned Robert not to tell Myrtle that our plans were already far advanced, but I had never dreamed that Tom would appear. He and Robert sat down and began openly to discuss our project.

If it had been possible for Myrtle to doubt our intention in the beginning, the possibility must have entirely disappeared in five minutes. I was too alarmed to say anything.

Tom had completed his five years of professional practice as an associate of the Institute of Chartered Accountants, and attached importance to being elected to fellowship. There had been a hitch because he had seen fit to quarrel with the senior partner of his firm; but he computed that the formalities would be complete by June. He proposed to leave England immediately afterwards.

The plan for me was to follow as soon as the summer school term ended. Robert had ordered himself to come last. Tom argued with Robert about cutting it fine. I watched Myrtle. I was more than surprised that Tom and Robert did not see the effect they were having on her. She was taking no part in the conversation, and it was plain that she was too wretched even to follow it properly.

They went on to argue about how Robert and I should earn our living, by writing or by teaching. Neither of us wanted to teach. Tom was slightly huffed and pointed out a paragraph in the *Sunday Times*, which we had already seen, about a slump in the book trade. 'One bookseller this week reports no sales whatever.'

Robert suggested that he and I might have to live on Tom to begin with: the whole talk had been high-spirited instead of grave, and now Robert induced an air of mischief and nonchalance. Myrtle looked as if she was going to burst into tears. She got up and went into the scullery.

I followed her, expecting to find her weeping. She was taking down cups and saucers.

'I thought I should like some tea,' she said, in a flat voice.

I stroked her hair. Suddenly she looked at me and I was accused of heartlessness and treachery. I turned away without speaking and went back to the others.

After tea Tom drove Robert away. Myrtle and I were left alone. I did not know how to look her in the face. There was nothing I could say. The damage was done. We cycled back into town without discussing it.

This was our last meeting before the Easter holidays. I arranged to ring up Myrtle as soon as I returned to the town. I told myself she might have got over the damage in the meantime. I was apprehensive.

PART TWO

CHAPTER I

UP AT THE GAMES FIELD

During the holiday I received no letter from Myrtle. And when I returned to the town she had gone away. I telephoned each day till she came back: it was a Friday, and she agreed to meet me on the following afternoon. I was down for duty at the school games field, so she said she would join me there. It did not seem a good arrangement to me, but before I could persuade her to do something else, she rang off. Whatever had gone wrong was not repaired.

Saturday afternoon came; and with it, for the opening of the school cricket season, a spell of cold drizzly weather. Usually I enjoyed my tour of duty. The boys played cricket in a comparatively orderly fashion, and those who were watching the match came and talked to me in a tone designed to shock less than usual. The field was attractive. At the gates there was a nicely planned tram-terminus and modern public lavatory, but neither was visible from inside. On the left of the pitch there was a line of poplars and on the right of sycamores and oaks; and straight ahead the ground fell away to a view of the town, with gasometers shimmering through the smoky haze of middle distance.

I stood in my overcoat pitying the boys in their blazers and white flannels. In a feeble effort to compensate for deficiency of social *cachet*, the headmaster insisted on the boys wearing white flannels whenever they went to the field in the summer term. It was about the only rule they kept, and they looked surprisingly presentable as a consequence.

On a summer evening, with golden light slanting through the trees on active little white-clad figures, it was easy to catch again the romantic air of boyhood – that air which every man delights to remember, whether he has ever breathed it or not. There was everything present: the heart-touching mixture of repose and vigour, the small sounds of the game, the occasional voice, the clapping of a few hands, the calm and movement, the green glow of the ground. On a cold drizzly Saturday afternoon they were present, but, it seemed, to a lesser degree.

Keeping my eye open for Myrtle, I shook off boys who were inclined to come and converse, and stood alone near the sightboards.

''Ello, Joe!' My interest in the match was cut short by Fred who had sidled up without my noticing.

Fred's white flannels were spotless. The green of his blazer was echoed in the greyish colour of his skin. His hair was dripping with brilliantine.

'You're looking very spruce, Fred.'

Fred grinned foolishly. 'Mr Chamberlain's got me!'

For a moment I could not think what he meant. He was referring to the prospect of conscription. The crisis had reached the boys. It came to me as a shock.

'He's got us all,' said Fred.

'He's welcome to you,' said I.

Fred stood still. It seemed as if my remark made its impression gradually. In the end he sighed and drifted away.

I sat down on the sub-structure of the sightboards. For me the match might not have been going on: Myrtle was late.

The sky began to cloud over a little more, but the drizzle ceased. The first innings ended unexpectedly, and I noticed Frank coming round the boundary towards me.

'Do you mind if I come and talk to you?'

I glanced up at him without enthusiasm.

'I'm sorry to bother you.' He paused: there was something the matter.

As he had seen me often enough with Myrtle, I told him I was waiting for her.

Frank sat down beside me. 'I'll go away as soon as she comes.'

We were both silent.

Frank said: 'It's about Trevor.' He was apparently watching the match.

'Oh?'

'I wish you could use your influence over him a bit.'

'What for?'

'To make him pull himself together.'

'What's the matter with him?'

'He isn't doing any work, for one thing.'

'He never did do much.'

'He's doing none, now.'

'I suppose he'll go in for art.' I glanced at Frank, slightly amused.

'He's not doing any work at that, either.'

My interest began to stir. 'What *is* he doing?' I stopped looking across the pitch and looked steadily at Frank.

'He's going to stupid parties, night after night, and getting drunk.' Frank's voice grew louder. 'He's doing himself no good.'

I did not care very much whether Trevor was doing himself good or ill; nor was I seriously troubled by Frank's alarm. I do not know why I persisted with the conversation. Somehow I was drawn on.

'What parties?' I said.

Frank muttered something about the School of Art. Immediately I knew why I had been drawn on.

'Who goes to them?'

Frank suddenly glanced at me. 'I've only been to one...'

'But you must know. Hasn't Trevor told you?'

'I don't think you'd know them. They're not the sort of people you'd know.'

'Not any of them?' I could not make my voice sound unconcerned.

'I think Myrtle goes, as a matter of fact.'

Frank looked at me, diffidently. I said nothing. I remembered Tom's solemn warnings about what Myrtle did when I would not have her.

'Does Tom go to these parties?' I said.

'No. But I think that friend of his called Steve does.'

I have to admit that I felt a gleam of satisfaction.

'They're very bohemian parties,' said Frank.

'What does that mean?'

'They drink a lot of beer and lie on the floor.'

I said nothing.

Frank said: 'I hope you don't think I'm a prude. I suppose it's all rather silly.'

I said: 'Who invites Myrtle?'

'A journalist on one of the evening papers. Called Haxby, or something. They say he's in love with her.' Frank's voice warmed to me. 'I know he doesn't stand a chance.'

I turned a little. 'Look, Frank,' I said. 'I'll have a word with Trevor.' I felt that everyone was the worse for going to such parties. I would have liked to stop them all, forthwith.

'It won't be easy. He's very flattered at being invited.'

'I'm surprised he's so popular. I thought you and I were the only people who liked him.'

'He's allowed to take the family car and drive people home afterwards.'

'Don't worry, Frank.' I tried to make the remark sound conclusive. I wanted to get rid of him. I felt uneasy and alarmed. Bohemian parties. Haxby. Vistas opened before me, thoroughly unpleasing vistas. I was not thinking for a moment about Trevor.

Neither of us spoke. There was a cry from the field as the bowler and his mates appealed for l.b.w. It was disallowed. Frank glanced at his watch, and then gave his collar a stylish look by pulling the points against his chin.

I was too proud to look at my own watch. I glanced at the sky, which was brightening.

'I think this is the cue for my exit,' said Frank.

Myrtle had just come through the gates at the far end of the field. I went to meet her.

'What a dreadful day!' Myrtle's first remark seemed to set the tone for us completely. Her voice sounded hollow and distant. I kissed her on the cheek.

'Not as bad as all that. I'm glad to see you, darling.'

Myrtle glanced at me, and then looked away. Some woe appeared to be weighing her down, though she was clearly making a gallant effort to bear up. I noticed that she was wearing a new coat. It was made of black persian lamb and suited her well. I commented upon it, and she drew it closely round her.

'I'm so cold.'

I suggested that we should stroll a little. After all, what better way is there of getting warm than exercise? Myrtle gave me a look to indicate that my imagination was inconceivably earth-bound. We strolled, all the same.

I was disturbed. A month of separation had elapsed, but we were just in the same state as before. Our first meeting for a month – how I had been looking forward to it! Myrtle was displeased with me. Absence had not lived up to its reputation.

Myrtle's presence beside me raised my spirits a little. In spite of her displeasure, her cheeks glowed prettily and her eyes were bright. I began to try and raise her spirits, too. I began to think about plans for the evening.

Myrtle gave me a sudden flickering look. This time I sensed not so much reproach as will. She intended to do something.

'What's the matter?' I asked.

'Nothing.' Myrtle turned away.

I suppose I might have pressed her. Instead I glanced idly across the field. I saw Bolshaw coming towards us.

I was surprised. Bolshaw rarely showed any sign of being interested in doing games duty when it was his own turn, let alone mine.

'Do you want to meet Bolshaw?' I asked Myrtle.

'If you like.'

She was looking so elegant and attractive that I would have liked. It would have given me innocent pleasure to show her to Bolshaw. His wife was bossy rather than pretty.

Myrtle was undecided, I wavered, and Bolshaw went past us. Myrtle, in spite of herself, glanced at him with furtive interest.

'You'd be amused by him,' I said.

'Would I?' She now glanced at me with furtive interest.

Encouraged, I began to tell her about Bolshaw's most

recent activities in the staff-room. I do not profess to be a mimic, but I did my best, saving my greatest efforts for a remark that had caught my fancy.

'When I look round me at my colleagues,' Bolshaw had said, 'I can always tell the married men.' Pause, while he looked round at his colleagues, most of whom actually were married. 'They have that *tamed* look!'

I can only repeat that the remark had caught my fancy. It did not catch Myrtle's. She did not say anything: she did not need to. In common language, the fat was in the fire.

I tried feebly to carry it off. I doubt if I should have redeemed myself if I had managed to achieve levitation. I did not achieve levitation.

Myrtle looked at her watch. She paused; and then she broke the news to me that she was not going to spend the evening with me.

I was astonished. I had sensed that she intended to do something, but not this.

'You didn't give me a chance to tell you,' she said.

'What are you going to do?'

'I've been invited to a party.'

I did not go on. I stared at Myrtle. Suddenly tears came into her eyes and disappeared again. I looked away, embarrassed and touched. I should have liked to put my arms round her. It was the moment to do it. But we were standing in the middle of the field with scores of boys watching.

Having broken the news to me, Myrtle seemed as if she could not bring herself to leave. I was certain that she did not really want to go to the party.

'Oh dear!' I sighed.

'What's the matter?' Myrtle was genuinely concerned.

'You've got to go.'

'Yes.' She dropped her head, and pulled her coat closely round her again.

Quietly I walked her to the gates. She hesitated.

'There's your tram,' I said.

Myrtle held out her hand and I took her fingers in mine. And then she went towards the tram. I watched it move clatteringly away. 'There goes sweetness and sadness,' I thought.

I speculated about the people, other than Haxby, who would be at the party. Saturday night – I did not doubt that it was one of the parties Trevor and Steve had started to go to. Frank had observed that they were not given by the sort of people I knew. That was true. Unhappily for me, the people who went to them got to know each other. Yet although I was jealous, I intended not to follow suit. I had several circles of friends in the town. This was a circle that I meant to keep out of. It was not my style.

Perhaps I ought to remind you that I had several circles of friends that were not necessarily shared by Myrtle and Tom. I had a circle of artistic friends made through my interest in writing: I had a circle of bourgeois friends made by letters of introduction from Robert: I had a couple of friends on the staff of the school: and in another town I had my family circle to which I was devoted. For the sake of describing myself completely, I should have to explore the lot. Let me give prompt assurance that I do not intend to do so.

Trollope discourses somewhere upon the difficulty that arises in novel-writing of disentangling men and women from their surroundings in order to isolate them as literary characters. A novel cannot contain everything. This novel is the story of Tom, Steve, Myrtle and me. In between us and the circles of friends I propose to leave out altogether, there are two people who played a part in our story whom I propose to leave half-in and half-out. Robert and Haxby.

Robert was a man of remarkable stature; to do him justice I should be inclined to give him the novel to himself, and that would make you feel he played a more important part than he actually did. On the other hand I never knew Haxby, so I cannot write about him: not being the kind of man who is impelled to establish intimate relations with his rival, I never tried to meet him. If you want to know more about Robert, ask me to write another novel: if you want to know more about Haxby, ask someone else.

Pondering on how little we can share of the sum of someone else's life, through not being present at the parties she goes to, for instance, I returned to my duty. I found Bolshaw walking in front of me again. This time he beckoned me.

'Come and have a chat with me,' he said.

We walked back to the pavilion. Bolshaw dislodged a row of small boys who were sitting on a bench in front of it. He ordered one of them to bring his attaché case out of the pavilion. I waited: I did not know what we were to talk about.

The afternoon had brightened a little. The cold breeze had dropped: the clouds had thinned and there was a glowing patch where the sun was. Many of the boys had gone home, and those who still played on moved in a tired, desolate fashion. Yet the growing light brought the green of the grass and trees to life again. The air was warmer.

Bolshaw opened his attaché case and pulled out a notebook and a sheaf of papers. He handed them to me.

'It's my research,' he said.

I was astonished. I had heard him mention his research, but I did not really believe in its existence. I had imagined him much too lazy.

I recovered from my astonishment while Bolshaw was explaining to me his problem. It was a piece of theoretical research in astrophysics. I can tell you that it was of practical importance to anyone interested in certain of the spiral nebulae.

'Of course, I don't expect you to understand it,' Bolshaw said.

I suppressed the desire to say: 'Then why are you showing it me?' Bolshaw was making a friendly gesture. I thought of his job. Even if I was leaving the school at the end of the term I wanted to be offered his job. Since the headmaster was likely to do what Bolshaw recommended, Bolshaw's friendly gesture had extraordinary, almost spiritual significance for me. 'What's the next move?' I asked myself.

'I can simplify it for you,' he went on.

I listened. He did simplify it. Whatever his failings, he had considerable intellectual power and acuity. He drew the skeleton of his work beautifully.

'And now,' he said, 'this is how I'm attacking it.'

I listened again. I did not understand it, of course. It was not in my line – a long way from it. Yet the principle of his attack was ingenious, and I grasped it just well enough to see that if it came off he could make an elegant coup. I admired. But listening and admiring were all very well – I did not know what he was leading up to.

'Now,' said Bolshaw, pointing with his pencil at the sheet of paper on which he had been writing down headings as he went along: 'Now, I may run into a bit of trouble here.'

'Trouble?' I looked closely at the paper, though I do not know how that could have helped me. 'A bit of trouble?' I said rashly. 'You mean a bit of hard work!'

Bolshaw's expression did not change by a flicker. 'Do you think so? Do you think you could see your way through it?'

I had been neatly trapped. I had meant what I said. He needed somebody to try out a number of tedious calculations. I could do nothing but nod my head.

'That's interesting.' Bolshaw spoke with weight, and then looked at me suddenly. 'Would you like to join me in this work?'

I could have kicked myself. 'I'd be delighted,' I said, and mumbled, 'Honoured.'

Bolshaw then said: 'Would you care to take the papers with you now?'

'Oh!' I stared at him with a pained expression, largely at the thought of having to do the work. 'I'm afraid I'm not free at the moment.' I saw what seemed a clever way of getting out of it. 'I'm just completing the manuscript of a book.'

Bolshaw looked at me.

'I've just received some extremely interesting suggestions from a distinguished critic,' I said, lying for the sake of verisimilitude. Of course Miss X.Y. had not returned the manuscript.

Bolshaw nodded his head understandingly. I wondered if

I had done right.

Bolshaw put his papers away with equanimity. I felt a slight exhilaration.

I changed the subject. 'By the way,' I said, 'what's the news of Simms?'

'He's very sensibly taking my advice,' said Bolshaw. 'He's putting in his resignation.'

Instead of saying, 'You'll be getting his job; what about me?' I kept my glance firmly fixed on the case containing the work he wanted me to do, and said in a solemn tone:

'I think it's the wisest course. For everyone.'

Bolshaw suddenly said:

'I intend to think about your position.'

It sounded like a remark from one of God's first conversations with Adam. I looked forward to the consequences just as hopefully. I went home, pondering them.

And then I rang up Myrtle again. I was told that she had gone out to a party. I felt gloomy and spent the evening alone.

CHAPTER II

NOT AS GOOD AS A PLAY

I bore Myrtle's new tactics with patience. The next time we spent an evening together there was no quarrel. To avoid it I took Myrtle to a cinema. We did not mention Haxby. On the other hand it was impossible to pretend that either of us was light-hearted. Myrtle's expression of unhappiness was deepening. Day by day I watched her sink into a bout of despair, and I concluded that it was my fault – had I not concluded that it was my fault, the looks Myrtle gave me would have rapidly concluded it for me.

The topic of conversation we avoided above all others was the project of going to America. Even a casual reference to Robert made Myrtle shy desperately. I cursed the tactlessness of Robert and Tom. I felt aggrieved, as one does after doing wrong and being discovered. I did not know what to do.

When you go to the theatre you see a number of characters caught in a dramatic situation. What happens next? They have a scene. From the scene springs action, such as somebody pooping off a revolver. And then everything is changed.

My life is different. Sometimes observant friends point out to me that I am actually in a dramatic situation. What happens next? I do not have a scene; or if I do, it is small and discouragingly undramatic. Practically no action arises. And nothing whatsoever is changed. My life is not as good as a play. Nothing like it.

All I did with my present situation was try and tide it over. I quail at the thought of tiding-over as a dramatic activity. Anybody could have done better than me. You, no doubt, could have offered me a dozen suggestions, all of them, as they were designed for someone else to follow, setting a high moral standard.

When Myrtle emerged from the deepest blackness of despair – after all, nobody could remain there indefinitely – I tried to comfort her. I gradually unfolded all my plans, including those for her. It produced no effect. She began to drink more. She began to go to parties very frequently. It was very soon clear that she had decided to see less of me.

I did not blame Myrtle. Had I been in her place I would have tried to do the same thing. Being in my own place I tried to prevent her. I knew what sort of parties she was going to: they were parties at which Haxby was present.

We now began to wrangle over going out with each other. She was never free at the times I suggested. Sometimes, usually on a Saturday night, she first arranged to meet me and then changed her mind: I called that rubbing it in a little too far. Here is a specimen of our conversation upon such an occasion, beginning with an irascible contribution by me.

'Where *are* you going?'

'Nowhere, darling.'

'Then why can't you meet me?'

'Because I've got to stay at home.'

'What *for*?'

'Some people are coming round to listen to gramophone records.'

'Gramophone records!' I knew what that meant. Haxby and his friends listened to gramophone records for hours on end.

'It was the only night they could. I'm sorry, darling.' Myrtle paused, and then said in half-hearted reassurance: 'I *am* going to see you tomorrow.'

'But what am I going to do tonight?' Saturday night.

Myrtle reminded me that my circle of bourgeois friends had invited me to a dance. She advised me to go.

'I said I wouldn't go because you wouldn't go with me.' Myrtle did not dance.

'They don't like me.' Myrtle's voice came over the

telephone like that of a soul in purgatory.

'You don't try with them,' I said, thinking, 'Why on earth can't she get on with my friends?'

There was a pause.

'You can come round to my place if you like.' Her voice trailed off.

'To listen to gramophone records!'

We had reached an impasse.

I decided to follow Myrtle's advice. As a matter of fact I greatly enjoyed dancing. I also enjoyed listening to gramophone records.

Myrtle's behaviour, I repeat, was perfectly sensible. By seeing less of me she stood a chance of finding somebody else, or of making me jealous, or of both. Either way she could not lose.

The impasse being reached, my behaviour became perfectly odious.

Myrtle said: 'I've just bought some records of the Emperor.'

'Good heavens! Where did you get the money from?'

'I earned it, darling.'

'I shouldn't have thought you could afford it.'

'I shall be broke for weeks.'

'What a prospect!' Some vestigial restraint prevented me from saying that I should have to pay for all her entertainments, which would have been quite false.

'Hadn't you got a record of the Emperor?'

'Yes, but this is a better one. I shall sell the old one.'
'Who to?'

'Somebody will buy it. A girl at the office.'
'Oh.'

I paused, seeking new fields for odiousness.

'What else are you going to play in the cause of culture?'
'I haven't thought.'

'Beethoven followed by Duke Ellington?' This was a hit at Haxby's friends who followed the high-brow cult of respectfully admiring jazz. Myrtle had told me.

'What's wrong with that, darling? I thought you liked the Duke?'

I said with rage: 'The Duke, indeed!'

Myrtle did not say anything. I had started off feeling righteous. Now my righteousness took control of me.

'I suppose,' I said, 'you've had to buy lashings of drink?'

'What makes you think that?'

'You don't appear to be able to take your culture without it.'

Myrtle actually laughed, or at least it sounded like it on the telephone. And it could only have been me she was laughing at.

'If you want to make yourself ill, I suppose you can,' I went on.

'I shan't drink it all, darling.'

'Other people will!'

'But if they drink it, I can't, darling.'

'I meant they'll make themselves ill.' My voice rose. 'At your expense!' I cannot think which appalled me more, the drunkenness or the cost of it.

'You're wrong,' said Myrtle.

'I'm not. After the last of these parties you looked like death, yourself.'

There was a long pause. Out of the silence I heard Myrtle simply say:

'I feel like death now.'

My righteousness was removed in a single twitch. I saw myself without it. I had nothing to say. The fact of the matter is that my righteousness and my odiousness were the same thing, and they were both something else. Plain jealousy.

On the following afternoon the weather had changed to something more nearly like what is expected of April. The sun was shining. I lay on the sofa in my lodgings, reading the *Observer* and wishing I were at the cottage. From where I was lying I could see some lilacs in the next-door garden: the buds were unopened, and they rocked gently in the breeze. I closed my eyes – it was after lunch and I was waiting for Myrtle.

I forgot that Sir Nevile Henderson had been to Berlin to

explain British plans before Parliament heard them: I forgot that Myrtle had probably been drinking herself silly with Haxby and others till two in the morning. I imagined piles of chestnut flowers, some of them tinged with pinky-brown now the leaves were unfolded; and ash trees in the lane, rustling with handsful of silver-green feathers. Red campions in the ditches: white and yellow stars all over the meadows: the hedges and the animals and the birds.

I was awakened by the landlady's niece showing in Myrtle. I rolled back lazily. Myrtle looked ravishing. Her cheeks were lightly coloured and her eyes bright golden brown: from where I lay her long nose looked shorter. Over the back of the sofa I took hold of her hand, and drew her down to look into her face. She smiled at me with gaiety and innocence. Her despair had vanished. There was no sign round her eyes of a drunken debauch. Her breath was clean and fresh. I could hardly believe it. I rose to the occasion like a shot.

'Kiss me, sweet,' I said, and she did.

'You lazy old thing, you were asleep!'

'I was dreaming about being at the cottage, darling.'

'You would!' Her look indicated what she thought I had been dreaming about – thus showing that a girl who is earthy in its most beautiful sense can be totally wrong about a man.

'I was dreaming about flowers,' I said.

Myrtle shook her head, smirking at the thought of how I could lie. She came and sat beside me on the sofa.

I caressed her. In this mood I did not intend to mention Haxby. As I touched the bloom of her skin and felt the warmth of her flesh, my jealousy disappeared. She smiled at me encouragingly. I knew and she knew – she was almost telling me – that Haxby was nowhere.

'Darling,' I whispered into her ear.

This went on for a little while. There were sounds outside the door and Myrtle sat up attentively.

Anyone who has ever lived in lodgings, especially respectable lodgings in a semi-detached house on the outskirts of a provincial town, will know the obstacles to enjoying illicit love therein.

We both listened.

'It's all right,' I said.

Myrtle was much too indirect to nod, but somehow I knew she concurred. We had heard sounds that we recognized.

By a stroke of good fortune the obstacles in our case removed themselves on Sunday afternoon. It was good and rather peculiar fortune, such as is not commonly associated with a semi-detached house in a provincial town. I can only describe it truthfully. Every Sunday afternoon, at precisely two-thirty, the landlady's niece was visited by a very respectable-looking middle-aged man, who lived higher up the street. The landlady was sent out for a two-hour walk with the dog, no matter what the weather; whereupon the niece and the respectable-looking middle-aged man promptly went upstairs.

'He's as regular as clockwork,' Myrtle whispered.

She was right. It was a singular performance and it fascinated us constantly. The explanation that had come first to our minds was that he was a married man. Not at all. I had drawn the landlady into conversation about him, and had discovered that he was a bachelor living quietly with his mother and father.

'Why doesn't he marry her?' Myrtle would ask.

'*I* don't know.' I felt that Myrtle was insensitive, putting such a question to me. Nevertheless I felt exactly as she did. One can always have the conventional response about somebody else. Why on earth did not he marry her?

The man was never referred to, by the landlady or her niece, as anything but Mr Chinnock. He was well built and rather handsome, in a solid, meaty way. The suit he wore on Sundays was made of hairy tweed: across the waistcoat was stretched a heavy gold chain with a framed golden sovereign dangling from the middle. In manner he was slow, gentle and more than a little stately.

I supposed Myrtle and I ought to have assumed that the niece and Mr Chinnock went upstairs for a Sunday afternoon nap. Going by the sounds, we should have thought them restless sleepers. I am afraid we judged their conduct by our own – in fact, we used to speculate on how far their conduct differed from ours. Myrtle imagined the niece called him Mr Chinnock in all circumstances. 'Now *then*, Mr Chinnock!' Or *'That's* it, Mr Chinnock!' I was beguiled by such invention, though Myrtle pretended to have no idea what it was about. She smirked at the ceiling. The thought of somebody else, in the room above, on a Sunday afternoon – the mystery of it! What man can honestly say he does not know what I mean?

The Sunday afternoon I began describing passed rapidly and delightfully. Myrtle and I stood beside the french window, arms round each other's waist, looking down the garden at the grass and budding plants and the smoke rising from chimneys of little houses like our own.

At exactly four-thirty we heard the niece and Mr Chinnock come downstairs. They went into the scullery.

'I'll be loving you, always,' sang the niece in a quavering soprano.

'With a love that's true, always,' sang Mr Chinnock in a full baritone.

'Phon and antiphon,' said I to Myrtle.

'Mr Chinnock's putting on the kettle,' said Myrtle to me.

All was right with the world.

It may seem strange that Myrtle and I could feel that all was right with our particular world. We ought not to have done. There was a dramatic situation; but nothing had happened. Myrtle had introduced Haxby into the situation. I was jealous of him. Still nothing had happened. Instead we were mysteriously enjoying an interlude in the same old way.

Only by strenuously searching my memory can I recall a novel incident. That night I broke my custom and visited Myrtle's home.

There was no one in the house and she took me up to her room. It was a pretty room, decorated by herself. With humility she had hung no drawings of her own on the walls. The colour scheme was warm and rosy. There were leopard-skin rugs, deep red curtains and looped muslin

over the windows. A little vulgar? I suppose it was. Myrtle
was a little vulgar, and I must say that I liked it. The room
was evidence that she could let herself go, and that was
what I liked. People who cannot let themselves go on
occasion will not do for me.

I sat down on the bed. Myrtle sat beside me. I put my
arm round her. The minutes passed.

Suddenly it felt as if she softly collapsed against me. I
was utterly seduced. It felt as if she had melted into the
marrow of my bones – my woman, my wife, my squaw. And
then –

'That *tamed* look!'

'By Heaven!' I thought. 'What am I doing with a
woman, a wife, a squaw?' I sprang off the bed. Tamed!

Myrtle looked up at me, startled. Our eyes met. There
was a fleeting moment of clairvoyance. She read my
thoughts.

'My foot's gone to sleep,' I said, and stamped it on the
ground.

Myrtle did not say anything. She knew, I was certain she
knew, that I had in some way recoiled from her. I sensed
the shock to her as clearly as I sensed the other shock to
myself.

I stretched out my hand and stroked her hair. Myrtle
remained still, with her head bent. She began making small
pleats in the bed-cover.

'Is it getting better?' she said, lightly.

'Yes, I think so.'

I looked down at her. I wondered what had happened.
She was apparently paying no attention to me. The air was
warm and scented; the light glowed on her hair; she was
breathing softly, all on her own. Suddenly I felt in touch
with something inexplicable, far beyond the place where
our thoughts revolved and our wills told us what to do. I
felt in touch with something like instinct. And I knew how
little, how hopelessly little our thoughts and wills affected us.
At the root of everything we did was . . . the unknowable.

'No wonder,' I thought, as I remembered to give my foot a
last shake, 'we go on doing such damned unknowable things.'

CHAPTER III

TWO DRAMATIC TURNS

The mysterious interlude with Myrtle lasted. There were no more incidents of recoil, no more intimations of anguish to come. Three weeks later I was spending Saturday at the cottage, happily looking forward to Myrtle's visit next day. From time to time I wondered where she was spending the night. I was not seriously worried: Haxby was nowhere, I thought.

It was a beautiful May afternoon. Our private lives were drifting inexorably towards dissolution, like the whole of Europe towards catastrophe: the weather was perfect. The sun was shining; cloud shadows passed slowly over the grass, dousing the glow of daisies and buttercups. I roamed over the meadows, half intending to pick some flowers to decorate the house, but really passing the time in aimless thought. I was wondering what to do about Miss X.Y. and my manuscript.

It was the time of year when the whole countryside seemed to be bursting into bloom. The hawthorn was not yet fully out, but the air was strong with the sweet light perfume of wild flowers. Under the hedges were campions and dead-nettles and bird's-eye, turning their petals to the sun: beside the brook there were some big late mayflowers: sprinkled over the slopes were a few cowslips, looking dusty and etiolated beside the brilliant buttercups. I picked a bunch of wild forget-me-nots and greeny-gold wild mignonette. I thought it really was time Miss X.Y. did something about it. I was going to America.

I sat on top of a gate, filled with the poignance of leaving such a lovely country. Where could America show anything to compare with this for delicate, sweet-smelling lushness? Where else could the sky be so luminous and yet so gentle, the flowers so bright and yet so freshly perfumed? Where else could I feel was home? The beauty of it shone over everything, like a shimmering haze – one could stretch out one's hand and seem to touch it with one's finger-tips. Where else, except over English meadows, does beauty leap so nearly to the verge of being palpable? Do not ask me. I do not know.

Idly I watched some lambs cropping the grass. They had grown to look more like sheep; but every now and then one of them reverted to earlier lambhood, tried to take a pull of mother's-milk, and got buffeted in the ribs for its pains. I wondered where their fathers were – over the hills and far away. Only the human male is tied to its female and its young, tied and tamed. Oh! to be a ram, I thought, and then be over the hills and far away: till it occurred to me that rams cannot write books or get drunk with their friends – and in fact only feel rammish for deplorably limited periods.

I climbed down from the gate. I had decided to write to Miss X.Y. If it irritated her, so much the worse. If she did not want to read my book the lapse of more weeks would not bring her round to it. I walked down to the cottage and wrote her a polite letter immediately: the letter could not be posted for another twenty-four hours, but I felt much better for having written it. I made myself some tea and lay in my armchair dreaming of Myrtle.

The door of the cottage was open, and a bluebottle buzzed in. Suddenly I realized that summer had come. The end of summer is signalized by the last rose: the beginning by the first bluebottle. My last summer in England, and here it was. I was roused from my dream. The beginning of the summer: the end of an epoch. The bluebottle buzzed round the room, and I felt very solitary. Restlessly I went and stood in the doorway.

To my surprise I saw Steve coming up the road, alone and on foot. He appeared to be swinging along steadily, judging by the way his dark head bobbed up and down above the hedgerows. When he came into the last stretch, and saw me watching, he began to drag his feet.

'I hope you don't mind me coming to see you, Joe.' He looked diffident and awkward. 'I came on a bus to the village. I won't stay long.'

'You're just in time for tea.'

'Good.' The diffident expression changed immediately to one of simple anticipation. Steve came into the cottage. 'I'll get the cup and saucer myself,' he mumbled. 'Please don't bother about me, Joe.'

I sat down. I did not intend to bother about him. 'Look after yourself,' I said in a tough, hearty tone.

Steve glanced at me, and then poured himself some tea. Then he helped himself to a single chocolate biscuit – a very unusual performance. I waited to see what he had come for. I felt sure from his manner that he was eluding Tom for the afternoon.

Steve drew a deep breath, and then said:

'Joe, I've just done something terrible.'

'Oh, what?'

'I suppose everybody will say it's terrible . . .' He glanced down.

'Come on – out with it, Steve.'

Steve looked at me with a solemn tragic expression. He said: 'I've volunteered for the Merchant Navy.'

'Good Lord!'

Though I did not exactly burst into laughter, I was not far from it. I said: 'Say it again!'

The reason I asked him to repeat it was that I did not for a moment believe him. By nature I am a credulous man, but with Steve I had been forced to see that credulity, admirable though it may be, rarely offers the best means of arriving at the truth.

'I've volunteered for the Merchant Navy.'

Steve's tone deferentially indicated that he thought it was rather captious of me to make him repeat a remark I must have already heard.

'You can't have,' I said. I supposed it was a cold, unfeeling way of receiving such a dramatic piece of news, such a solemn, tragic, false, dramatic piece of news.

'But I really have, Joe.' Steve put down his cup and saucer, and looked at me with an anxious, imploring expression. Although Steve was given to egregious lying, he never took umbrage at being accused of it.

I knew nothing about the normal age of entry to the Merchant Navy, but I recollected reading parliamentary discussions about the age at which young men might be called up for compulsory military training.

'You're too young,' I said, on the off chance of defeating him.

'I'm not, Joe. Not for the Merchant Navy.' Steve was too tactful to make any such remark as 'You don't seem to believe me'.

'Have you actually signed on?' I said.

'Of course.'

'When?'

'This morning.'

'Is the office open on Saturdays?'

'Yes. How could I have signed on if it weren't?'

Steve sometimes broke down if you asked him enough questions. This time I saw that he was patiently going to prove that he had done it. I paused. During the pause Steve helped himself to another chocolate biscuit. He munched it. Then he poured out another cup of tea. Naturally I had not varied a hair's breadth from my original disbelief. I was inclined to think he had *thought of* volunteering: there were some handsome recruiting posters plastered about the town. In fact I thought he might have visited the recruiting office and made some inquiries. I took another biscuit myself. I said:

'What made you decide on this powerful step?'

'I've got to do something.'

'Going to sea is a bit drastic, isn't it?'

'It's the only way of escaping, Joe.'

'Escaping from what?'

'Tom, I suppose.'

'Good Lord!'

Steve glanced at me seriously. I turned to face him.

'Do you really want to escape from Tom?' I said, in the shrewd, penetrating manner of a psychologist.

'I don't want to be an accountant!'

'Is the Merchant Navy the only alternative to accountancy?'

'You don't understand, Joe.'

'What?'

Steve looked at me. 'Imagine what it's like to be in my place.'

'For once, Steve, my imagination boggles.'

Steve had been on the point of assuming his suffering look, but a smile supervened.

'I've always wondered,' I said, 'exactly what caused technical boggling of the imagination. Now I know.'

'It's nothing to laugh about. It's terrible.' Steve stood up. He walked across to the doorway, picking up another biscuit as he went.

'I'm sorry, Steve,' I followed him, pushing the plate of biscuits out of sight as I passed.

'Anyway, I've taken the step now, haven't I?'

'*You* know that, Steve.'

'You don't blame me, do you?'

'Blame you, Steve? Of course not.'

'Other people will.'

'Blaming is one of the favourite human occupations. People blame you whatever you do.'

'You are the first person I've told. I daren't tell my mother and father.'

'I think,' I said, 'you can expect Tom to do that.'

'Joe!'

We strolled across the road and leaned against a gate, looking idly at the cottage.

'I had to do it, Joe. I can't go on being an accountant.' Steve looked at me. 'It's the arithmetic. It's torment. And Tom wants me to go round to his house for a lesson three evenings a week.' His voice rose. 'Three evenings a week!'

'That certainly is torment,' I agreed, disloyally to Tom.

Steve paused. 'Anyway, it will be over now.' He pondered. 'I won't have to do any arithmetic in the Merchant

Navy, will I?'

'Not much.' I grinned. 'I guess you've already received enough training for the Merchant Navy in arithmetic. As in certain other basic subjects, too.'

An amused flicker appeared in Steve's eye, in spite of his agonized expression: it was merely momentary. He said:

'You don't understand, Joe.'

'What?'

Steve suddenly spoke with force. 'I want to sleep with women.'

'You get that as well in the Merchant Navy. While you're in port.'

'I mean it seriously.'

I looked away. 'I did realize that.' There was a long silence broken only by the occasional chirping and flutter of birds in the hedge. Steve stirred – I imagined he must be turning to look at me more closely as he spoke.

'Do you think it's silly of me? I mean, I'm only seventeen.'

'I don't think it's silly at all, Steve. No more than the things we all do are silly.'

'I want to get to know some girls.'

I nodded my head.

'I suppose you think I'm being stupid and conventional, Joe.'

I could not help smiling. 'No, Steve.'

'Sometimes I want to be just ordinary, Joe. Terribly ordinary.'

'I think you'll find it terribly tame.'

'I suppose I would. That's the trouble.'

'Don't let that put you off, Steve!'

'It doesn't. I want to start going out with girls, even if it is tame.'

This was not what I meant, but I did not propose to argue.

'I wish Tom would realize this,' Steve said.

It seemed to me that if Tom was trying to make Steve go round to his house three evenings a week he must have a pretty shrewd idea.

'I don't seem to be able to talk to him about it, Joe.'

I foresaw the day when he would, but held my tongue.

Steve turned and leaned his chest against the gate, looking up the field. The movement attracted the attention of some bullocks, who began to advance under the impression that we were going to feed them. Steve picked up a boulder and rolled it towards them.

'It's a relief to have told someone about it.'

I did not know whether he meant the relief of having told me about his signing-on for the Merchant Navy, which was fantasy, or of having told me about his adolescent woes, which were real. It is possible to get a deep relief from confessing something that is untrue: Steve got it frequently.

I said: 'These things work themselves out, you know.' I did not know what it meant, but I had learnt that meaningless remarks of this kind give a bit of comfort.

Steve said: 'I suppose I ought to be going back. Is there a bus?' He gave me a helpless look.

'There's a timetable on the desk. You know where it is.'

Steve slouched across the road and disappeared into the cottage. I began to meditate, on Steve and Tom, on Myrtle and me; and on the difficulty, the transience, the poignance of all human relationships.

I was roused from my meditation by the arrival of Tom's car. As an arrival it was sudden, noisy, unexpected and menacing.

'Have you seen Steve?'

'Yes. He's here.'

'Where?'

'In the cottage.'

Tom got out of the car. I did not move from where I was leaning against the gate. There were signs of passion in his face, a slight goggling of the eyes.

'I thought I'd find him here.'

I was puzzled. The cottage seemed an odd place for Tom to look for Steve – I began to wonder if it might have been pre-arranged.

Tom came and stood beside me, making an effort to look

unconcerned. He straightened his tie, which was wine-coloured – a mistake, in my opinion, since it enhanced the contrast between the gingery redness of his hair and the purplish redness of his face.

'It's been a beautiful day.' Tom glanced at the sky, which was melting into the tender shades of twilight; at the hedgerows, leafily stirring in the evening breeze. Glanced is the word for it: before I could expatiate on the charms of the flora, Tom said:

'Shall we go indoors?'

As if to convince me that he was not making a beeline for indoors to discover what Steve was doing, Tom said in a weighty, pompous tone:

'I have an announcement to make.'

We went into the cottage. Tom stared at Steve. Steve fluttered the pages of the bus timetable furtively.

Tom sat down. We all sat down.

'I have some news for both of you,' said Tom. 'I've had a most satisfactory talk with our senior partner this lunch-time, about my fellowship of the I.C.A. That's all settled –'

'Good,' I interrupted, thinking this was the announcement.

'Consequently,' Tom went on, 'I've decided my date of departure for the U.S.A. I've just ordered my tickets. I leave this country on June 15th.'

Steve and I were completely silent, I with surprise and Steve with shock. Tom had his eyes fixed on Steve.

It was useless to pretend the news had not induced a high state of tension, but I said, 'Well, well,' in a light easy tone, hoping to reduce it thereby.

Steve had his eyes fixed on the ground. Tom looked strong and determined.

'It means a break,' Tom said, 'but it's got to be done. Thank God we shall do it in time!' He looked at me. 'Robert says we must decide when you're to go.'

I nodded. I must say that I felt a pang. I thought Tom's tone was bullying. It is all very well to agree on the analysis of a situation; but to act upon it does not follow so readily for every man. Tom sensed my failing enthusiasm.

'It would be most unwise to delay it any longer.'

'I agree.'

My failing enthusiasm sprang from reluctance to leave England, not from lack of faith in our historical prophecy. I had great faith in our historical prophecy, based as it was on the word of Robert.

Tom and I exchanged our interpretations of the latest European events. I will not record them because they will make you think us feebler prophets than we really were – this may be called omission of true facts in the cause of art. Anyway, I think our motives were far from contemptible. Sympathy, I beg, for those who were wrong before the event instead of right after it.

The exchange of interpretations was brief, because Tom's interest was focused entirely on Steve's reaction. I felt embarrassed. It seemed to me the odds were now at least ten to one on Steve's producing his story about the Merchant Navy. There was a peculiar silence. I said:

'Would you like some sherry?'

Tom accepted, with a strained over-polite smile. Steve shrugged his shoulders. While I was taking the bottle out of the cupboard, Tom looked at my letters; that is, he examined the envelopes on my desk, in the cause of not flinching from the attempt to understand human nature. I had taken the precaution of sealing them.

'I see you've written to Miss X.Y.' He paused. 'Of course, if it had been me I should have gone up to London and seen her, weeks ago.'

I poured out the glasses of sherry, and we raised them to our lips. Tom and I drank ours. Steve, instead of drinking, said:

'Tom, I've volunteered for the Merchant Navy.'

The result was devastating. Either from the sherry going down the wrong way or from pure rage, Tom's face turned purple.

'What!' he shouted, in a great splutter.

He stood up. 'You silly little fool!' He went across to Steve, and Steve looked frightened as if he thought Tom were going to beat him. Steve was the taller but Tom easily the stronger. 'Tell me exactly what you've done!'

'I've volunteered for the Merchant Navy.'

'The details! I want the details!' shouted Tom.

I say that Steve looked frightened: he did – and yet I got a distinct impression that at the same time he was enjoying himself.

'When? Where?' Tom was asking him.

And Steve was replying, in spite of his supposed fright, in an easy, provocative manner. His small eyes were lazy and bright. Suddenly I felt sorry for Tom, who was beside himself with passion. I should have felt sorrier still for Tom if I had thought there was a word of truth in what Steve was saying.

'It's got to be stopped, immediately,' Tom said.

'It can't, Tom,' said Steve.

'I'll *buy* you out!' shouted Tom.

Steve was taken aback. His signing-on had now become so real to him, from the inflating power of Tom's belief in it, that he was taking Tom as seriously as Tom was taking him.

'You're under age,' Tom repeated. 'I'll buy you out!'

'But the money?' said Steve, in a tone of anguish.

Tom looked round him. 'If we go straight away and withdraw your signature it may not be too late.'

I could see that he knew no more about the legal side of it than I did. He took hold of Steve's arm.

'Now?' said Steve incredulously.

'Of course.'

'But I don't want to.'

'Don't you see what it means, you little fool!' Tom glared at him, and explained slowly, like a corporal explaining slowly to a private. 'If there isn't a war I shall go to America. And if there is a war you'll be at sea. In either case we shall be separated for ever!'

Steve displayed a mixture of superficial discomfort and basic equanimity.

'For ever!' Tom shouted.

I thought, 'Poor old Tom.' I saw this scene going on for a long time: Steve was lying back in his chair, and Tom was tireless.

They paused, so I intervened in a reasonable tone.

'It probably could be stopped if you acted rapidly.' Tom could never resist action, and I saw it as a means of getting them out of the house and back to the town.

'Exactly,' said Tom, seizing Steve's arm, and hauling him up.

'Not now, Tom,' said Steve. 'It's too late tonight. The office will be closed. We can't go now. I don't want to.'

'Come on!'

Steve had been pulled out of his chair. 'Let me drink my sherry first,' he cried.

Tom paid no heed. Steve was torn away from his sherry. I thought 'You worthless boy, that serves you right.' Tom dragged him into the car, and pressed the self-starter.

There was a mysterious clanking noise under the car and then silence.

The car would not start.

Tom tried again and again. He got out and lifted up the bonnet. Then he got back again. There were a few more sporadic noises, and then silence of striking permanence. Steve sat, hunched up and silent, inside the car. Tom, powerful and purple, engaged in action such as cranking the engine and stalking to and fro. I did nothing: I have occasionally felt like a professional scientist but never like a motor mechanic.

Tom muttered some kind of explanation. 'She won't start.'

And then the same thought struck both of us. 'We shall have to stay the night,' Tom said, in a masterful tone.

I was about to say there was another bus, and then remembered the wretched man had only till June 15th – I never doubted that Tom would leave for ever on June 15th. 'Who am I,' I asked myself, 'to stop him getting the most out of his last month, however singular that most may be?' I was not expecting Myrtle till the following afternoon.

'All right,' I said. 'I was going over to the pub later on.'

Tom nodded. 'We'll go for a stroll in the meantime.' He turned to the car: 'Now, Steve, you'd better get your coat.'

Reluctantly Steve got out of the car, went into the cottage, and emerged with his coat. Tom's eyes followed him. Then Tom and he walked away up the lane. I heard Tom's voice rising in power as it moved into the distance. The scene was going on.

I went indoors, and poured myself another glass of sherry. And I noticed that Steve's glass was empty – in the few seconds he had spent fetching his coat Steve had swigged off his sherry. I could not help smiling.

CHAPTER IV
NIGHT ON THE PARK

I was invited to have supper with Bolshaw and his wife at their house. I had taken care to meet Myrtle first of all. The interlude was over. Our situation had sprung up again: this time it was worse.

Myrtle lived in a street that debouched on the park. I was just entering it – I was a little late – when I met her, apparently already on her way to wherever she was seeing fit to go.

It was a light evening, and I could see from a long way off that she was in a state of abysmal depression. She had begun to look sadder and sadder during the last days. I suppose I was unfeeling and detached: I thought of it as her 'I'll-never-smile-again' expression. Really, she overdid it. I felt genuinely upset and, such was the weakness of my nature, faintly irritated by remorse. I kissed her warmly on the cheek.

'I'm sorry I'm late, darling.' I had a perfectly satisfactory excuse.

'It's all right,' she said, in a distant tone.

'Where are you going?'

Myrtle put her hand to her forehead. 'My dressmaker's.'

'Oh,' I said helpfully, 'that's nice.'

Myrtle looked at me. I knew it was not nice at all. I put my arm round her waist – when anyone looks woebegone I cannot help trying to cheer them up.

'I'm sorry you're feeling so low, darling.'

I suppose Myrtle thought the remark became me ill when my conduct was at the root of her depression.

'Have you been sleeping badly?'

Myrtle nodded her head.

'Nightmares?'

Myrtle nodded again. She roused herself sufficiently to make a tragic revelation. 'I dream that I'm *two people*.'

Satan entered into me. 'Two?' I said. 'There's no cause for alarm till it gets to ten.'

Cheering people up may be good-natured: it appears that making jokes is sadistic. All I can say is that if somebody had said it to me I should have been amused.

We were at the top of the street. Tramcars passed between us and the park. Beyond the railings we could see couples lying under the trees, and little boys playing cricket. I observed two youths from the school approaching us on bicycles: I recognized them by their blazers. They turned out to be Benny and his younger brother. They took off their caps very politely; and rode on without staring, though they missed no detail of Myrtle's appearance.

I may say that despite Myrtle's obvious misery she was beautifully dressed. I gave her great credit for that. She was wearing a new summer frock, made of material prettily printed in a pattern of greens and bright yellow and covered all over with handwriting. Her shoes were American. Her hair was dressed in the latest style.

'That's Benny,' I said encouragingly. 'I've told you about him. Do you remember?'

'I didn't know he was so old.'

I had frequently told her he was nineteen.

'He looks quite well-behaved,' she went on, apparently remembering at least that I had told her definitely that he was not well-behaved.

'He's a menace,' I said, with conviction. 'Some day one of Benny's tricks will get him thrown out. And me too, probably. I shall heave a great sigh of relief when he leaves.'

Myrtle had ceased to listen: it made me feel as if I were babbling.

I touched the material of her dress. 'Where did this come from?'

She told me without interest.

I kept my finger inside her sleeve, so that it touched her flesh.

'Darling,' I said, looking at her face.

Myrtle looked back at me. For a moment I thought she was going to weep.

'Darling,' I said, 'I do wish I could think of something to say.'

Myrtle made a perceptible effort to smile, but failed.

I wanted to take her into my arms and comfort her. The trouble was that I could only have comforted her by taking her into a registry office.

I realized that I was now late for my next appointment. Myrtle showed no signs of moving. More trams passed with a cheerful clang: I ought to have been on one of them. At last I said: 'I must go now, darling.'

Myrtle looked down. I took hold of her hand, and held on to it tenderly. There was something else I had to say before I could go.

'Are you coming out to the cottage this week-end?'

Myrtle did not reply.

I felt embarrassed, ashamed, apprehensive and determined.

'Are you, darling?'

Myrtle looked at me, absolutely blank-faced: 'Do you want me to?'

'Of course.' There was a pause. 'Will you?' I held her fingers tighter.

Myrtle made the faintest possible gesture that could be recognized as assent.

I kissed her and we parted. I took a tram down to the station and there changed to a bus. Throughout the journey my thoughts turned round and round. Why? how? and why? again. I knew by experience that she suffered this mysterious ebb and flow of mood, but I felt slightly reassured if I could link it with some external event. I had told her that Tom was due to leave England on June 15th. No event seemed too irrelevant for me to strive fatuously to make it relevant. I had not told her about Steve's signing-on for the Merchant Navy, because he never had signed-on:

Tom found that out by a dramatic visit to the recruiting office. I tried to think what precisely I had said or done.

My efforts led me nowhere, and I joined the evening's entertainment in a mildly abstracted fashion.

Just as I was about to leave Bolshaw's house there was a telephone call for me. I knew what it was going to be. Myrtle wanted me to meet her again, on my way home.

Myrtle met me at the station. It was after eleven o'clock. She was already standing there, waiting, when I arrived. She had been home for a coat to put over her summer frock.

'What is it, darling?' I said.

By the light of the street lamps I could see faint signs of animation in her face.

'I wanted to see you again.'

I stared at her anxiously. Somehow I had wanted to see her as well. It felt inevitable, as if we had been drawn together. I did not speak.

We stood on the edge of the pavement, facing each other. Myrtle said:

'I wanted to say I was sorry for being rude to you earlier this evening.'

I felt a sudden stab of pain as I recognized the words – apology of one who is in love to one who is loved. How well I recognized it! You apologize to the one who ought to apologize to you – to such straits does love reduce dignity and common sense.

The one who is loved invariably behaves badly, and I was no exception. I thought, 'Oh God! She's in love with me.'

'That's all right, darling,' I said. Fortunately I did not utter the most cruel remark the loved one can utter in these circumstances – 'Forget it!' The result was more or less the same.

Myrtle drew away from me. It was not all right.

I put my arm round her waist, and began to lead her along the road.

'I realized you weren't feeling well, darling,' I said.

'Well?'

'It's a sort of malaise you're having. Being touchy is part

of it.'

'Is it?' There was a faint edge to her voice.

I said comfortably: 'I wasn't perturbed.'

'Then you ought to have been!'

I was alarmed. Purposely I pretended not to have caught on. 'It wouldn't do for us both to be touchy at the same time, or else...'

'Yes,' Myrtle breathed. 'Or else?...'

'It just wouldn't,' I said. 'Clearly.'

We were silent for a while.

Myrtle was walking slowly. I suppose she must have felt me tending to go faster: I found it hard to get along at Myrtle's pace.

'Do you want to go home?' she said.

'No. What makes you think that?'

'It's getting late.' A tram lumbered past us, dimly lit and filled with people who had been to the cinemas. 'You mustn't miss your last tram.'

I said I was going to take her home before I left her.

Myrtle said: 'I suppose they were angry when I rang you up tonight.'

'Angry,' I said, in astonishment. 'Why should they be? I think Bolshaw thought you must be slightly eccentric, that's all.'

'Were you angry?'

'Not at all. I'm glad you rang.'

'Why?'

'I don't know. I think I wanted to see you again, because...'

'Because of what?'

'I don't know, darling.' I felt embarrassed. 'Because of the way we parted.'

'What was wrong with that? I thought you seemed satisfied.'

'Really!'

I stopped. Myrtle stopped and we stared at each other. We were quite near the end of her street, but there was no street lamp and we could not see each other very well.

'What's the matter?' said Myrtle.

'You say I seemed satisfied. You can't have any idea, darling. How could I have been satisfied?'

'I said I would see you at the week-end.'

'I thought you didn't want to come.'

Myrtle burst out with great emotion:

'It didn't seem to matter to you if I didn't!'

'Of course it does.'

'I seem to see less and less of you!'

I did not know what to say. She had seen me at the cottage just as often.

'Oh, I don't know,' Myrtle went on, passionately. 'Here we are now ... Why is it like this, darling? You go out to see your friends and I spend the evening with my dressmaker.' She looked at me. 'I spend hours and hours with people I don't really want to be with!'

People she did not want to be with – Haxby, she must be including Haxby.

'Darling ...' I began.

'It's true. You're always somewhere else.'

'It isn't true. I have to go and see other people sometimes.' I was on the point of saying 'You could always come with me if you would' but it seemed cruel: also it was not quite true. Even had she felt at ease with all my friends, I should have wanted to see them alone sometimes.

We then began a futile argument about how often I ought to spend evenings with different friends and acquaintances. Myrtle was facing the road, and as a tram swayed past the light crossed her face. I was relieved to see no tears.

'Since Easter I seem to have seen absolutely nothing of you.'

I enumerated meetings missed through accidents chiefly on her part. I brought up the Saturday afternoon at the games field when she had dropped me. My list was impressive – impressive as a list of facts, but not as the truth.

'And it doesn't seem to matter to you,' Myrtle said, as if she had not heard.

There was a pause. We were still standing in the same

place. People were passing us. I said:

'Let's go on the park!'

I knew that it was a useless thing to say, that the scene could only go on and produce no result.

We walked through the gates, and turned off along a narrow path beside some shrubbery, disturbing a boy and girl who were locked in each other's arms against the railings. They seemed curiously remote from us, as if love-making were of no interest.

We resumed our argument about how I should dispose of my evenings.

At last we came to a seat. Arid though the argument was, we could not leave it. Anyone who has ever been involved in this kind of scene will recall the peculiar boredom of it, the peculiar boredom that ties both of you together, like twine round a parcel.

There were long periods between each remark, enormously long. For me they were often spent in reframing my next remark, trying to take off the edge of my words, trying to transmute them into something of whose hardness I should be less ashamed afterwards – I could not forget that Myrtle was a tender girl and so very young. On the other hand some of the periods were spent in thinking how late it was; and others in watching car-headlamps moving along the main road – something obscured the lower part of them, a palisading, possibly. It is hard to keep one's concentration up to concert pitch in this sort of scene.

As a minor counter-attack I put forward the proposition that I never seemed to go anywhere myself nowadays. If I was not seeing Myrtle it was not because I was seeing someone else. Naturally this did not please: second only to my offence of seeing other friends was my offence of spending evenings alone.

At last, in desperation, I gave the argument a heave which overturned it on to a deeper plane. I said gently:

'Aren't we getting into this mess because I'm going to America and we shall be separated?'

Myrtle softened a little. 'Well, it is really....'

'What can we do, darling? I shall have to go.'

Myrtle's emotion broke out again. 'You don't seem to mind! You want to go!'

'I don't want to go.'

'You said you did.'

'There are some things I want to do most. To do them I shall have to get out.'

'But that needn't mean being separated. That's what I don't see. You never mention me going!'

I was astounded. After all the time I had spent persuading her to think about taking a job in America, it seemed incredible. She had never listened to me. Her going to America meant only one thing – being married to me. She was unable to listen if I talked of anything else.

Hastily I began to invent reasons why she could not go to America in a state of dependence on me. I should have no money, no job.

'I don't see that it matters,' said Myrtle. 'If you were fond of somebody you'd want them to be there all the time.'

'But not in those circumstances!'

'Why not?' said Myrtle, inexorably, there being a good deal in what she said. 'I should have thought it meant assured happiness.'

'Assured happiness!'

'And you could *work*!'

Heaven help me! I thought. By work she must mean school-teaching. I realized what I had always suspected – that not for a moment did she take my writing seriously. Assured happiness!

'You'd be settled,' said Myrtle, in a tone that was not the tone of a tender girl or a very young one either.

'Tamed!' said I, in an anguished voice. I saw myself settled, with someone I was fond of there all the time. There all the time, mark you! How could I write books about people? How could I go out and discover what they were like? How could I support my curiosity about them? How could I watch what they were doing, have long intimate talks with them – and, if it came to that, get into bed with some of them? How indeed?

'What's wrong with being settled?' Myrtle ignored my

interjection. 'Everybody else is.'

I fell straight into the trap.

'I'm not like everybody else!'

'But you could be!' Myrtle went on. 'If only you'd – if only you'd...' She gave the sentence up, but not the meaning. The latter was only too clear to me.

Myrtle could not utter the word 'marry'. In the whole conversation neither of us had used it. I could not bring myself to utter it, as a child will not utter the name of something it does not want to happen. And I seemed to have hypnotized Myrtle into doing the same thing.

Myrtle was not entirely wrong about me: that was the trouble. Somewhere she touched in me a vestigial romantic belief that if I were abandonedly in love I should want her to be there all the time. For a moment I sensed what her idea of permanence could mean, what it could mean to me if I were somebody else.

'We can't go on talking like this, darling.' I shook my head. 'There is something deeper than these tedious mechanical reasons. I just can't have anyone about me. Somehow I do know that I want –' I searched for a phrase – 'I want to go on alone.'

It was an unusual phrase, that must have made it sound as if I were aiming at the North Pole. Myrtle said nothing.

'I've always felt like that, darling,' I said.

'Yes,' said Myrtle. 'You were careful to tell me that at the beginning.'

'Didn't you think I meant it?'

'Yes. Then.'

'Why not now?'

'It was different. We weren't so fond of each other then.'

'That doesn't alter it. Darling,' I said, 'my personality's stuck. It can't be changed.'

Myrtle had stopped listening, and I said under my breath, 'Even under the regenerating influence of a woman!'

We were silent. I felt cold. It was a dark night, with a clouded sky – no wind, yet coldish. It must have been the first time I had ever noticed the cold before Myrtle did. I took hold of her hand, and helped her up from the seat. We began to walk. Myrtle began to walk away from the direction of her home, but I gradually steered her round.

'What are we to do?'

Myrtle's voice was soft and melancholy, and she looked at the sky. Yet there was a reasonable note in it, as if she were facing the problem realistically. Still looking away, she repeated it. We were sufficiently in tune for me to know that she was raising the question of whether we should part.

I shrank from it.

'What do you think we ought to do?' I asked.

I heard her draw in her breath sharply. She knew it was not really a question.

I said: 'Darling, do you think I ought – do you think it would be better if I started keeping out of the way?'

'We couldn't not see each other!' Her voice was louder and more passionate. I thought this affair would have to end.

'I ought not to have let this happen,' I said.

'I don't see that we *shall* have to!' said Myrtle, cutting into my maunderings.

'But what else?' I began a long speech. We were standing at a cross-roads, and a tram-repair lorry came up, with a violent clatter of loose tools and implements. We were in the middle of the night.

Myrtle said something.

'What did you say?'

'Only more protestations.'

We were both silent, worn out. Aimlessly we watched two young policemen in mackintoshes shut themselves up in their little police telephone-box: a small red light flashed on the top of it.

'I think you'll have to think of it like that,' I said.

'Well, I can't . . . And I don't suppose I ever shall!'

We moved to go home. Nothing was decided. We stopped and looked at each other. When were we to meet again? I could not bring myself to ask her.

'Do you want me to come on Sunday?' Myrtle asked gently.

'Yes. But darling, I can't ask you like that. Not now. . . .'
We were holding each other's fingers.
At last I mumbled: 'I shall be there. . . .'
'Then of course I shall come.'
We whispered good night.

I walked home by the road along which I had been used to cycle so joyously on Sunday nights. I felt utterly empty. I wondered what Myrtle thought was the outcome of our scene. I asked myself how much good it had done. I thought I saw now that an end of it all was appointed for us. I could have wept.

CHAPTER V

IN DISGRACE

At this point I began to look forward much less equivocally to my departure for the U.S.A.

For the time being I looked secure in my pedagogue's niche. Ever since our talk at the games field, Bolshaw and I had been on good terms; so I judged the headmaster was hearing less about my irresponsibility, laziness and other forms of moral delinquency. All the same, I thought with unrestrained pleasure about giving in my notice at the end of the term. It would be a real coup to walk out when I was obviously in no danger of being pushed out.

One fine Monday morning I sat in the playground, counting the accumulation of worries that rose from my enforced vocation. There was a row of ancient lime trees growing up through the asphalt, and I used to let the sixth form boys sit under them to work during the summer term. It was pleasant: the sun shone down; girls in summer frocks walked briskly past the railings; scarlet buses ran to and fro.

While waiting for Frank and the others to come from prayers I was making a list of physics questions likely to be set in the coming Higher School Certificate examination. I was very adept at what the boys called 'spotting'. My skill was widely recognized, and the boys had suggested, with the intention of helping me on my way, that instead of dispensing my information free to a whole form I should sell it to them individually.

Suddenly I stared at my divining-chart. 'Why am I working on this? Why am I not writing a masterpiece?' The answer was that I had written a masterpiece; but my letter to Miss X.Y. had produced only the information that she was touring in the Balkans. 'Why am I working on this chart?' No answer, except that it fell within the scope of duties I had to perform in order to buy myself food and lodging.

From the building came the sound of the boys at their devotions. The organ chimed out and they began to sing 'Blest are the pure in heart'. Strangely enough, in spite of all they did, many of them managed to remain pure in heart. From plain observation I decided that superficially innocent they were not: yet it was quite easy to see them as surprisingly free from contamination. Pureness of heart is an odd thing, rarely comprehended by the righteous. I could write a lot more about it.

Frank came out to me, with a firm, graceful tread.

'I wanted to see you before the others come.' I saw him looking diffidently along his nose. 'Have you heard what happened on Saturday night? Trevor was run in for dangerous driving.'

Now you see the sort of worries that rose from my enforced vocation.

Frank shook his head lugubriously. 'It's a sod, isn't it?'

'What'll happen to him?'

'He'll probably get his licence endorsed.'

'The rows there'll be!'

Frank and I stared at each other.

'Hello!' Trevor had quietly joined us. The sun lit up his golden hair. Sometimes his small pale face looked debauched, sometimes angelic. This morning, when it would have been helpful to look angelic, it looked irritatingly debauched. 'I suppose you've heard?' he said, spinning out the last words with a nasal emphasis.

'Were you drunk?' I said.

'I wish I had been. I didn't do anything wrong. I think the cop was just bored. He said I jumped the traffic-light at the corner of Park Road.'

'Were there any witnesses?'

'Yes. Another cop coming off the park. One of those officious cops that goes round preventing people from copulating on the grass.'

'For Pete's sake!' Frank seized him by the back of the neck to shake him.

'Were you alone?'

'No. I'd got a girl.' Trevor languidly pushed back the hair that had fallen when Frank shook him, but there was an unmistakable look of bravado and provocative triumph in his face.

I had always known we should have trouble with Trevor.

'I didn't even jump the traffic-light.'

Frank interrupted. 'Look out! Here comes Benny and Fred.'

With their faces shining like the bright sky, the other pair joined us. Fred was soppily singing, to the tune of 'Blest are the pure in heart', some words he was making up as he went along. 'I do not want to work ... pom, pom ... I'd rather sit and dream ...' He stopped singing: 'About luv....'

Benny jumped behind my chair. 'What are you doing, sir? Making us a list of questions?' He breathed heavily down the back of my neck.

'I'm goin' to make a list,' said Fred, 'of questions we *won't* get. And then I won't 'ave to learn them.'

I ought to say they had all passed the examination the previous year and pretended they were going to fail it this.

Frank and Trevor had taken out their pocket-combs and were combing their hair. Benny and Fred made some show of composing themselves, since they were on view to the public. I began to collect the written work they had done over the week-end.

Out of the corner of my eye I saw Bolshaw crossing the yard. He beckoned to me. I had to go.

I followed Bolshaw into the laboratory. His form of silent oafs looked up and then down again. Bolshaw's forms spent the whole of the summer term in silent revision for the examinations.

From Bolshaw's serious statesman-like expression I deduced that he had some project in hand. I was afraid he might be going to try and lure me into his research again.

He sat down at his desk with a heavy shambling movement. It occurred to me that he was looking older; his eyes looked faintly bleary, and his false teeth a trifle greener – though why false teeth turning green should be a sign of age I did not know.

'I've been working!' Bolshaw blew through his whiskers. 'I enjoy it.'

I concealed my astonishment.

Bolshaw opened his case and pulled out the folder containing some of his research papers. 'I should like you to have a look at this.'

I realized that nothing could stop him. He repeated his earlier propositon. He held up his hand as if he were going to give me his blessing.

'I think the time has come,' he said.

The time had indeed come. Simms could not delay his retirement beyond the end of the term. In our present stable condition of amity, Bolshaw was bound to nominate me as his own successor.

My heart sank at the prospect of having to do his computations for him. Till suddenly it occurred to me that I could take away the papers, so satisfying him, and not do the computations, so satisfying myself.

My inspiration was not, of course, an original one. Miss X.Y. had had it long before me, and hosts of people before her. I could have kicked myself for not having accepted in the first instance. To give the maximum satisfaction one should always accept people's papers, whether one ever intends to read them or not.

As I assented I gave Bolshaw a look of restrained enthusiasm. He was too shrewd for me to risk anything really effusive.

Bolshaw appeared to be satisfied. 'I always admire a man,' he said, with characteristic impartiality, 'who recognizes when the time has come.'

I did not feel called upon to reply.

'I wish our headmaster,' he went on, 'gave me cause for this type of admiration.' Every word echoed down the room.

'It's a pity,' said Bolshaw, 'that I'm not the headmaster. A genuine pity.' He blew through his whiskers again. 'What?'

It was more than I could do to keep any trace of glimmer out of my eye. As he noticed it an answering glimmer came into his eye as well. I would not have thought him capable of it. I suddenly saw a clever, sensitive man behind this ludicrous façade. There was a moment of *rapport*. I thought 'Bolshaw's not a bad chap,' and I thought he was thinking the same about me.

I went back to my pupils. I found Trevor calculating quietly, like an angel-child, with his slide-rule; and Benny absorbed in tracing out a simple wireless circuit. Perhaps I was wrong to let other people's doings oppress me. It was highly satisfactory to be secure in my job. After all, I had got to consider the eventuality of my trip to America not coming off.

A few days later I was teaching a form of junior boys in the laboratory. I had them at the end of the afternoon for two consecutive periods, in which they were supposed to do experiments. They were tired. So was I. In the·last two periods of the afternoon everybody was slack, and on this occasion the weather was warm and humid and oppressive. Across the playground I could see shapeless grey clouds, apparently hanging round the tops of the lime trees: I felt as if they were hanging round the top of my head as well.

I decided to ease my state by taking a leaf out of Bolshaw's book. Instead of trying to teach them anything, I commanded the boys to open their note-books and do silent revision for the examinations. Then I slumped down into my chair.

For a while I was occupied with reflections on my private affairs. The room was silent. I thought about Myrtle and America – a cloud of claustrophobic reflections hung like a veil between me and the light of happiness. There were clouds everywhere. The boys began to whisper to each other: silent revision had begun to pall.

I walked round the room, threading my way methodically between the benches. Sweat glistened on the boys' foreheads. Their hair was slightly matted and their collars soiled. Some of those who had really been revising, and so had no cause to feel guilty, looked up at me reproachfully. With a blank expression I moved on. There were toffee-papers on the floor. I inspected a boy's note-book at random, and brought to light a drawing that must have been on its way round the class. The drawing was quite unconnected with the subject the boys were revising. I tore it up and left the bits on the bench. Then I sat down again.

I began to think about the drawing. 'Why,' I asked myself, 'were they passing that round instead of studying a diagram of the earth's magnetic field?' 'Because,' I answered myself, 'it was much, much more interesting.' The subject of the drawing had fascinated the human race since the beginning of time. The earth's magnetic field had not. The boys' heads were bent silently again over their note-books. Poor little devils!

A bell rang for the end of the first period. The boys looked up. In a mood of compassion, I suddenly said:

'Who'd like to go for a walk round the yard?'

I could not have said anything sillier in the circumstances. Any schoolmaster will tell you, even I can tell you, that you should always let sleeping boys lie. I deliberately woke mine up. The idea was reasonable enough, and certainly it was kindly: not two minutes had elapsed before I regretted it.

There were cries of delighted surprise. It was the first time such a thing had ever happened. The rest of the school was bathed in a droning silence. I specified one circuit of the playground and immediate return to the class-room.

The boys rushed out. Through the window I watched them happily make their circuit. And then they embarked on a second circuit. They did not return. And the noise they made echoed wildly back to the building.

I strode out into the playground. 'Come back!' I shouted furiously.

The boys stopped. They looked up at me. I glanced up at the windows of the school. From every class-room stared the face of a master: from the headmaster's window stared the face of the headmaster. Instantly I thought: 'There's going to be a row about this!'

The boys went back into the class-room and spent the rest of the afternoon in apprehensive, agitated silence. I did the same. They were afraid I was going to punish them. I was much too preoccupied to bother. I was expecting a visit from the headmaster. The only way I could have punished them was by keeping them in after school, and I had every intention of making myself scarce the moment the last bell sounded.

I escaped, that afternoon. I received a letter from the headmaster next morning. It began:

Dear Mr Lunn: I really think I must ask you to reconsider your choice of vocation as a teacher. After...

That is enough. I was not exactly sacked; I was not exactly anything. Yet in no sense was it possible to interpret the letter as favourable to my career in pedagogy. I viewed it with alarm. 'One more letter like this,' I thought, 'and things will be serious!'

I could not blame Bolshaw for intervening, because he was away ill. It was entirely my own fault. And yet, it seemed to me that my crime was not great. In the past I had committed greater. Why had the headmaster seen fit to act on this one?

From questioning the headmaster's actions, I went on to question my own. I was soon immersed in serious philosophical doubts. Perhaps the headmaster was right. It might well be that a schoolmaster really ought to behave like a schoolmaster. If I could not behave like a schoolmaster, perhaps I ought not to be one.

This left me faced with the most alarming question of all.

'What *can* I behave like?'

PART THREE

CHAPTER I

FALSE ALARM

The next few times we met, Myrtle and I were chiefly concerned with talking about the headmaster's letter. I am afraid we were taking an opportunity of not talking about ourselves. A week-end at the cottage had restored us, and our night on the park was not mentioned again. Nothing had been resolved: our fate still hung over us, but in tacit agreement we were ignoring it. I asked myself why we should not go on ignoring it. I was willing to ask anyone else – except Tom.

'You're behaving like ostriches,' he said.

'And what's wrong with the ostrich?' I asked. 'It's despised very unjustly. I've a great fellow-feeling for the ostrich. An ostrich doesn't look things in the face.'

Tom made an indecent rejoiner.

'I can see that looking things in the face is a moral exercise,' I said. 'But does it do the slightest good? Sometimes it does not. Some things are much better not looked in the face. You ought to know that.' I paused. 'Anyone with a grain of tact and kindliness knows it.'

Tom was silenced. I considered that I had won a small victory. I was willing to call a small victory anything which prolonged my pleasant relations with Myrtle.

In the meantime I responded with perverse anger to the prospect of being asked to resign. Out of pride mingled with political ineptitude I refused to go and see the headmaster.

Myrtle, with commendable common sense, advised me to placate the headmaster: she did not want me to move to a job somewhere else. Tom strongly advised me to go and denounce him. Neither of them understood or sympathized with my passivity. To me it seemed the way of the world. Nobody could know as well as I, who, whatever else I might be, was not a prig, the roll of my manifold offences against society.

'Darling, you didn't do anything wrong!' Myrtle said, one evening as we sat in a public-house. Outside it was raining.

'I know,' I said obtusely, 'but that doesn't have anything to do with it. As you see, my sweet.' I shaped a small pool of beer on the table into a pattern. 'You talk,' I said, getting the argument on to a really abstract footing, 'as if there were a connection between crime and punishment. I can see practically none.'

Poor Myrtle had no idea what I was talking about. She could break social conventions without a qualm; but that did not stop her feeling they were right and pretending she had not broken them.

'Darling,' she said, 'sometimes I really don't know what to make of you.' She was reproachful and cross.

'All right,' I said, relenting. I smiled. 'I'll do something about it.'

Myrtle was right. The headmaster, out of weakness and exasperation, had allowed himself to be provoked beyond the limits other people would admit.

Myrtle took a small sip of beer thoughtfully.

'What will you do, darling?' she said, looking at me. Reflection was over for her, if not for me. We were on common ground again.

I decided to consult Bolshaw.

'I thought Bolshaw wanted the headmaster to get rid of you, darling.'

I explained to Myrtle about my part in Bolshaw's research. She listened with interest. I could see that she now saw much stronger reasons why Bolshaw might want me to stay. I cannot say she looked shrewd or calculating – she was too young for that. Yet her soft pink cheeks had a brighter tinge, and her brown eyes shone with a more hopeful light.

The landlord switched on the wireless, and the din made

it hard for us to converse. Outside, it was still raining. We sat quietly holding each other's hand.

Next morning I saw Bolshaw. For once I had done the right thing. It happened to be Bolshaw's first morning at school after being away ill. He did not know about the headmaster's letter to me. It was a surprise to him. Bolshaw was always surprised if anyone did anything without having previously been advised to do so by him.

'Fancy him writing you a letter!' said Bolshaw, in a grand, slow manner, as if it were scarcely credible that the headmaster's hand was strong enough to hold a pen.

I showed him the letter. Bolshaw read it carefully. He was sitting in the staff-room at the time. He lifted his head, and the light gleamed on the steel frames of his spectacles. He kept his head lifted: I thought he was not going to bring it down again.

'What is it supposed to mean?' he asked.

I shrugged my shoulders, and looked at him with the nearest I could muster to a solemn, repentant expression. I described the occasion which had provoked the letter. I have to admit that I did not describe it to Bolshaw as I have described it to you. I doubt if you would recognize the description I gave Bolshaw.

On the other hand Bolshaw was not a fool. He knew me well enough. I tried to maintain my solemn, repentant expression for the sake of keeping up the appearances to which he attached so much importance, but I did not for a moment assess them at more than a marginal value in the balance he was weighing up. How much did he want me to be sacked? How much did he need me to assist in his research? How much did he deplore independent action on the part of the headmaster? I do not know. I stood waiting while he swept across some kind of balance-sheet that was beyond my comprehension. All I cared for was to know whether the total for me was printed in black or red. It came out black.

Bolshaw handed me back the letter. 'A silly letter,' he said. 'A silly letter.'

I put it in my pocket.

'Let me give you some advice, Lunn!'

I knew I was safe. I nodded meekly.

Bolshaw threw back his blond head again. His voice resounded like that of a mythical god.

'Keep your nose to the grindstone!'

Later in the morning I rang up Myrtle. I repeated the conversation verbatim.

'Then it's all right, darling?'

'Bolshaw's going to see the headmaster today.'

I went back again into the school. In a sense it was all right. At least I was going to escape being asked to resign.

Though Myrtle and I were going together again, she did not give up Haxby. He existed as a perpetual reminder to me that all was not well – and I was damnably jealous of him.

I never knew Haxby, but I can tell you what he looked like. He was tall, dark and skinny; and he had a friend who was slightly less tall, dark and skinny. They had intense black eyes and jerky movements. I thought their appearance was mildly degraded, and I called them the Crows. I could see that Myrtle was wounded. I called them the Crows in a careless, natural, confident tone, as if it would never occur to anybody to call them anything else.

You may think I was being cruel to Myrtle: I can only say that Myrtle was deliberately tormenting me.

Myrtle frequently made it clear that she preferred the Crows' company to mine. They were always available; and they were young, inexperienced, never likely to give her good advice, ready to lead her into things she really liked – such as playing inane games at parties, listening to gramophone records, showing devotion to culture by long pretentious discussions, and staying up half the night.

Myrtle knew that I disliked her preference thoroughly. It was not in my style. It went further than that. It was a powerful affront to some of my deepest feelings. At this time my deepest feelings circulated round two activities – one was writing books, the other making love to Myrtle. I thought she made it only too clear that she did not care at all for the first. I would gladly have thrashed her for it. Unfortunately, thrashing your young woman does not make her admire you more as a novelist. I felt frustrated, angry and hurt. When I thought of marrying Myrtle – yes, there were many, many moments when I did think of marrying her – this angry hurt recurred. I could not get over it. It stuck, as they say, in my craw. And my *cri-de-cœur* was one of such anguish that it must be recorded.

'*She doesn't believe in me as a writer!*'

And so I ask you not to be too hard on me for condemning the Crows. But a veil over *cris-de-cœur*! They are embarrassing.

'How are the Crows?' I would say lightly.

'All right,' Myrtle would reply in a distant unhappy voice, indicating that she was too far borne down to argue with me.

And she would look at me with a soft, appealing, reproachful expression, as much as to say she would never go near them if she could be with me all the time. It was the soft, appealing, reproachful expression of blackmail.

One Sunday morning Myrtle arrived at the cottage with a hangover, after an evening with the Crows.

'Bohemianism!' I cried, in a righteous tone to which print can never do justice.

You may think I had no room to express moral indignation. No more I had. No more have you, I suspect, half the time you express moral indignation – but does that stop you any more than it stopped me?

'Bohemianism!' I repeated, as if once were not enough.

Myrtle was appropriately flabbergasted.

I took Myrtle, figuratively speaking, by the scruff of the neck. I took her to the Dog and Duck for lunch, and back again in double-quick time.

The same night I asked Myrtle if she would like to go to Oxford with me the following week-end to see Robert. Myrtle was pleased with the idea. I thought if she was in Oxford she could not be with Haxby. I was pleased with the idea myself. And then I noticed an unmistakable smile of satisfaction on Myrtle's face. I had been led into doing just what she wanted. So much for the soft, appealing, reproachful looks given you by beautiful, ill-used girls!

Yet when the next week-end came near, Myrtle's enthusiasm vanished. She was afraid of meeting Robert; and she feared more discussion of our plans for going to America.

However, Myrtle did not flinch. When we met at the railway station on Saturday afternoon she was showing a brave front. She was dressed elegantly and a trifle theatrically. She had a very pretty dress and a new hat, with which she had seen fit to wear an Edwardian veil. Anyone could see the veil was becoming, but the effect was eccentric. I smiled to myself, thinking that girls of twenty-two can never help overdoing it. I was touched, and kissed her, through the veil, with great feeling.

And as I kissed Myrtle I noticed that her breath smelt odd. I looked at her closely. Her cheeks were highly coloured, and her eyes looked bright and strained. Her breath smelt of gin.

'What's the matter?' I asked.

Myrtle looked at me. 'Darling,' she said, '*you* know.'

My knees knocked together. 'Oh!' I cried. I knew exactly what she meant.

We were standing in the station entrance. The sun was shining brightly through the glass roof. A taxi drew up beside us, and a porter pushed us out of the way. I took hold of Myrtle's arm to hold her up. What a way to begin a week-end!

I led Myrtle towards the ticket office. I questioned her, but I did not doubt that she was speaking the truth. In spite of all I might have said or thought about her, I really trusted her completely. We were passing a glass case containing a model locomotive, brilliantly illuminated. The Flying Scotsman.

As usual on such occasions, I assumed a knowing matter-of-fact expression.

Myrtle's expression was less knowing, less matter-of-fact.

I said: 'It's happened before, you know.' My voice sounded clear and firm. It was the only thing about me that was clear and firm. 'There's no need to worry.'

I bought the tickets.

'Perhaps I ought not to go,' said Myrtle, looking up at me in great anxiety. 'You go by yourself.'

I glanced at her in surprise and refused to go without her. She took hold of my arm. 'You won't tell Robert, will you, darling?'

'Of course not.' I thought I should have to tell Robert quickly enough it if turned out not to be a false alarm. He would have to lend me money.

Myrtle sat opposite to me in the railway carriage, looking meek and distracted, inside an Edwardian veil.

At Bletchley, when we changed trains, I bought Myrtle a glass of gin.

When we reached Oxford we went straight to our hotel. Myrtle stood in the middle of the stuffy little bedroom, which smelt as if people had been sleeping in it for years.

'Could you buy me a bottle of Kuyper's, darling?'

'Of course.' I did not know why I had so much faith in the efficacy of gin. I suppose the less idea you have of what to do the more readily you take over someone else's faith.

I made off to my old wine merchant's with an energetic, resourceful stride. How can men who do not know what they are about walk with an energetic, resourceful stride? They do, shams that they are.

The weather had changed. The sun had disappeared, leaving a grey, drizzly afternoon. I stood on the street corner, waiting for a stream of bicycles to pass, and I was poignantly beset by nostalgia for my undergraduate days.

I turned into Broad Street, and ran into Tom.

I was astonished. Tom was supposed to be enjoying his turn at the cottage.

'What are you doing here?'

'I got a letter this morning from the American Institute of Chartered Accountants,' Tom said, with a bland, pompous gesture. 'I thought it wise to consult Robert immediately.'

I thought 'Liar – you knew Myrtle and I were here and didn't want to miss anything.'

'We won't interfere with any of your plans,' Tom went on, in the tone of a psychiatrist reassuring a lunatic. Then he glanced at me suspiciously: 'By the way, where is Myrtle?'

'In the hotel. She isn't well.'

I could see that Tom did not believe me. He obviously thought there was a domestic quarrel brewing. He looked more suspicious when I shook him off in order to do my shopping. He bustled away down the Broad, to report the news directly to Robert.

I felt depressed and anxious and worried. 'If only I can get out of it just this once,' I kept thinking. And I kept telling myself it was a false alarm – possibly brought on, I was inspired to diagnose, by being afraid to meet Robert. One inspired diagnosis led to another: for once I found the psychology of the unconscious useful and consoling. The one diagnosis I did not face was that it might have been brought on by a desire for holy matrimony.

My consolation did not last long: if it were not a false alarm there was no need for the psychology of the unconscious at all.

On my return I found Myrtle sitting in ,an armchair quietly reading *Vogue*. Her apparent anxiety had entirely disappeared. I did not know whether to be pleased or alarmed. She measured out a very healthy dose of gin in the single tooth glass provided by the hotel, and proceeded to drink it with signs of enjoyment.

'You have some, darling,' she said, holding out the glass.

'I don't need it.'

Myrtle smiled. 'Have some instead of tea.' She giggled.

We sat on the edge of the bed, and passed the glass to and fro. I could not help noticing that Myrtle was becoming high-spirited.

'That can only lead to trouble,' I said.

Myrtle looked at me with a wide-eyed, furtive glance, and drank some more gin.

I too drank some more gin. I had begun to feel the situation slipping outside the bounds of my comprehension. I was, quite frankly, beginning to feel amorous.

'Will you take me to see the statue of Shelley?' Myrtle said. What she was thinking about was written all over her face.

'If you want to gaze at a man with no clothes,' I said, 'there's no need to go chasing down to Univ.'

Myrtle looked deeply shocked. 'He was a poet,' she said. 'I love poetry.' She began to finger the buttons on my shirt. I could smell the warm air near to her.

'Give me some more liquor!'

'You've had quite enough, darling.'

'Then you have some.' I paused. 'How about me posing as Shelley?'

'Darling!' Myrtle pushed me away.

'Then you pose as Shelley!'

'Really, darling!'

'Then,' I said, triumphantly getting the better of my shame altogether, 'we'll both pose as Shelley!'

Myrtle stopped fingering the buttons on my shirt. As if she were thinking of something quite different, she put down her glass on the bedside-table. Her eyes looked smaller with excitement. I pushed her back on to the pillows. She made a feeble resistive movement. I was deciding I might as well be hung for a sheep as a lamb – when there was a knock on the door.

It was a chambermaid telling me I was wanted on the telephone.

Robert wanted to know if he should cancel our dinner-party. With badly concealed impatience I told him not to cancel it.

In surprise he asked if Myrtle was better.

'Yes,' I said, and rang off.

When I got back to the room Myrtle's high spirits had disappeared. She was now depressed, standing beside the window and looking out over the dreary back of the hotel. The drizzle had thickened into rain.

I was suddenly overwhelmed by the seriousness of our predicament. I put my arm round her, to comfort her. Neither of us spoke for a long time.

'Would you rather not dine with Robert?' I said.

Myrtle looked at me reproachfully. 'We must.'

I felt apprehensive. I felt the dinner-party was going to be disastrous.

'I think I'll change my dress,' said Myrtle.

'You look perfect as you are.'

Myrtle was not listening.

I sat down beside the dressing-table. Myrtle had brought with her a copy of a book by a successful American humorist. She sometimes read me passages which she found exceptionally funny, presumably to show me how it ought to be done. I now picked up the book and began masochistically to read it myself.

Myrtle remained in low spirits, but the dinner-party went off well, and next day her behaviour was normal.

I watched her anxiously, more anxiously, I think, than she watched herself. I did not tell Robert what was the matter, and I felt still less inclined to tell Tom. I knew that Tom, with his down-to-earth understanding, would tell me that Myrtle was trying to force me to marry her.

We returned to the town, with no sign of relief, and I spent a sleepless night.

I spent two sleepless nights – and ought to have spent three, but I was too tired for even the deepest anxiety to keep me awake.

Then Myrtle rang me up to tell me that all was well. I ought to have felt overcome with relief. I ought to have gone out and celebrated.

I was relieved, of course; and yet I felt no desire to celebrate. Myrtle's voice came to me through the telephone as if she were speaking from a long way off.

'I'm glad,' I said.

Yet I knew that I felt as if something had been lost. These things are very strange.

CHAPTER II

BESIDE THE SWIMMING-POOL

There was a short spell of hot weather and we began to frequent the local swimming-pool when we came out of work. It was an agreeable place, with a high entrance fee imposed to keep out the lower orders. Young men with rich fathers in the boot-and-shoe trade brought their girls in M.G. sports cars: we came on our bicycles. There were half a dozen showy young divers, and at least a couple of young men who could swim more than two lengths in very fast free style. The girls wore bathing-costumes made of what they called the latest thing in two-way stretch. You could not have wished for more in the way of provincial chic.

I usually arrived first, having a greater passion than the others for swimming and lying in the sun. On the evening when the course of our lives perceptibly took a new turn I had arranged to be joined by Myrtle and Tom. While I sat waiting for them I enjoyed the scene.

The owners of the pool had clearly had in view, when choosing their design, something colourful. They had got what they wanted. The bath, through which constantly flowed heavily chlorinated water, was lined with glittering cobalt-blue tiles, which gave the water a quite unearthly look. The white surface of new concrete changing-sheds glared brilliantly in the afternoon sunlight, and against it were lined deckchairs made with orange and green striped canvas. There were two plots of grass, from the centres of which sprang fountains of pink rambler roses.

Against this background, to my surprise, appeared Steve. When he was stripped Steve looked much more bony and boyish than when he was dressed: he hunched his shoulders and walked flat-footedly. He tended to hang about on the edge of the bath, though he was a fair swimmer, with his arms crossed over his chest, apparently shivering. He saw me, and came and sat on the grass beside me.

'Where's Tom?' I asked.

'I don't know.'

There was a peculiar silence, to which my contribution was more surprise.

'I suppose you know he's coming, Steve?'

'Is he?' Steve turned quickly in agitation. 'Honestly, Joe, I didn't know. What shall I do?' Steve's face assumed an expression of frantic alarm. 'What shall I do? I've arranged to meet a *girl* here!'

'Really!' I said, not committing myself immediately to unqualified belief.

'What shall I do?'

'I don't know, Steve.' Then I said helpfully: 'Perhaps love will find a way.'

'It couldn't get past Tom!' Steve hunched his shoulders. 'Honestly, Joe, it wouldn't stand a chance.'

'Oh!'

'This is terrible, Joe. Honestly, you don't understand.'

'Are you sure you didn't know Tom was coming?' Somehow I could not help feeling that in spite of his frantic alarm Steve was looking forward to a scene with Tom.

'Of course not. He'll go mad when he finds out.'

'He'll get over it.'

Steve gave me a look that was cold and cross. 'What will happen to me in the meantime?' he asked.

That question I was unable to answer. I suggested that we should go and swim, but Steve shook his head.

'I want to think,' he said. So he thought for a while. 'I want to talk.'

'What about?'

Steve turned to look at me. 'I really did like it, Joe ...'

'What?' I had no idea what he meant.

'Taking this girl out, of course. I took her to the pictures last night. You may think it sounds silly, Joe, but it wasn't! I liked it. It made me feel I was doing something that was real and true. It made me feel like other boys. Other boys take their girls to the pictures.'

'What film did you see?'

Steve's air of passionate sincerity vanished: he looked nettled.

'We went to the Odeon. It was a terrible film, I know. But she wanted to see it.'

'That's nothing, in the course of love, Steve. You must be prepared for greater sacrifices than that.'

'But it really was terrible. It was excruciating. All about a *sheep-dog*.'

'As you grow older, Steve, you'll realize that love is inseparable from suffering,' I said. 'Myrtle once made me go to Stratford-on-Avon to see *A Comedy of Errors*.'

'No!'

'If girls aren't ignorant, they're cultured,' I said. 'You can't avoid suffering.'

Steve spread out his towel over the grass and lay down on his stomach.

'Tell me about your girl,' I said.

'There's not very much to tell. I met her here last week. She's only a schoolgirl. Quite pretty, though. A bit silly, but I don't mind that. It makes me feel older than her, and I like that.'

'How old is she?'

'Fifteen. Nearly sixteen.'

'That's a bit young.'

'That's what I want, Joe. It's innocent, and I want to keep it innocent.'

'If she's only fifteen you're likely to succeed for a good many years.'

'Years!' said Steve, obviously presented with a new concept. He pondered it with chagrin. 'Won't it be terribly monotonous?'

'Not exactly,' I said. 'But it won't have the ups and downs of the other state.'

Steve was silent for a while.

'I did try to kiss her on the way home,' he said. 'Actually I didn't particularly want to. But I thought she'd expect it. One has to be conventional.'

'That seemed to be the aim.'

Steve turned his head up to see how I was taking it. 'She let me kiss her on the cheek.'

I maintained a serious expression. 'And then?'

A glint came into the corners of his eyes. 'She said: "Aren't I pretty!" and touched her hair.'

'But Steve!' I burst out: 'That wouldn't do for you at all!' I knew Tom constantly told him he was Adonis and this was not a whit too much or too often.

'It made a change,' said Steve, grinning, 'but not a nice one.'

Some people who were camped a little way off turned to listen to us. We stopped talking. Steve laid his face on the ground. I looked at the crowd – and saw Tom coming, bearing down like a battleship on Steve.

I greeted Tom, who spread out his towel and sat down beside us. Steve kept his face on the turf, and Tom glared at him. Steve was deliberately behaving badly. Thinking of Myrtle I asked Tom what time it was. He looked at his watch and told me. Immediately Steve heard the time he roused himself and stood up. He must have been due for his rendezvous.

'Steve, where are you going?'

'To get a handkerchief out of my locker.'

'What for?'

'I need it.'

'I've got a spare one.'

'I want my own.'

With bulging eyes Tom was watching Steve, whose errand sounded most improbable. Steve was furtively looking round at the crowd.

Tom shrugged his shoulders, and Steve shambled away, clearly searching for his schoolgirl. I glanced at Tom. It was the signal for him to plunge immediately into intimate conversation about Steve. In a moment he was asking me questions – Where was Steve going? What was he doing? How long had he been there? Had he been with me all the time? What had we been talking about?

I answered the questions as truthfully as I could without making matters worse. My heart sank as I followed the boring routine of jealousy in someone else.

'I don't know, Tom,' I found myself saying. 'How can I know?' I paused. 'And even if I did know it wouldn't make you any more satisfied if I told you.'

'I should want to know all the same,' Tom said, rebuking me.

I shrugged my shoulders. I knew he was in no mood for seeing Steve's latest manœuvres in their true ridiculous light.

'You forget that I'm in love,' said Tom.

'At least you're jealous,' said I.

'The two things don't necessarily mean the same thing,' said Tom, 'as you ought to know, Joe.' Tom could never resist the satisfaction of teaching his grandmother to suck eggs.

'One can be jealous without being in love,' he went on; 'but one can't be in love without being jealous.'

He gave me a sidelong glance, so I presumed he was referring to me. I had been too ashamed of my own jealousy to confide in him: consequently he found my display of that emotion suspiciously inadequate.

We were silent for a while.

Then Tom said, with great feeling: 'I'm afraid this is beginning to get me down, Joe.'

My sympathy quickened. 'Can't you begin to – I don't know – pull out?'

'Of course not.'

I felt inclined to shrug my shoulders. However, I simply said: 'I'm sorry.'

'I've never been able to withdraw,' said Tom, with some truth. 'I have to go on.' He paused. 'I'm afraid this time it may drive me mad.'

'That appears to be what Steve's aiming at.'

'Not at all, Joe. He can't help it,' said Tom.

'Oh.'

'That's what makes it so moving. That's why he needs me.'

Thinking of cash I said: 'He certainly needs you, Tom.'

'I don't know what he would do without me.'

'He'd lead a life of vastly restricted enterprise.'

Tom indicated that my remark showed lack of understanding.

'I think he's devoted to me.'

'He is, Tom.'

'If only I could feel sure of him.' Tom shook his head.
'That's the trouble with love, Joe. If only one could feel sure
... If only I could be sure this was going to last even another
year.'

For the moment I forgot, just as Tom did, that he was
supposed to be leaving the country in another three weeks. He
was speaking from his heart, and I was moved. I believed the
kind of love he felt for Steve could rouse as deep feeling, could
cause as sudden happiness and as sharp anguish, as any other
kind. But I had no faith in its lasting: I could no more believe it
would last than I could believe water would flow uphill.

'But it may last six months,' said Tom, and I swear that his
tone was that of a man who is announcing a not unsatisfactory
compromise.

Tom was a powerful swimmer: he had a good layer of fat
which kept him afloat, and strong muscles well-suited for
propulsion. We dived into the bright blue waves, and came up
blinking chlorinated water out of our eyes. Tom followed his
usual practice of setting out to swim many consecutive lengths
at a slow, steady pace. I swam beside him for a while and then
changed my mind. I climbed out of the bath and looked
round.

I was not the only person who knew Tom's usual practice.
Steve, confident that Tom's head would be under water for
most of the next fifteen minutes, was standing in full view of
everybody present conversing gaily with two schoolgirls.

I did not know what to do. Intervention of any kind seemed
to me fatal. I could only stand watching, while drops of water
trickled down from my hair on to my shoulders, hoping for the
best.

Now hoping for the best is one of the most feeble of human
activities, and I ought to have known better: especially as I
knew that one of the most obvious characteristics of showy
divers is entire disregard for the comfort of swimmers. I

glanced back and forth, from Steve and his lively, leggy, young girls to Tom's carroty head thrusting steadfastly across the bath. And I was just in time to see two boys in a double dive enter the water a yard ahead of Tom. He was immediately brought to a standstill bouncing angrily in the wash. He spat water from his mouth, and rubbed it out of his eyes; and looked all round. The first thing he saw was Steve.

In half a dozen strokes Tom was at the side of the bath, climbing out, and marching up to Steve. I saw the startled look on Steve's face as Tom tapped him on the shoulder. There was a brief exchange of words, and then they both came away together, leaving the young girls looking at each other speechlessly. Tom strode in front with the sunlight glistening in the fuzz of red hair on his chest: Steve reluctantly brought up the rear.

I went to collect my towel, and we all fetched up simultaneously at the same spot. Tom's eyes looked startling, the irises greener with rage and the whites bloodshot with chlorine.

'You're driving me mad, Steve!' he said, hurriedly wiping his face. His passionate tone was somewhat muffled by the towel.

Steve said nothing, and began ineffectually to dry the inside of his leg, where the water was dripping from his trunks.

'Do you hear?' said Tom. 'You're driving me mad.'

'What?' said Steve. 'I can't hear because of your towel.'

'You're driving me mad!'

Steve said sulkily: 'I wasn't doing anything wrong. Don't be silly, Tom.'

I thought it was time to remove myself, although I knew that Tom had no objection to my presence during his domestic rows – in fact I suspected that he rather liked me to be there, adding to the drama.

I turned away and began to dry myself. I heard Steve say: 'Here's Myrtle.'

It was a great relief. I saw Myrtle sauntering towards us, looking fresh and bright.

'You do look funny, all standing like that, drying yourselves. Like a picture by Duncan Grant.' She smiled to herself.

'Only his young men weren't wearing . . .' Her voice faded out, suggestively.

'Myrtle, you've not changed your dress,' said Tom, peremptorily. 'Aren't you going to bathe?'

I thought he was trying to get rid of her.

'No, I don't think I will,' said Myrtle and sat down on the grass. I sat down beside her. She did not often swim: I thought she was shy of appearing in a bathing-costume because she was so slender and small-breasted. And of course she always felt cold. 'I don't think I can.'

I glanced at her. She looked at me with round, apologetic eyes: 'I'm sorry, darling. I can't stay and go home with you. I want to go somewhere later. Do you mind?'

It was my turn to be alarmed and irritated. 'Not at all,' I said.

There was a pause. Myrtle was watching Tom and Steve. I was thinking. It reminded me of other occasions when she had behaved like this. My mind went back over many events during the past year, and suddenly I saw their pattern. Provocation, leading to an outburst, leading to reconciliation – and then the cycle all over again. We were just entering the first round once more.

'You sound cross,' she said.

'I'm not cross at all.'

Tom sat down on his towel beside her, with his back to Steve. He glanced at me, and said to Myrtle:

'Joe, saying he's not cross, has a wonderfully unconvincing sound.'

'I know.' Myrtle smoothed her dress over her knees. 'He's always cross. He's always cross with me.'

Tom's anger with Steve had faded or else he was concealing it well. He smirked warmly at Myrtle.

'These introverts,' he said to her.

Myrtle shook her head. 'I suppose I must be an extravert.'

'You are, my dear,' said Tom.

Myrtle gave him a sad-eyed, appealing look.

'You're like me.' Tom returned her look. 'That's why we understand each other so well.'

Myrtle did not reply.

'That's why you'd find me so much easier to live with.' He now turned all his attention upon her, as if neither Steve nor I were there. 'You like to feel relaxed, don't you? You like to do things when you want to do them – when you *feel* like it. When the *spirit* moves you, my dear. Not when Joe does. . . .'

Myrtle looked thoughtful. I cannot say I was pleased. I felt like saying: 'That's a bit thick', or 'Come off it, Tom'.

'We're easy persons to live with,' Tom went on. 'In fact I think we above all are the easiest. We go' – he paused, before shamelessly introducing my own phrase for it – 'by atmosphere.' And he waved his hand gracefully through the air.

Myrtle put on the expression of a young girl listening to revelations. I may say that there was nothing false about it. Both she and Tom were in a sense carried away by what they were saying to each other. I may say also that I was not carried away, and what is more my high resolve to be patient and forbearing had wilted disastrously. The only thing that stopped me intervening now was a feeling that Tom might make a fool of himself. I was waiting.

Myrtle nodded her head.

'Ah, Myrtle!' Tom put his hand on hers. 'There isn't anything you couldn't tell me, is there?' He looked into her eyes.

Myrtle blinked. I could have sworn Tom had gone a step too far. I think she must have moved her hand, because Tom took his away.

There was a pause. Myrtle said, in a friendly tone of observation:

'You're getting fat, Tom.'

This was not at all what Tom wanted her to tell him. Tom looked down at his chest, with the tufts of red hair that I personally found repellent, and inflated it.

'I like getting fat,' he said.

'Joe's always exercising,' Myrtle said. 'So boring.'

'It has its rewards,' I said, in a cross, meaningful tone.

Tom shook his head at Myrtle. 'He doesn't understand us, does he?' He stroked his diaphragm. 'If you and I settled down together, Myrtle, you'd fall into my easy ways, just like that' – he snapped his finger and thumb together – 'and you'd get fat as well.'

This was not at all what Myrtle wanted Tom to tell her. I was pleased.

'I couldn't, Tom,' she said, faintly despairing.

'You would, my dear. And you'd love it. You wouldn't feel so cold.'

I watched Myrtle's expression with acute interest and pleasure. Naturally in the past I had not failed to tell her that she always felt cold because she had too thin a layer of subcutaneous fat. This explanation she regarded as mechanical and soul-less in the highest degree. Myrtle knew that her feeling cold arose from distress of the heart. Tom had missed it. She sighed painfully.

Tom apparently did not notice. After all it must have been slightly distracting for him to have my eye fixed on him while he was making up to Myrtle, and to have Steve sulkily listening to him behind his back.

'I shall always feel cold,' Myrtle said.

'Not if I were looking after you, my dear. I should know exactly how you were feeling all the time.'

Myrtle looked distinctly worried at this prospect. I sympathized with her.

'And I should know' – Tom gave a clever, shrewd glance at me – 'how to give you good advice.'

It was one of Tom's theses that I did not know how to handle Myrtle, particularly in the way of giving her good advice. He appeared not to know that Myrtle hated advice of all kinds, good, bad and indifferent.

'Would you?' she said, looking at him with a soft lack of enthusiasm.

Tom was silent. He stared at her with his confident, understanding expression. He appeared to be judging, out of love and sympathy, her present state of health.

'You're tired, my dear,' he said, presumably finding shadows round her eyes.

'I am.'

Tom glanced at me again, as much as to say: 'This is how it ought to be done.' He leaned towards her, and said:

'You should go to bed earlier.'

If there was one thing Myrtle hated it was to be told she

ought to go to bed earlier: in one simple move it negated her love of life, her profundity of soul and, more important still, her determination to do as she pleased.

Myrtle did not speak. She was feeling much too sad.

There is a dazzling reward for allowing your best friend to make advances to your young woman in your presence – the dazzling reward of seeing him put his foot in it.

In my opinion Tom had put his foot in it up to the knee, up to the hip.

At the same time I was a little surprised: my faith in extraverts was very strong. It did not occur to me that it was in very bad taste for Tom to talk to Myrtle in this way: I was concerned that he had not made a better job of it. I concluded that he must really be distracted by thoughts of the impression it must be making on Steve.

I glanced at Steve: it was impossible to tell what he was thinking. His dark hair had dried in a soft mop that was falling over his eyes. He appeared to have lost interest in the schoolgirls. I think he was simply bored.

The sun was beginning to go down. Myrtle stirred uneasily, and Tom began to study the people round about.

'Joe, look over there!'

I looked. Tom was pointing towards the bathing sheds. Myrtle and Steve roused themselves.

It was Trevor and a girl. I have already remarked that Trevor was unusually small, that he was small-boned and altogether made on miniature lines. I now have to remark that Trevor's girl was unusually big.

We were startled. They came forward together, Trevor stepping firmly and delicately, and his girl walking with powerful tread. He was talking animatedly, and smiling up at her. She was listening in a big, proprietorial way. She was wearing a perfectly plain, light green bathing-dress, and a white rubber cap concealed her hair: nothing for one instant distracted one's attention from her physical form. It was a form not to be despised – far, far from it.

'She looks like Genesis,' said Tom, laughing.

'My dear Tom, you don't know anything about Genesis,' said Myrtle; and then suddenly blushed.

'The bulges!' said Tom. 'It's stupendous.'

We watched them, fascinated, as they strolled away and ensconced themselves privately in the furthest corner of the compound.

'After that,' I said, 'I think it's time for us to go.'

Tom and Steve went indoors to dress, and I bade goodbye to Myrtle. I thought she must be going to see Haxby but I refused to ask her. She held out her cheek and I kissed it lightly. As she walked lazily away I felt sad and irritated.

I found Steve standing in the doorway of a cubicle, rubbing himself perfunctorily with a towel. I stood in the doorway of mine, next to him. Tom was having a shower.

'Is that Trevor's regular girl-friend?' I said.

'I think so.'

'Was that the one he had in his car the night he was run in for jumping the traffic-lights?'

'I don't know.' He sounded uninterested.

There was a pause.

'Joe!' Steve called.

There was an odd tone in his voice. I stepped out into the aisle to look at him. His face had a curiously worried expression. He stopped rubbing himself.

'What's the matter, Steve?'

'Has Myrtle gone?'

'Yes.' I was puzzled by the question.

'Of course, she's gone. That's silly of me . . . Listen, Joe, you know why Tom was making those advances to her? . . .' His speech came in staccato bursts. 'I know you won't believe me, when I tell you this . . . Do you know Tom's latest idea? He's planning to marry Myrtle!'

I was astounded. I stared at Steve.

'Incredible! He can't! It's ludicrous!'

It was the most incredible story Steve had ever told me, and for the first time I had not accused him of lying.

'You're not supposed to know, Joe.'

'I should think not.'

'He talked to Robert about it last week-end. That's why he was in Oxford.'

It may seem absurd, but I was believing him.

Somebody came out of an adjacent cubicle, and we had to stop talking while he pushed past me. Looking down the aisle I saw Tom, with a towel round his waist, combing his hair in front of a mirror.

'Please don't tell him I told you, Joe.'

'Don't be ridiculous, Steve.'

'But you mustn't, Joe! Please don't let him know you even suspect until he tells you. Otherwise I shall have terrible scenes.'

'Look, Steve, you'd better – '

'He's coming! I can't tell you any more.' Steve backed into the cubicle and hastily flung his shirt over his head. His elbow stuck in the sleeve.

Tom came along.

'Now Steve, hurry up!' He glanced at Steve. 'If you put on your shirt the way I showed you, Steve, you'd find it would slip straight on.'

I retired to my cubicle.

And after we parted I went to my house. I had something new to think about.

I was utterly astounded. Apparently nothing was too ridiculous for Tom to do. First of all he professed to be wrapped up in Steve; secondly he knew Myrtle was in love with me; thirdly he was due to leave the country in less than three weeks anyway. I could not make sense of it; but I knew only too well that a situation was not less likely to arise because I was unable to make sense of it. Few situations, especially those precipitated by Tom, made sense.

'Steve must be lying,' I said to myself that night when I went to bed.

CHAPTER III

TWO SCENES OF CRISIS

It was early in the morning, and I was sitting in the school playground, waiting for Frank and company to join me. I was not preparing a lesson: I was not preparing anything. I was thinking. It seemed to me that my affairs had become desperately complicated. In fact I said to myself that they were in a hell of a mess. It was the morning after Steve had confided Tom's latest idea. I had a headache and felt curiously tense.

The sky was clouded over, and during the night there must have been some rain. Every now and then drops of water fell from the leaves of the lime tree under which I was sitting: the ground was damp, and the atmosphere carried a warm, pervasive smell of dust. Birds fluttered to and fro between the trees. Everything seemed unusually quiet.

My morning newspaper lay folded in my lap, and I noticed part of the headline. I had already read it. The fate of Europe was rolling on, but I had begun to lose any accurate sense of what it was rolling towards. I was aware to my shame that I had become less interested.

Sometimes I tried to link the disintegration of our private lives with the disintegration of affairs in the world. I saw us all being carried along into some nameless chaos. Yet it rang false. In spite of what the headlines told me every morning, in spite of what I reasoned must happen to the world, I was really preoccupied most deeply with what was going on between me and Myrtle and between Tom and Steve. People can concentrate on their private lives, I thought, in the middle of anything.

I had written to the American Consulate in London

about a visa for myself. My slackness in *Weltanschauung* had not robbed me entirely of the capacity for action.

I had made a beginning with Bolshaw's computation. I had to do something. There was no reply from Miss X.Y., and I needed to know the fate of my last book before I could begin a new one. Suppose she never came back from the Balkans, suppose I were kept waiting a lifetime! My anxiety had become completely unreasonable. Small wonder I took to computation.

The idea that my true love was being pursued by my best friend did not cause me an entirely sleepless night. It was far too ridiculous. And as it had been conveyed to me by a notable liar, I reserved my right to make a scene. However, Tom's new gambit had brought me to one important conclusion; namely, that if I did not intend to marry Myrtle myself I ought not to stop anyone else marrying her.

This conclusion was important to me, and it was only afterwards that I learnt it was incomprehensible to everyone else. I must make it clear now that I not only came to the conclusion: I stuck to it. To understand it entails harking back to a revelation I made earlier on, that, feeling myself not to have been born a good man, I often sought to try and behave like one. Alas! I accepted that all was fair in love and war as far as primary things went; but if I could show a bit of decency in secondary ones, so much the better, I thought.

That was my aim. Nobody understood it. And I might have known that the result, if it was anything like the result of my previous attempts in this direction, was likely to be farcical. With my usual optimism, determination or crassness, I did not foresee it. I sat alone under the lime trees fascinated by the general concept rather than practical results. And of course I had a headache.

The boys came out and drew up their chairs beside me. I noticed that Trevor was missing and asked Frank where he was. Frank did not know.

'I saw him last night,' I said.

I thought Frank gave me an odd look.

'With 'is girl?' said Fred, getting down immediately to

his favourite topic of conversation.

I did not reply.

'Wish I'd got a girl,' said Fred. 'I've been reading Freud. It's bad not to 'ave a girl.'

Had Trevor been present he would have lured Fred into an innocent, half-baked disquisition on psychoanalysis. As it was, Fred was ignored. He sighed and began to work.

A little while later a boy came out to me with a chit from the headmaster. It forbade the holding of lessons in the playground.

I was amazed. 'Look at this,' I said to Frank and passed it to him. Fred and Benny read it over his shoulder.

'What a sod!' said Frank. 'Oo-ya bugger,' said Fred.

The messenger, who had read it himself, sniggered cheerfully. I handed back the slip of paper and sent him on his way.

'What are you going to do, sir?' said Benny. It was a trivial annoyance. The practice of holding lessons in the yard was of long standing. The senior boys regarded it as one of their privileges.

'I don't propose to move now.'

I happened to look up, and saw the face of the headmaster peeping at me through his window.

Then I made a silly mistake. I decided to go and talk to Bolshaw. I thought he would be only too ready to gossip about the latest *démarche* of the headmaster. I walked into the school, and found him sitting in his room with the door open. He came out into the corridor to talk to me.

There was no excuse for me. I knew well enough that Bolshaw was unpredictable. His having recently been my ally did not make him approve of me any the more. To imagine that he would agree with me was walking into danger in the most imbecile fashion. Into it I walked, and a moment later found myself in the midst of a violent quarrel.

'I've just come out of the yard,' I said.

'Free period?'

'No. Teaching the sixth. I got the headmaster's note.'

'Have you taken them into the small lab?'

'Not on your life.'

'What do you mean, Lunn?'

'I don't propose to do anything about it.'

'Why not?'

'It's too silly.'

Bolshaw stood peering at me in the semi-darkness of the corridor, with his heavy shoulders rounded and his hands in his pockets.

'Why have you come to me?'

I ought to have known there was something wrong. To me the incident was trivial, and I was blind to his view of it. I replied:

'To see what we can do about it.'

Bolshaw raised his voice. 'Surprising as it may seem, I agree with the head for once. It's time this unconventional behaviour stopped. Look here, my good fellow, I told you that you'd got to put your nose to the grindstone. That meant this kind of thing has got to stop.'

I was furious. It crossed my mind that he had put the headmaster up to it.

'It's becoming increasingly clear to me,' Bolshaw said, 'that there's no room on this staff for people who flout the conventions.'

'What the hell's it got to do with you?'

I had been trapped into losing my temper.

'Everything. I know what the conventions are.'

'Do you indeed? Do you know that I and other masters have been taking lessons in the playground for the last seven years? When everybody does a thing – then it is conventional!'

Bolshaw snorted.

'That's what being conventional means!' I said. 'It's got nothing to do with whether they're good, bad, moral, wicked, useful or just damned lazy!'

'Listen to me, my good fellow! I don't propose to argue with you about what it means to be conventional. I *know*! And I can tell you this. Sooner or later the members of this staff who flout the conventions are going to find themselves' – he paused – 'outside!' He took a blustering breath. 'It may interest you to know that it was I who decided the chit should be circulated. The headmaster agreed with me, that more persons than one have got to put their noses to the grindstone!'

It was too much for me. I shouted angrily. 'What about yourself?'

And Bolshaw clearly had not the slightest idea what I meant.

'My function is to see that the noses, having been put to the grindstone, are kept there.' He gave a braying, self-satisfied laugh. 'The proper place for them!'

'It's the proper place for yours,' I said. 'You may appoint yourself to be keeper of the conventions, but I notice you don't appoint yourself to do any teaching.'

'I do more teaching than anyone else in this school.'

'You certainly teach fewer periods.'

'That's because I have the power of imparting knowledge more rapidly than others.'

'I don't know how you manage it from the staff-room. Do you teach by telepathy?'

Bolshaw looked away in a dignified fashion.

'It's a pity that you find it necessary to quarrel with me, Lunn. It's most unwise.'

I was alarmed. I knew that he was speaking the truth. Unfortunately he had spoken it too late. I had already done myself damage.

'I don't want,' he said, 'to have our collaboration disturbed.' He paused to allow the effect to sink in.

I could have cried out with rage. I had been thinking this quarrel would mean my labours in his research coming to an end. Now I saw that he was going to use it to force me to go on. I had played into his hands.

I was silent. Nothing could be unsaid.

Bolshaw rattled the change in his pockets, and glanced into the class-room. Then he turned back to me.

'I think it's a very good rule,' he said, 'never to quarrel with one's superior in authority.' He paused. 'I'm happy to say I've always kept to that rule. Except, of course, on rare occasions when I deemed it wiser to break it.'

There was nothing for me to say.

Immediately school was over on that afternoon I went to the café to meet Tom. I felt unusually agitated, and hardly noticed when I splashed through puddles of water lying in the cobbled market-place. I was thinking the sooner I was in America the better.

Tom was not there. I sat in our customary place, watching for him through the window. I suppose the sky was still grey and damp, but I do not recall it. There must have been delphiniums and lilies on the stalls. What I do remember, and strangely enough the recollection is vivid to this day, is that the waitresses were wearing a new uniform. They had previously worn black with white aprons: now they were in brown with aprons the colour of pale *café-au-lait*. Our waitress had blonde hair, and the new colours made her look very pretty.

Tom came in.

'You're looking worried,' he said. 'Have you had bad news from Miss X.Y.?'

I shook my head. Tom ordered tea. The ritual of ordering a meal was very important, whatever else was going on.

I described my quarrel with Bolshaw.

Tom listened with patience and sympathy. I was just coming to the end of it when the waitress brought the tea. We paused.

Tom poured out some tea and gave it to me, saying: 'It probably won't be serious.'

'It's maddening. There was no need for it whatsoever. I just took leave of my senses.'

Tom smiled. Instead of saying 'You introverts,' he said:

'I do it frequently.' He looked at me with concentrated interest. 'If you lost your temper as frequently as I do, Joe, you wouldn't be so upset by it. You don't seem to realize how often other people do lose their tempers.'

'Bolshaw didn't really lose his.'

'No. He was satisfied with you losing yours. Are you under the impression there's no emotion flying about between you and Bolshaw? The two of you aren't counters in a complicated puzzle. You're both human. At this moment Bolshaw's probably feeling a glow of satisfaction, instead of feeling frustrated irritation.' Tom called the waitress: 'I should like another meringue, please.'

I confess to being comforted by this revelation of truth. Tom was speaking precisely in the tone he copied from Robert.

The next thing he said was, 'I think you'll find it cleared the air.' It might have been Robert speaking, had the remark not been so absurd.

'Cleared the air!' I cried. 'It's probably cleared me out of my job!'

Tom shrugged his shoulders.

There was a pause, and I said: 'I think the sooner I'm in America the better.'

'Yes.'

Something made me glance at Tom – he met my glance with patent evasion.

'I've been thinking about my own plans,' he said.

'Yes?' I should hope he had.

Tom adopted his weightiest manner. 'I may possibly postpone my departure.' He spread out his hands. 'Just by a fortnight.'

I was brought up sharply. 'Why?' I said.

'Certain affairs at the office are running behind time.'

I did not believe him. 'Is it Steve or Myrtle?' I asked myself. I was just framing an oblique question, when we were interrupted. There was a stir beside us, and I looked up to see Frank.

I was startled. I had not asked him to come. Occasionally we invited him to have a drink with us in a public-house, but neither he nor any of the other boys was supposed to join us without being asked. Tom looked surprised.

'I thought I should find you here.' Frank looked very embarrassed. He had naturally pleasant manners.

'Sit down,' said Tom.

Frank drew up another chair to our table. He sat down and nervously straightened his tie, which was already tied to perfection.

'I know I'm intruding,' he said, 'but I had to come.' He addressed himself to Tom. 'I hope Joe won't mind.' He pointed his nose diffidently towards me.

I shook my head.

Frank said: 'It's about Trevor.' He glanced round. 'I suppose you know he's been having an affair with a girl? Well, he's... you know... got her into trouble.'

I exclaimed in surprise.

Tom said: 'He'll have to marry her.'

At this moment the waitress came up to ask if Frank wanted anything. 'Bring some more tea,' Tom said to her commandingly.

I was silent. I was seeing us all ruined by a scandal.

'He'll have to marry her,' Tom repeated.

'That's out of the question,' said Frank.

'Nonsense. How old is he?'

'Nineteen.'

'Then why can't he marry her?'

'*She* doesn't want to marry *him*!' Frank replied, with great seriousness.

'Good gracious!' said Tom, and added: 'I can't say that I blame her.'

'That isn't the point,' said Frank.

'Why doesn't she want to marry him?'

'She wants to be a sculptor.' It appeared that all parties concerned thought sculpture and wedlock were mutually exclusive.

Tom laughed. 'She looks as if she's sculpted herself!'

I said: 'Is it that big woman we saw him with last night?'

'That's right,' said Frank. 'She's huge.'

Tom said: 'He's proved his manhood, anyway.' He smiled flickeringly: 'I suppose he thought the bigger the woman he took on the surer the proof.'

Frank laughed ruefully. 'Poor little Trev!' Tom gave him a knowing glance.

Frank's expression changed suddenly. 'But what are we to do, Tom?'

'What's Trevor doing?'

'Nothing. He's terrified. He doesn't get on with his

family. He nearly got chucked out after the trouble over the car. If they hear about this . . .'

'Is it quite certain?' I asked – a question appropriate to me.

Frank looked at me. 'It's quite certain. This is the third month.'

'The little fool!' said Tom.

I said: 'It's no use taking that attitude.'

'I feel it,' said Tom. 'I feel healthy rage, Joe.'

The waitress brought us a fresh pot of tea, and a cup and saucer for Frank. Tom poured the tea.

Frank said to me: 'I'm sorry I came to you, Joe. We couldn't think of anyone else.'

'That's all right.'

Tom said: 'We must make some plans.' He paused. 'First of all we'd better get the situation clear.' He paused again. 'They ought to get married.'

'They can't,' said Frank.

'If she doesn't want to marry him, then she ought to have the child without.'

'There'd be a terrific scandal. It would ruin Trev's career.'

Tom pursed his lips. 'Then there's only one solution.'

'Trev says she's willing . . .'

In alarm I pushed my chair away from the table.

'Look!' I cried. 'I can't possibly be mixed up in this!'

'There's no need!' With a grandiose gesture Tom swept me aside. 'I'll handle it.'

His voice was full and resonant. He meant what he said. It was just the generous, disinterested action of which he was capable: he would plunge in without counting the risk – and also, as a matter of fact, he would enjoy himself. I forgot his bustling absurdity and felt great affection for his good heart.

'I'm afraid in my position at the school . . . ' I began, feeling ashamed.

Tom interrupted. 'You'd better keep out of this.'

I nodded my head, thinking of the trouble I was in already at the school. I said: 'I think it would be best if I'd heard nothing about it.'

Frank looked worried. 'I won't say that I've told you.'

I smiled at him. 'It isn't your fault, Frank.'

Frank smiled back, readily restored.

I prepared to leave them. First of all I took out my wallet, and counted the pound notes in it. I handed them all to Tom, thinking it was rather handsome of me.

'You'll probably need these,' I said, in a solemn tone.

Tom accepted them, clearly thinking there were not enough. I was ruffled. I felt in my pockets for small change and found insufficient to pay for my tea.

'You'll have to let me have one of them back again,' I said.

'I'll lend you half a crown,' said Tom, not intending to part.

I walked away through the market-place. I realized that I had lost my resilience. I felt as touchy and cross as Myrtle accused me of being. I was inclined to ask myself rhetorical questions, such as: 'Why do I get involved with people?' and 'Why don't I leave them all?' It seemed to be that in some distant way Trevor was responsible for my having quarrelled with Bolshaw.

America, I thought, was the place for me. Land of liberty, where my pupils would not get their girls in trouble. Or would they? Exactly what sort of liberty was it? My speculations were suddenly interrupted by recalling that Tom had postponed his setting sail for the land of liberty.

My speculations changed to suspicions. 'What,' I asked myself, in a question that was far from rhetorical, 'is Tom up to now?'

CHAPTER IV
CONCLUSION IN A PUBLIC-HOUSE

It was evening and I was waiting apprehensively for Myrtle to come. We had just had a strange conversation over the telephone. For the last few days I had seen nothing of her; things were going wrong again. She had rung up to tell me she was going to a midnight matinée.

'Midnight matinée!' I had cried, in surprise. 'What on earth of?'

'Of a film.'

'You didn't tell me, darling.'

'I didn't think you'd be interested.' Her voice sounded desolate and reproachful.

As she did not tell me the name of the film I gathered it must be 'Turksib' or 'Earth'. I said: 'Who are you going with? The Crows?'

Myrtle did not reply. I thought: 'So much for that!' and began a gossipy conversation to divert her.

'I've got an excellent story about Tom,' I said. 'He told me he'd postponed going to America so I sent a postcard to Robert, asking if it was true. And got a postcard back from Tom himself.'

'How queer,' said Myrtle.

'Not queer at all. He was in Oxford, and must have been in Robert's rooms, reading through his correspondence while he was out – saw my postcard, and just replied to it.' I thought the story was funny. 'What could be simpler?'

'How queer,' Myrtle said again, rather as if she had not been listening.

I tried another tack. I said:

'I'm feeling slightly more cheerful about school. There's

a bit of intrigue going on in the staff-room against Bolshaw. I'm not taking part because it won't succeed. Shall I tell you about it? It's interesting because I could reasonably support Bolshaw for once.'

'How queer.'

It was the third time. Her voice sounded distant and lifeless, as if it were repeating the phrase from some worn-out groove.

'What is the matter, darling?' I said. 'You keep on saying "How queer" in an extraordinary way.'

'Do I?'

'You do.'

'I don't know ...'

'In that case, I might just as well have been talking about the weather.'

'I suppose it's because I'm so empty-headed!'

'Myrtle, what *is* the matter?'

'I often wonder how I compare with Robert and Tom!'

I gave up. I had a sudden vision of her desperate unhappiness.

'I want to see you,' I said. 'Will you meet me, darling?'

'I'm going to a film!...' Her voice trailed off in pain.

'Let's have a drink before you go. Will you? Please, darling!'

At last Myrtle agreed, though her tone remained lifeless.

And so it came about that I was waiting apprehensively for her to come and join me in a public-house near my lodgings.

I sat in the public bar, which I had chosen instead of the saloon because it was always empty. The floors were made of uncovered boards, and the table-tops were not scrubbed very often. The wall-paper had been given a coat of shiny brown varnish: over the fireplace there was a dusty mirror with a knot of red Flanders poppies twisted into one corner of the frame: on the opposite wall was an oilcloth chart showing the town Association football team's fixtures of three years ago, surrounded by advertisements for hairdressing, sausages and furniture removals.

On the mantelshelf stood a fortune-telling machine

shaped like a miniature wireless set. You put in a penny and selected a button to press, whereupon a coloured light flickered, and the machine delivered a pasteboard card with your fortune inscribed upon it.

I put in a penny. The card said:

YOU ARE SUNNY AND GOOD-NATURED.
BEWARE THE INFLUENCE OF OTHERS.

'Dammit!' I said aloud. I took the card between my first and second fingers and flicked it, as I used to flick cigarette cards when I was a boy, into the empty fireplace.

The door opened and Tom's red head looked in. I was astonished.

'Ah! I thought I might find you here.' Tom came towards me. 'I've just called at your house.' The latter sentence was uttered in a vaguely apologetic tone.

'Did you know I was meeting Myrtle?'

'Are you?'

I looked at him. Tom had a remarkable talent for turning up at rendezvous I had made with someone else. His instinct for not missing anything amounted to second sight. I said:

'Yes. You can push off when she comes.'

'Of course,' said Tom, as if I had offended his taste for old-world courtesy.

'Did you want to see me about anything special?'

'No.' Tom stood on his dignity for a moment. Then he went across to the service hatch, where he bought a pint of beer for himself and another one for me.

'How is Myrtle?' he asked.

I told him. I was so worried about her that I paid no attention to my suspicions of him. I confided my fears and my self-reproaches.

Tom reassured me.

'It wouldn't make the slightest difference if you married her,' he said. 'It's the ebb and flow of her nature.' He spoke with great authority, though not necessarily with great truth. 'If you married her she'd still have those bouts of accidie. It's the ebb and flow you know.' He was pleased with the phrase and illustrated it with his hands.

It seemed to me that we had too much ebb and not enough flow. 'Poor Myrtle,' I said, with a deep stir of sympathy for her. She had a lightly balanced emotional nature – that was what made her so attractive to me – but for some reason or other, alas! it tipped over too readily in the downward direction.

'I shouldn't take it very seriously,' said Tom. 'It really is her temperament, and fundamentally, you know, she's accommodated to it.' He smiled at me. 'I understand these things, Joe.'

I knew perfectly well that when he was alone with her instead of with me he approached the problem in a very different tone.

'I'm much nearer to her in this way than you are,' he said.

This remark, on the other hand, Myrtle must have had addressed to her very frequently in their *tête-à-tête*.

'Much nearer, you know,' Tom repeated.

I did not mention any steps he might be proposing to take on the basis of this peculiar nearness – time would display them soon enough.

And then I said, honestly: 'You give me great comfort, Tom.'

'That's what one's friends are for,' said Tom.

'God knows, I'm in need of it.'

Tom shook his head. 'It's time this affair was over,' he said, in the tone of great wisdom that he used when he spoke from the depths of his soul – you remember, the very old soul. I recalled Bolshaw saying: 'The time has come.' I wondered how on earth everybody but me recognized the time with such certainty. I decided it was because they lacked the capacity for recognizing anything else.

Tom drank off about a third of a pint, and sighed with satisfaction. I noticed the barman had appeared at the service-hatch: he was polishing glasses which he placed on a shelf out of sight.

Suddenly the door opened. I thought it was Myrtle and my heart jumped. It was a seedy-looking man wearing a peaked cap and a muffler. He glanced at Tom and me, apparently did not care for the look of us, and went out again. We heard him go into the saloon.

We were silent. It was a warm evening, and an invisible fly buzzed round the ceiling. 'Have some more beer?' said Tom.

'It's my round.'

Suddenly I remembered Trevor's crisis. I asked Tom what had happened.

Tom smiled blandly. 'I think everything will be... managed,' he said. 'Apparently we have to wait. The timing is important, you know.' He stopped. 'I think it would be wise for you to be ignorant of it.'

'Will you need more money?'

Tom shrugged his shoulders. I stood up to buy the next round of drinks. Myrtle came in.

Myrtle saw me first and made no effort to raise the light of recognition. Then she saw Tom, and smiled tremulously.

'Ah, Myrtle,' said Tom, in an effusively sympathetic tone.

'Tom was just going,' I said to Myrtle, malevolently recalling the times Tom had got rid of me or of her.

Tom shrugged his shoulders, and smiled at Myrtle. 'Joe behaving as usual.'

The remark unaccountably plunged Myrtle into despair. She made it very plain and Tom was not at all pleased.

'I think I'll go,' he said.

I watched him leave while Myrtle settled herself beside me. I was suddenly overwhelmed by apprehension. I thought, 'This is going to be the worst scene.'

Myrtle and I looked into each other's eyes. It was a light evening, but the room was dark and we were sitting with our backs to the window.

I saw written in Myrtle's face all the things I wished not to see. Fear and shame suddenly rose up in me, mingled with a deep poignant sympathy. Myrtle did not speak. She sat there, just letting me look at her. Not a word had been passed between us, not a touch, and yet I felt as if the whole scene were already over. 'This is the end.'

'How are you feeling now, darling?' I could not help myself from speaking as if she were in the grip of an illness from which she might already be recovering.

'I don't know.'

I looked at her closely. Her eyes looked bigger, and the bright patches of colour in her cheeks had spread out more widely. Under her eyes there were brown stains. She seemed to be breathing with a deeper movement of her heart.

'Darling.' I took hold of her hand. She let it lie in mine.

'This can't go on,' she said.

I said nothing. I felt as if I had been struck.

There was a long pause. 'Can it?' she said, and looked at me.

I did not possess the courage to say 'no'. I said, nearly inaudibly: 'I don't know. If you don't think...'

There was a movement and the barman appeared in the hatch to see if we wanted anything.

Myrtle asked for a double whisky.

Out of surprise I bought her one, and I thought I had better have one myself. I set the two glasses on the wooden table in front of us.

We each drank a little. Neither of us said anything. We drank some more. The minutes passed by us, like the flies buzzing across the room. The flies congregated at the mirror.

'How *can* it go on?' Myrtle spoke without looking at me now.

'I don't know.'

We were silent again. I drank some more whisky. I could not tell what I was feeling or thinking. I was overwhelmed by recollections of the past.

I noticed her gulp down her drink. The expression on her face remained exactly the same. She said:

'I think about nothing else, nowadays.'

I said: 'Nor I.'

There was a pause. And I said: 'Do you want it to end?'

'How could I?' Faint life came into her voice.

'Then how?...'

'I love you.' She suddenly looked at me.

'Oh God!'

Myrtle drew in her breath sharply. She was holding the glass quite close to her lips, looking into it.

'What's the matter?'

'You don't want to marry me!' No sooner had she uttered the words than she burst into tears.

I was faced with the truth, with the core of my own obstinacy. I could have stretched out my hand and whispered, 'I'll marry you.' She was so near to me. It was so little to say.

I shook my head. 'No.'

Myrtle sobbed quietly. I watched her. I finished my glass of whisky. Do not think I was not caught in the throes of self-reproach and remorse. I was. I was confronted with the core of my own obstinacy, and it was a hateful thing. Yet I neither could nor would break it. Not for a moment did I see that she had a core of obstinacy too. Everything that was causing her pain was my fault. I tortured myself – because I would not give in.

We sat for a long time thus, concerned, each of us, with ourselves: and the bonds between us were snapping. We had reached the final question and the final answer – what seemed the final question and answer to us – and there was nowhere further to go.

Myrtle took out a handkerchief and tried to wipe her eyes. She glanced at the stains on it of mascara. Quietly I went and fetched us another double whisky apiece. I dropped too much water into Myrtle's. She picked it up and absent-mindedly began to drink it as if it were lemonade. I stared at my own glass. We could not speak.

In the saloon bar someone switched on a wireless set, and I heard a voice inexorably reading out cricket scores. Myrtle appeared not to hear it. We were still entirely alone in the bar. At last she looked up.

'I must go away,' she said.

'Don't go yet, darling.'

'I must ...'

It seemed unbearable to let her go. I put my arm round

her, as if to comfort her.

'My own darling!' I cried, hiding my face against her neck. I felt as if I possessed her completely, and it touched me so that I could have burst into tears. I felt another living creature, closer to me than I had ever felt anyone before, now, at the moment when we were going to part.

Myrtle uttered a great sigh. I picked up her glass, and held it for her to drink out of it. Then I had a drink.

'I'm late already,' Myrtle said.

'Never mind.'

'But I've got an appointment.'

'Are you going with Haxby?'

'Yes.'

'He can wait.'

Myrtle freed herself from my arm in order to turn to me. 'Don't you care about anybody?'

'I don't understand what you mean.'

'Of course, you don't.' She began to show signs of life. 'You don't care if he waits. You don't care if I go.'

'That's all you know about it.'

'How can I tell? You never say anything. Other people do, but you never do. *You* never say anything one way or the other. You talk about Haxby as if he didn't matter.' She rounded upon me with impressive force. 'Do you know he wants to shoot you?'

'Good gracious!' I exclaimed.

'He's jealous!' said Myrtle.

'I suppose he must be.'

'There you go! You just put yourself in *his* place!'

'How can I be a writer if I don't?'

'I don't know *how* you can do it. You don't care about me.'

'If you mean that I don't know what it is to be jealous, then you're...'

'Do you? Do you?' Myrtle faced me. 'Then why didn't you tell me?'

'Because I don't tell anybody. Because jealousy's hateful!' I cried. 'I hate being jealous of Haxby. I wish I'd never heard of him!'

'There's a way out, isn't there?' She meant by marrying her.

I stood up. 'No!' I cried. 'I won't take it.'

Myrtle watched me. 'No, I realize that now. Tom made that pretty clear to me.'

'Tom?' I said. 'You've been talking to Tom about this.'

'Of course. Who am I to talk to? I haven't got any friends. And Tom understands you.'

'Says he does.'

'He understands you better than you think.'

'There's no truer word than that!'

'How horrible you are!'

I sat down again.

We were silent for a while.

'Does Tom think he understands you?' I said.

Myrtle did not reply.

I said: 'I'm sorry, darling.'

Myrtle looked at me, this time gently. 'You don't understand how I have no one to turn to. Tom is being kind to me, that's all. He's wonderfully sympathetic.'

I wondered if she had any inkling of Tom's motive in being wonderfully sympathetic, and decided not. It was not for me to enlighten her – anyway I was not sure myself.

I put my arm round her again, in a friendly way. My anger was subsiding and so was hers.

'Please, don't let's quarrel, darling.'

Myrtle was suddenly silent. It must have crossed both our minds simultaneously that I meant 'Don't let's quarrel before we part.'

'Don't say that!' she cried.

There was a pause. I finished my drink. Myrtle left hers. She sat looking at it, as if she wanted never to go any further with it, so as never to move from where she was now sitting with my arm round her.

The room was in twilight, and the barman unexpectedly switched on the light. We hid our faces.

Myrtle stood up, and I did the same.

'I must go,' she said.

We looked into each other's eyes. 'What is it to be?'

Neither of us could utter the question.

'I'll put you on the bus,' I said.

Myrtle nodded, and we went into the street. It was less dusky than we had imagined. The air was warm on our cheeks. The street was wide, and lined with trees. We strolled to the bus-stop and waited.

I stood beside Myrtle for a while and suddenly looked at her. I saw that her expression had changed completely. Even though I was determined not to take the lead, I could not let the moment pass again without asking her:

'What do you want me to do?'

Her voice sounded hollow and distant as she said: 'I suppose we ought to stop seeing each other?'

I made no pretence of not accepting it.

'I'm terribly sorry,' I murmured, finding words feeble and hopeless. Myrtle appeared not to hear.

We saw a bus approaching.

'Goodbye, darling.'

Suddenly we were in each other's arms. I kissed her and she clung to me.

The bus passed us without stopping. We were at a request stop and had failed to hold up our hands.

'You'll have to wait for the next.'

Myrtle drew away from me. She was crying. 'Goodbye darling.'

'I'll wait with you.'

'No, don't; please don't! Go now!'

'I can't leave you.'

'I beg you to go!' She spoke with force and anguish.

I took hold of her hands for a moment, and then turned away.

I walked along the road, which sloped upwards and curved away to the right. As I reached the bend, I looked back. I saw Myrtle standing alone. Tears welled up into my eyes, so that I could not see where I was going. But I went on.

I went back to my house. The landlady and her niece were out, and the place was completely empty. I switched on the light in my room, and my glance fell on the telephone. I felt unutterably lonely.

I sat down in my chair, and began to think. The break had come at last. Yet there was something strange about it. Myrtle had said: 'I suppose we ought to stop seeing each other'; but she had framed it as a question, so as to leave it open for me to say, 'No, no!' I felt very confused. Had we parted or not? It seemed like it, yet somehow I felt sure that Myrtle had not. It takes two to make even a parting.

Gradually I became calmer. My mood changed. I went over the scene again and again; and I found it beginning to strike me differently. My confusion was disappearing and something definite was being revealed to me. I received the revelation with a bitter kind of resistance, because it made me feel cold and heartless.

I knew now that whatever Myrtle did in the future, for me the affair was irrevocably over.

CHAPTER V

VERTIGINOUS DEVELOPMENTS

Each time the telephone rang during the next few days I thought it would be Myrtle. It was not. I kept away from places where I might meet her and arranged to go and spend the week-end in Oxford. I felt uneasy and miserable, and at the same time convinced that something was going to happen.

I diverted myself with tedious business-like activities. The American Consulate in London had told me it was necessary to go to the Consulate in Birmingham to obtain my visa, so I arranged to collect it on Friday afternoon, when the school had a half-holiday. And I wrote again to Miss X.Y. about my manuscript.

On the day after my ambiguous parting with Myrtle Tom rang up, aiming to discover what had happened. I made him come round to my lodgings to find out.

I was sitting in my room, beside the open french window, eating tinned-salmon sandwiches for tea, when Tom arrived.

'I see you haven't lost your appetite,' he observed.

I thought the remark was in bad taste. 'I'll ask the landlady to make some more for you.' He was very fond of salmon sandwiches. 'I hope she hasn't run out of salmon,' I added, to frighten him.

Tom greedily ate a couple of mine, just in case. He glanced over the cake-stand. 'Very nice cakes she makes you. She's very devoted to you.'

'The niece makes them.'

'Ah! She made them for Mr Chinnock, of course.' He wagged his head sagely, at the thought of more devotion in a different guise.

I took the last sandwich, and went to order more. I met the landlady bringing them of her own accord. Tom saluted her in a flowery fashion, which clearly pleased her. She was a lean, middle-aged woman, with a pale, indrawn face and narrow, dark eyes. Tom made a gleam appear in her eyes. When she had gone out of the room Tom said:

'Now she'll be more devoted to you than ever.'

As there had been numerous quarrels over Myrtle visiting me late at night, I thought a little more devotion would do me no harm. Up to date I had seen no signs of it. Possessiveness, yes: devotion, no.

Tom said: 'I hear that Myrtle was looking dreadfully unhappy at the film show last night.'

'Who told you?'

'Steve went to it. He saw her. She was with Haxby.'

I did not say anything.

'What happened after I'd left you?' Tom asked. 'Did you break if off?'

'Break it off!' I exclaimed. 'It's not a stick of toffee. You don't break things off just like that.'

Tom's disapproval was evident. In my place he would have broken it off. However he said amiably: 'Then it's still on?'

'Not exactly,' I replied. 'That's the trouble.'

'Poor girl!'

'You told me yesterday she wasn't such a poor girl.'

'Is that how you left it?'

'Well, yes.'

Tom shook his head. 'I don't understand how you can leave it neither one way nor the other. I couldn't. I should have forced a decision.'

I was feeling in no mood to be amused. 'In a sense I did. I forced one from myself – afterwards. It's over as far as I'm concerned.'

'That's better. You'll feel much better for it.'

'I don't. I feel worse.'

'Purely transient,' said Tom.

There was a pause. Tom helped himself to the last of the

resh batch of salmon sandwiches.

I decided to tell him what had happened as honestly as I
ould. I repeated most of the conversation verbatim. I
lescribed Myrtle's tears and our last embrace at the bus-
top.

'My dear Joe,' said Tom, 'how you make the poor girl
uffer!'

I said: 'How she makes me suffer, if it comes to that!'

'She probably thinks you don't intend to see her again.'

'That's just what you advised me to do.'

'It's positively brutal!' said Tom, paying no attention
vhatsoever. 'How you make her suffer!' His voice rose with
nger. 'You treat her appallingly!'

You may find Tom's behaviour mildly contradictory:
hat is nothing to what I found it. In my own behaviour I
imed at some sort of consistency, and until I knew Tom I
vas under the impression that other people did the same.
Not a bit of it! Tom was a revelation to me, and through
im others were revealed. Only through observing Tom, I
lecided, could one understand the human race.

Tom denounced me for several minutes. After counsel-
ing me to break off the affair, he now abused me
passionately for doing it – and at the same time managed to
convey additional contempt for my pusillanimity in not
naking the break sharper. His face got redder and his eyes
began to glare. He was carried away by his sympathy for
Myrtle.

'You've ruined her life!' he cried.

I said nothing. Tom let the torrent carry him on. He
urned his attention to my failings. While he ate my cakes
ne denounced my self-centredness, my coldness of heart,
ny unawareness of the feelings of others, my lack of passion
– my complete unsatisfactoriness as man, thinker and lover.
A few years earlier I should have lost my temper and
argued furiously.

'What are you going to do next?' Tom demanded to
know.

'Nothing,' I muttered.

'That's just like you.'

I did have a faint sensation of not knowing whether I was on my head or my heels. However, I pulled myself together and said ingeniously:

'What are *you* going to do next?'

Tom was brought momentarily to a standstill.

'I shall have to consider that,' he said.

I thought: 'That's unusual.'

'Myrtle has suffered terribly,' he said, more quietly. 'I think I'm the only person who understands exactly what it must have meant to her.'

'She told me you understood.'

'She said that, did she?' Tom suddenly looked at me quite naively.

I nodded my head.

'We've both suffered,' said Tom.

I nodded again. It seemed the only appropriate gesture to such monumental nonsense.

'I've been thinking about Myrtle for some time, Joe.'

'Oh?' I pricked up my ears.

Tom looked at me with a changed, unidentifiable expression. 'I've been thinking,' he said, 'that if you don't marry her, it might be a good idea for me to.'

I received the suggestion without a tremor. I was proud of having identified his expression – it was that of a man who is confident that he has introduced a delicate topic with unequalled tact and dexterity.

I made a non-commital murmuring noise. I think Tom had expected more. He was clearly puzzled that I showed no surprise, let alone passion. He said:

'What do you think?'

I said: 'I've been thinking about it, from a different point of view, of course, for some time.' I paused. 'The trouble about finding a husband for one's mistress, is that no other man seems quite good enough.'

Tom was extremely cross. He laughed, but a purple flush suddenly passed over his face, making his hair look yellower and his eyes greener.

'Witty as usual,' he said.

Whenever anyone says I am something or other 'as

usual', it means he is disapproving of me.

'Perhaps,' he went on, 'we ought to talk just a little more seriously.'

'Would you like some more tea?' I said.

'Thank you.'

A stately air had now come over the proceedings. Tom accepted a cup of tea, and then said with great politeness and consideration:

'I take it that you would have no objection?'

'To your marrying Myrtle? I'm in no position to object.' I changed my tone to one of seriousness. 'I resolved some time ago that if I wasn't going to marry her myself I ought not to stop anyone else marrying her. Of course I don't want to let anyone else – or anything like it. But I shall make myself do it.'

'I see. It seems quite incomprehensible to me, of course.'

I bowed.

Tom said: 'This makes matters a little easier than I'd expected.'

'Easier?' I exclaimed. Perhaps I ought to interpolate that, even after having been prepared for it by Steve, I still thought I had never heard such a silly idea in my life as Tom's proposition. Also I thought Myrtle would see it in exactly the same light.

Tom pursed his lips and smiled.

The telephone rang. Tom and I glanced at each other, each thinking it was Myrtle. I closed the french window and took off the receiver. Tom waited to see if I wanted him to leave the room. I heard the voice of Steve.

'Joe, is Tom there?' He sounded worried.

'Yes.' I handed the receiver to Tom.

They conversed for a few moments, making arrangements to meet in half an hour. Tom put down the receiver, and turned to me with a self-satisfied smile.

'How are you getting on with Steve?' I asked.

'Perfectly well, Joe.' There was an amused glint in his eye, as much as to say: 'If you understood us you would not be alarmed.'

I called the landlady to clear away the tea.

'How's he getting on with his schoolgirls?' I said.

'I don't know. I don't really ask him.' Tom had now taken to setting me an example.

Recalling the scene at the swimming-pool, I said: 'That's wise of you.'

Tom sat in his chair again. 'He's growing up, of course. I realize that he's bound to grow away from me. It's very natural.' Tom paused. 'I encourage him. I don't want him to feel tied.'

I could not help being interested by this crescendo of lies, which, seemingly, we were only half-way through, as he said next: 'The important thing is to avoid scenes, Joe.'

'Don't you have any?' I could hardly believe my ears.

'No, Joe.'

We were interruped by the landlady. Tom lit a cigarette. When she had gone he leaned forward confidently, and said:

'Of course, Steve doesn't know anything about my intentions towards Myrtle.'

'No,' I said. 'No.' I accepted this last, most glorious lie, with a recrudescence of the head-or-heels sensation.

'I hope you won't mention it to him.'

'If Steve doesn't know,' I said, 'you can rely upon me not to tell him, Tom.'

'I know you're one of the discreetest of men, Joe.'

Tom rose to go away, and on this happy, fraudulent note our conversation ended.

Tom had only left the house a minute or two when the telephone rang once more.

'It's Steve again. Has Tom gone? I wanted to speak to you, not him, when I rang before.' Steve's voice was agitated. 'I want to see you, Joe.'

'What for, Steve?'

'I can't tell you now. There isn't time. Tom will be here any moment. I want to see you, Joe.'

I had taken care to have all my time booked up until I went to Oxford. Steve was insistent, and at last I agreed that we might meet in the station refreshment room while I waited for my train. He rang off promptly.

I was mystified.

On Saturday morning I received a letter in unfamiliar handwriting. It was from Miss X.Y. and she said:

Dear Mr. Lunn: I do not know how to begin this letter, as I feel I am at a terrible disadvantage. I quite understand your anxiety about your manuscript, and of course I forgive you for writing a third time. I am afraid I have to ask *you* to forgive *me*, because the manuscript has unfortunately been mislaid. The reason I have delayed so long in writing to you is because I hoped it might turn up. Of course I was looking forward immensely to reading it ...

I burst into a shout of mingled laughter and rage. Miss X.Y. had wasted five months of my time at a most critical point in my career; I was exactly where I started. The letter ended with an offer to read the novel, if I would send another copy, within a week.

At first I was too annoyed to accept, but in due course common sense supervened. I remained convinced, however, that should disasters of any magnitude be possible they would certainly befall me. In this mood I went off to meet Steve.

I hurried down to the platform and into the refreshment room. Steve was nowhere to be seen. I bought a bottle of beer and a cheese roll, and began to eat, keeping my eyes fixed on the door. I finished the cheese roll and I finished the beer. Still no sign of Steve. Suddenly it occurred to me that Steve was in a refreshment room on the wrong platform. I ran across the bridge, and searched for him on the other side. I found him. He was quietly reading a volume of poems by Baudelaire.

'Come out, Steve!' I said impatiently. 'You're in the wrong refreshment room.'

Steve looked injured. 'But I'm not, Joe! This is the right platform.'

'The right platform for somebody else's train, but not mine,' I said, taking him by the elbow and dragging him out. He stuck to his argument. There were two alternative

routes to Oxford: he had chosen the platform for a train
that left three hours later. I realized to my horror that I was
behaving rather like Tom. I decided that Tom had great
provocation.

'Do you want a bottle of beer?' I said, when I had safely
installed him in the right place.

'Yes, please.' Steve wore the expression of a saint on the
eve of martyrdom. This expression did not prevent him
putting down half a Bass in one breath. 'I got very thirsty,
waiting for you,' he said.

'Now, what do you want to tell me?'

We were leaning against the marble-topped counter,
looking outwards at the platform. Behind us were two glass
domes, containing buns, which served as a screen between
us and the waitress. Steve glanced at his glass, and
restrained himself out of politeness from drinking the rest of
the beer before beginning his story.

'I found out that Tom's postponed his trip to America.'

'I know that.'

'I mean *again*, Joe. He's not going till the end of July
now.'

This was news to me.

Steve said nothing. With a mixture of injured dignity and
triumph he now finished his beer.

I was lost for a moment in alarm.

'What's his excuse now?' I asked.

'The job we're doing in the office.'

'I don't believe it.'

'That's what he's going to tell you anyway,' said Steve.

'What's his real reason? Do you know?'

'How should I know? He tells me so many things.'

'Repeat some of them.'

'I wasn't supposed to tell you.'

'Repeat them all the same.'

'He doesn't want to arrive ahead of you and Robert. He
says you intend to send him first to do all the work.'

'But we're tied till the end of July.'

'You told him you were going to make him support you.'

'That's absurd – it was a joke,' I said. 'Robert said we

were going to settle on him like Russian relations.' I smiled at the thought of it. 'And then treat him badly, as if he were a servant.'

'He took it seriously.'

'He's got some other reason, I'll be bound.'

'You mean it's part of his plan for marrying Myrtle?'

'Nonsense! He can't marry Myrtle. It's idiotic!'

'He's trying to make me believe it,' said Steve. 'And he's made himself believe it.'

'That's as may be. It does seem to me that his principal obstacle is making Myrtle believe it.'

Steve looked at me with shrewd grey eyes. 'She's seeing him a lot more than you think.'

I was slightly taken aback. 'Really,' I said.

There was a pause. I sipped a little beer. Steve eyed his empty glass, having no money to buy any more.

'And where do you come into this, Steve? Is Tom's devotion to you correspondingly weaker?'

'Weaker?' said Steve. 'Did you say weaker, Joe? It's stronger. Honestly, it's terrible! I can't get away from it for a moment. He tells me I'm growing away from him, and he doesn't want me to feel I'm tied to him – and then he refuses to let me out of his sight! Last night I wanted to stay at home. To work on my poetry. Honestly, I didn't want to go out with anyone else. I just wanted to stay at home. But he came round to the house. He stood in the middle of the room and said: "I want to know. Are you coming or aren't you?" In front of my father and mother!'

I imagined the scene well, with Tom glaring across the room. 'What did you say?'

Steve shrugged his shoulders. 'I had to go with him.'

'Extraordinary,' I said.

'He's terrified of me being unfaithful.'

I could not help laughing, though it hurt Steve's feelings. 'What about when he goes to America?'

'He expects me to join him in two or three years.'

This was more news to me. 'Indeed!'

'Yes,' said Steve. 'As far as I can see, he intends to marry Myrtle and take her to America; and me to stay here and be faithful to him. For three years!'

I was speechless from the staggering imbecility of it.

'Think of it, Joe!' Steve said, in tones of anguish.

'I'm thinking of what's supposed to happen at the end of three years, Steve, when you join the happy couple in America.'

Steve said: 'I don't think he's got as far as that.'

'It seems a very arbitrary place to draw the line.' I glanced at him, and just at that moment he happened to glance at me. We caught each other's eye, and burst into helpless laughter. All the other people in the refreshment room turned and stared at us.

I glanced at the clock, and realized that the train which was drawing in was the one I had to catch.

'You need another drink, Steve,' I said. 'Goodbye!'

I threw down some money on the counter to pay for a bottle of beer, and left him to drink it.

I reported Tom's latest manoeuvres to Robert, who was alarmed. I could see quite clearly that he thought Tom would never go to America on his own: I think he really doubted whether Tom would ever go at all. We decided to concentrate on our own plans. I now had my visa, and Robert had applied for his. Escaping from the atmosphere of the town for a few hours enabled me to see our affairs in some sort of perspective. I became aware of how events were rolling on. It was June.

We dined in the college, and afterwards went back to Robert's rooms feeling a little more relaxed. We talked about our books, and Robert laughed somewhat unkindly over Miss X.Y.'s letter. As the evening passed I confided more freely my emotions about Myrtle.

'In ten years' time I shall wish I'd married her,' I said, bitterly.

Robert made no comment.

I had begun to feel tired and I launched a boring tirade about remorse, the gist of it being that after doing what you wanted to do it was hypocritical to express remorse.

I noticed Robert looking at the clock. It was after eleven.

The telephone rang.

Robert crossed the room to answer it. I picked up something to read. It was a trunk call for me.

I was frightened: I took over the receiver, certain that I was going to hear of some tragedy.

I heard the distant voice of Myrtle.

'Is that Joe?'

'Yes.'

'It's me, Myrtle.'

'Oh.'

'Darling, I've got a dog!'

'What!'

'I've got a dog, darling. A *dog*!' Her voice sounded excited. Either her depression had been dissipated or she had been drinking.

'Isn't it wonderful?'

'Yes.' First of all I had found it impossible to believe she was saying it was a dog she had got: now I found it impossible to understand what was going on at all.

'I said, "Isn't it wonderful?"'

'I said, "Yes."'

Myrtle's voice came to me with reproach. 'You don't sound very enthusiastic!'

There is only one phrase for expressing what I felt. It was a bit much.

'I'm sorry,' I muttered.

Were it possible to hear anyone's spirits fall, I should have heard Myrtle's fall with an echoing 'woomph!'

'I'm glad,' I said, with as much enthusiasm as I could summon – very little, as a matter of fact.

'It's a red setter.'

'Good,' I said.

'It answers to the name of Brian.'

'What?'

'Brian, B-r-i-a-n.'

'Good heavens!'

'I can't hear you.'

'I said, "How are you?"'

'All right. I'm feeling wonderful. Brian and I went for a

walk in the park this afternoon. We had a wonderful time.'

I could think of nothing to say. I just listened to her voice, which expressed pure happiness.

'You must come and see him.' She paused. 'When do you come back?'

I was suspicious. I said:

'Tomorrow evening.'

'Will you come and see Brian and me?'

'If you'd really like me to . . .' My spirits now fell.

'I'll expect you tomorrow night. Goodbye, darling.'

'Goodbye.'

I glanced at Robert, who had been standing by the fireplace listening.

There was short silence. Then I said:

'Are we all going off our heads?'

I really meant it.

PART FOUR

CHAPTER I
IN AN INTERLUDE

I sat in the open doorway of my cottage, listening to the noise of the rain on the leaves. The hedgerows and trees had come to their full summer thickness. The may was all gone, and green berries were already showing, standing up instead of hanging down; and the ash trees had put out tufts of seeds with beautiful little wings on them. It was nearly the end of June. The first date of Tom's departure had passed, and we were soon to pass the second. In spite of the rain, yellow-hammers were diving like chaser-planes from the tree immediately opposite, and magpies strutted in the field. It was Saturday morning and I was expecting Myrtle.

Yes, incredible though it may seem, Myrtle was coming to spend the afternoon, and apparently she was coming to spend it in the highest of spirits. Ever since the arrival of her dog she had shown no signs other than those of happiness. Tom spoke with enormous portentous knowledge about ebb and flow. I doubted him. Through her gaiety sounded a faintly crazed note that reminded me of hysteria. I thought this kind of happiness must be unstable – just as suddenly as it had come it would collapse and plunge her into deeper despair. Tom thought I was making too much of it.

'You take your responsibilities too heavily,' he said.

I thought it over and decided that perhaps I did. I studied Myrtle, and half-reassured myself. Our meetings were sunny and light-hearted, and apparently quite casual. Of course I asked myself what Myrtle thought she was doing. Nobody could accuse me of not asking myself innumerable, internal questions. But you are more interested in the answer? I have to confess that I expressed my answer in a most undesirable form, the form of a business phrase. Myrtle was continuing our relationship on a day-to-day basis. I presume that a man who is about to go bankrupt still continues to visit his office, use the telephone, and enjoy the creative act of composing business letters. So, Myrtle, before bankrupt love.

On a day-to-day basis, Myrtle was delightful company. Having done justice to my conscience, I began to do justice to myself as a whole again. It was Myrtle's choice. 'Remember that!' I kept saying to myself: 'It's her choice.' I got a consolation from the concept of Myrtle's choice.

The rain ceased and I went out into the lane to pick some flowers. In the hedges there were two kinds of dog-roses, white and pink, and the pink ones had deep carmine buds. Though I knew it was useless I picked a bud, and it unfolded, like a living creature, immediately. I was looking for honeysuckle. In the ditch the campions and cow-parsley had gone. At last I found some honeysuckle that was nearly in bloom: it was growing up a big tree; the stem was old and twined like bast. In the warmth of the bedroom the flowers would open. Ah! Myrtle, I thought.

I returned slowly to the cottage, kicking a loose stone along the road.

I began to think about Tom. During the week there had been a crisis with Steve. As yet I had heard only Tom's side of it, but that was enough to trouble me.

Tom and I had met by chance in the central lending library. It was a large hall with a gallery running round it. The floor was highly polished, and the room always smelt of beeswax and turpentine. Bookshelves were built out from the walls at regular intervals dividing the space into a number of alcoves. These alcoves were used by serious-minded people for silent reading, and by the young for whispered flirtation. I found the mingled amorous cum literary tone of the place most estimable, since it encouraged the serious-minded to flirt and the flirtatious to read.

I had a suspicion that Tom was trying to avoid me. However in the course of moving round the shelves we met face to face. Caught unawares he had an unusual expression. His features looked set, and his skin showed a greyish tinge.

'What's the matter?' I asked.

'I'm a little disturbed. That's all.'

'What about?'

Tom did not reply. I followed him as he went to have his book stamped, and we left together. In the street he paused uncertainly.

'I'll walk along with you,' I said. It was about half-past six and the streets were empty: everyone was having an evening meal. The air was luminous and cool, and our reflections flashed by in the shop-windows.

'What's Steve been doing?' I asked.

'How did you know it was Steve?'

I did not imagine it was Myrtle because I believed his feeling for her to be thorougly bogus. 'I guessed.'

Tom said: 'He told me last night that he was going on holiday with his father and mother.'

I was puzzled. 'What does that matter to you?'

'It matters to me because I was going to take him away myself.'

'But you're going to America, Tom.'

'Before I go to America.'

I was silent for a moment, distracted by confirmation of our suspicions that he did not intend to go. I remembered what Steve had told me in the refreshment room.

'When *are* you going?'

'Later.' He waved his hand impatiently. 'Later ... my dear Joe, don't let your anxiety run away with you.'

'I see,' I said. 'Where were you taking him?'

'To France. He wants to improve his accent.'

Often I had seen the comic side of the patron-protégé relationship. I now saw the reverse. When Tom said Steve wanted to improve his French accent he was speaking with heart-felt seriousness. A vivid picture sprang up in my mind of Steve lounging in a Parisian bistro, probably drinking Pernod and trying to get himself seduced by the woman behind the cash-desk – improving his

French accent.

'I promised to take him,' said Tom. And added: 'He promised he'd go' – thus giving the show away completely.

'Poor old Tom!' I said.

Tom glanced at me, but did not understand why I was smiling. I was thinking of the lectures I had received from him, Tom, the worldly-wise, on how little importance one should attach to people's promises.

'Of course, I could insist,' said Tom. 'His parents would back me up.'

'Good gracious!'

'They're ambitious for his future,' said Tom, reprovingly.

I thought: 'As if Steve hadn't got his eye on the main chance!' I said:

'Where are they going?'

'Grimsby,' said Tom, with distaste.

I said: 'I suppose he'll have to make his own choice.'

'Exactly. It would be disastrous for him to feel tied to me.'

It must have been the tenth time I had heard this phrase, from one or the other of them. Why, I wondered, did nobody point out that Steve had never been tied to anyone but himself, nor was ever likely to be? I contented myself with saying:

'Won't he feel tied to his parents?'

'Certainly! It's very foolish of him.'

It had occurred to me, as no doubt it had to Steve, that escaping from his father and mother in Grimsby would be child's play compared with escaping from his patron in Paris.

'I'm afraid,' said Tom, 'he's going off the rails.'

'Alas! he's not the only one,' said I.

We had come to a crossing of the main streets, and we stopped. In day-time the crossing was the busiest in the town: now it was deserted. In the centre, where the policeman stood on point duty, there remained his pedestal with nobody on it. We were silent. Tom suddenly lowered his head, and I saw a look of misery on his face.

'I'm awfully sorry, Tom.'

'It's my last chance. It means more to me than anything has ever done.' He looked up at me with strained eyes. 'Do you think I ought to buy a new car?'

It was a totally unexpected question. I saw quickly enough what he meant. He had so far lost control that he could envisage trying to bribe Steve with a new car. I wanted to cry 'no'. I said:

'I doubt if it would really help.'

Tom's voice suddenly went dead. 'I didn't think it would. I'm not a fool.'

We both knew the conversation had ended, and we went away immediately in different directions. Something made me look back, and I saw Tom walking with a changed gait. Instead of propelling himself along with his diaphragm thrust out and his shoulders swinging to and fro, he was walking with the slow, stiff movements of an automaton. I had never before realized he was capable of the change. I was shocked and touched.

This sight continued to haunt me in recollection. It came back to me while I was kicking the loose stone along the road up to the cottage. I thought of Tom's predicament, and of all the other people who had found themselves in it. 'Ought I to buy a new car?' Other people; other vehicles – such as steam yachts.

'Ought I to buy him a steam yacht?'

Bearing Steve in mind, I felt the answer was almost certainly 'yes'. Amusement led me to wonder if I was taking Tom's responsibilities too heavily. Indoors, I laid down the bunch of honeysuckle.

My reflections were cut short by the sound of a bicycle bell.

'Darling!' shouted Myrtle's voice from the roadway. 'Come and see who I've brought!'

'Who?' I cried, in mixed incredulity, disappointment and anger. I went outside to see.

'Doesn't he look beautiful!' In the basket on the front of Myrtle's bicycle sat the dog.

'Well!' I exclaimed, in unmixed relief.

Myrtle's face was alight with pleasure. I kissed her. She was wearing a new kind of scent. I kissed her again, and slid my hand warmly over her back.

She made me hold the bicycle, while she set down the animal.

'Brian! Brian!' she called, without the slightest appearance of noticing the inappositeness of its name.

The animal bounded and fussed around. It was a pretty red colour, and it had a charmingly silly, affectionate expression. It kept leaving a little watery trail behind it. I led Myrtle indoors.

Myrtle stirred beside me.

'I thought you were asleep,' I murmured.

'I thought you were!'

We were quiet. The smell of honeysuckle had begun to fill the room.

'Can you hear something?' said Myrtle.

I could. It was the animal whining downstairs.

'Brian wants to come up,' said Myrtle.

'Well, he can't,' said I.

'Oh darling, why not?'

I did not want to get out of bed to open the door. 'You don't have to have dogs in the bedroom.'

'But he's crying. He's only a puppy.'

'All the more reason,' I said. 'We should make him feel shy.'

Myrtle took hold of me gently. 'Please go and fetch him, darling.'

I did as she asked me.

With a flustering patter the animal ran upstairs. Myrtle was delighted. We persuaded it to lie down on one of the mats while I got back into bed.

Myrtle began to chatter happily. She told me about the latest events in her firm. She was doing well. One of her ideas had got the firm a valuable contract from a new client in London. Her employer had promised a rise as well as commission.

I listened with entirely unselfish pleasure, hearing the

voice not of hysteria but of clear-headedness and resource.

After outlining her idea with undisguised competence, Myrtle suddenly felt it was time to retrench behind her true maidenly modesty. 'Of course, it's all luck,' she said. 'I think the people in London just wanted to be nice to me.'

I took hold of her.

Myrtle fluttered her eyelids. 'Don't be silly, darling.'

I began to feel rather more attentive. 'How's your boss getting on with his mistress?' I said, leaning over her.

Myrtle frowned. 'About the same.'

'And how are you getting on with her?'

Myrtle's frown changed to a look of sadness. 'Not very well. I don't think she likes me getting on in the firm.'

'Oh dear.'

Myrtle said with absurd innocence: 'What does it matter to her if I make an extra £5 a week? She can have another £5 any time she likes, without doing any *extra* work. . . .'

'Don't you see,' I said, 'she knows everyone says she's planted there because she's the boss's mistress? She probably takes her position in the firm very seriously.'

'Do you really think so, darling?' Myrtle pondered this new idea. 'She did try to prevent him taking this contract – because it would mean too much reorganization for her! . . . He didn't give in, but he forbade me to go to London again and went himself.'

I laughed quietly.

Myrtle settled herself comfortably against me. 'Ah well,' she said, with a modest smirk, 'I'll find some way of getting round him.'

We were on the verge of beginning to make plans, but something stopped us.

And it turned out that this was her most sensible stretch of conversation. My feeling that the crazed note had disappeared from her gaiety was soon dispelled. A little while later she was talking about cars.

'. . . like the one I shall have next year.'

'Myrtle!' I said. 'Are you going to have a car?'

'Next year.' She paused. 'I'm not going to have the money and not have a car.'

'Why do you want one?'

'For getting about.'

I let her run on. The next time I listened she was saying: 'My gun's come.'

'Your what?' I was constantly finding it impossible to believe my ears.

'My gun. Didn't I tell you I was getting a gun? It came yesterday.'

I felt dizzy – a dog, and a car, and now a gun. I thought she must be going mad. A gun! I suddenly connected, with emotion not far from terror. It may seem very unsoldierly of me. When girls get guns I am convinced it is time for me to go.

'What ever do you want a gun for?'

Myrtle looked thoughtfully at the ceiling. 'To shoot with.'

'Shoot what?'

'Rabbits and things.'

'But where?'

'Oh, in the fields ... woods ...'

I laughed. 'Good heavens! I didn't know you could shoot. Have you learnt?'

'Not yet.'

'Then how on earth? ...'

Myrtle sounded dignified and reproachful. 'The husband of a girl down at the printer's is going to teach me.'

'And then?'

'Then,' said Myrtle in a reasonable tone, 'if I see a rabbit, I shall take a pot at it.'

My fear that she was suffering from hysteria came back in a single bounce. Also, I must add, a certain fear that her gun might fall into the hands of Haxby.

'I rather look forward to potting at rabbits,' she said.

No, I decided: if I had to choose between her potting at rabbits and Haxby potting at me, I should probably be safer to choose the latter.

'There's a warren, or whatever it is, just before we get to the Dog and Duck.'

I suddenly realized what she was thinking.

Myrtle went on, with a giggle: 'I've ordered some tweeds for the autumn.'

I thought: 'You won't be coming here.' It was quite simple. I had no doubt of it.

Even while she was lying beside me I did not doubt the affair was over. This afternoon, for the first time for months, we had been easy and harmonious together. I had felt simple, kind, ready to please; I had said nothing to torment her – because my mind was no longer divided. I felt no temptation to jump out of bed for fear of being tamed. There was no question of my trying to live the rest of my life with someone who did not believe in me as a writer. No *cris-de-cœur*! The struggle was over. I was in the clear.

Myrtle appeared to notice nothing. She prattled on. At last she said gaily: 'Now I'll have to leave you, darling. I'm going to a party, tonight.'

I laughed, as if it were really a joke. 'With the Crows?'

'Given by them!' said Myrtle. 'And Tom's going to be there too.'

'Tut-tut,' I said, lightly smacking her.

'And Brian as well,' said Myrtle. 'Can you imagine it!' She began to play with the dog. 'Come on, Brian! . . .'

In the end she persuaded the animal to sit in the basket, and prepared to leave. I noticed that in the excitement we did not arrange to meet again. We kissed and she rode off, down the lane.

As she disappeared round the corner, I could hear her talking animatedly. 'Look! Brian. Are we going to see some rabbits? Brian? . . .'

I went indoors. I began to read. I failed. I found it was impossible to concentrate. I kept thinking of Myrtle, and thinking: 'It won't do.'

My spirits switched over completely. I had not relaxed when it was time to go to bed, and I found myself unable to sleep. It was light very late, and there was one of the loveliest of sunsets. The trees were quite still and the sky was glowing. I kept getting out of bed to look. Each time the rising moon was a little brighter. The flowers began to smell in the hedgerow opposite, and the birds to be quiet. It was exquisite.

Suddenly, through the open doorway, I noticed a vague patch of moonlight on the wall. I fancied it was a girl, standing soft and naked. When I looked it was nothing like it, of course. I smiled at myself. And from the window came a gust of air, blowing over my body. My imagination stirred violently, and a new thought burst in like a shooting-star.

'I must look for someone else.'

CHAPTER II

SPORTS DAY

The school sports had been postponed because of bad weather. Nobody wanted them now. Sports day was the sort of climax you could not approach twice and the headmaster's second choice of date lighted on the coldest day of summer. After morning prayers he called attention to the temperature – as if the boys were not shivering already.

'Now don't let me see any boy this afternoon without his overcoat!'

The boys listened in a docile fashion.

'Now don't let me see any boy . . .' His particular form of injunction always sounded less like an order to obey than an invitation to deceive. He descended from the rostrum, clutching his gown tightly round him. Daily he was embarrassed by little boys who waylaid him.

'Well, what is it?' This morning he had to stop because there was a long queue of them. I sauntered by. Each little boy appeared to be asking the same question.

'Please sir, will a mackintosh do?'

I moved away. I was concerned with the part I had to play in the sports. The arrangements were in the hands of Bolshaw, and in the previous year I had found myself down on his list as telegraph-steward. This meant that I was on duty beside the cricket scoreboard, thirty yards in front of the distinguished spectators' row of chairs, for the whole of the afternoon. I thought telegraph-steward was an intolerable rôle, suited only to someone who felt a pathological desire to be in the public eye. I aspired to be the prize-steward, since this appeared to involve no duties at all. I told Bolshaw that I thought if I were only given a chance I could make an exceptionally good prize-steward. I tried to convey that I could care for the prizes as if they were my own children.

I went to the field early in the afternoon. Bolshaw had failed to circulate his list in the morning, and I was hopeful. I decided to install myself as prize-steward before he arrived. The games master was already there. Bolshaw did the organizing: the games master did the work. The weather was wretched and I was wearing an overcoat. There was a wind blowing, no blustering winter wind, but a summer one that insinuated its iciness. The games master came out of the pavilion, wearing a high-necked sweater and a pair of gym shoes.

'Come on, Joe!' he said. 'Come an' 'elp me with the prizes, before the nobs come.'

The games master was a friend of mine. He was a middle-aged family man, an ex-sergeant-major, unlettered, cheerful and fond of boys. I helped him unpack the prizes. The wind rustled the pieces of tissue paper out of our fingers.

'Brr,' said the games master, jumping springily from one foot to the other. 'The ruddy Lord Mayor'll 'ave to be set up like a brass monkey for this. 'E'll need 'is gold chain to tie 'em on with.'

We surveyed the table, and the desired objects for which, like children of my own, I was to care. There were electro-plated cups of different sizes, accompanied by a collection of teaspoons, cruets, rose-bowls with wire across the top and jam-pots with electro-plated lids.

''Ere, what's this?' said the games master. 'Not something useful?' It was a safety-razor: I read the card, on which was written:

JUNIOR 100 YARDS

'Good God!' I said, and rapidly went through the other cards. Someone had playfully exchanged them all. A handsome case of silver teaspoons was going to the winner of the junior egg-and-spoon race, while the victor ludorum was going to get a plastic serviette-ring for his efforts.

We began a hasty redistribution. The Lord Mayor arrived. He was going to give away the prizes. He was a short, vigorous, red-faced man, with a bay-window and a powerful glare. He looked as if he had high blood pressure. He also looked as if he thought the games master and I were trying to steal the prizes. He stationed himself very close to the table and glared at us. We retired to the pavilion, which was filled with boys in different stages of undress, chattering at the top of their voices.

The games master pushed his way in.

'Now then! Listen to me! You all know what a cold afternoon it is. Well, we're going to get it over at the double. I'm not going to 'ave you all standing there, doing sweet fanny adams and catching your death. Understand this, now! Any boy who isn't ready for 'is race loses 'is chance!' There was a hush. 'What's more, I'll run 'im round the gym tomorrow morning with the slipper be'ind 'im.' The hush turned to laughter. 'Who's not brought 'is overcoat or 'is mac?' The laughter turned back into a hush. 'All right!'

We were about to begin what promised to be the fastest sports meeting in the history of athletics.

Many of the boys were excellent untrained athletes, and the school games record was highly creditable. But the Greek spirit burned with the lowest possible flame in the staff. Those given official duties walked about with their collars turned up and a look of hard-boiled irritation: as prize-steward, I was sorry for them.

As I walked across the field I met Bolshaw.

'Lunn,' he said, 'Lunn!'

'Yes.'

Bolshaw stared at me, with his shoulders hunched inside an old-fashioned overcoat. His hat was pulled down to his spectacles.

'Lunn,' he said, 'I've rearranged the duties. I've got a different one for you.'

'What?'

'Telegraph-steward.'

I thought: 'It's not different at all!' I said: 'But the prizes,

Bolshaw. Who's to look after the prizes?' At that moment I felt devoted to the prizes.

'I've thought of that,' said Bolshaw. 'I'll keep an eye on the prizes myself.'

'Myself.' I could not argue. I turned up the collar of my overcoat and made for the telegraph-post.

At the post I found Trevor and Benny waiting to assist me. I looked at Benny. 'What are you doing here?' I said loudly.

Benny's face took on a grossly pathetic expression.

Trevor said: 'He's a menace. Send him away!' He disliked Benny.

This made me feel inclined to let Benny stay. Like a dog Benny sensed it.

'Don't listen to him, sir.'

I hesitated. Benny's expression was poised on the edge of a ludicrous, grateful smile. There was a loud bang. The first race had begun. It occurred to me that if I sent Benny away I should have to take a hand in the work myself. That settled it.

Soon I was delighted by the way things were going. I normally found sports meetings tedious: today's performance began at the pace of a smart revue – it was perfect.

As usual, perfection did not last. Bolshaw had instructed the starter not to wait for boys who were late for the start. Naturally it was not long before a wretched little boy ran up as the gun went off. The starter shouted at him. The boy jumped like a rabbit and started to run down the track. The effect was dramatic. The spectators immediately came to life.

'Go it, the little 'un!' they shouted. He did not catch up but they cheered him loudly as he walked off the field.

Races followed each other at a pace more suited to Americans than Greeks. And then the weather took a hand. The clouds had been lowering, the wind dropped, and now there came a shower of icy rain. Immediately the spectators made for the lines of thick leafy trees on each side of the field.

The boys in the middle ran towards the pavilion. On the

way they surged past the distinguished spectators, and saw
the headmaster beside himself with alarm because rain-
drops were falling on the prizes.

'Look after the prizes!' he was crying. He stripped off his
overcoat and laid it over them. 'Give me some more coats!
You there, boy! Give me your overcoat. Boy! Boy!'

The Lord Mayor was struggling to undo his chain. The
boys swarmed round, and in a few seconds the table was
covered with a mountain of clothes.

'That's enough!' cried the headmaster. 'Enough!
Enough! Don't be silly!' He furtively cuffed a boy who was
taking no notice and the Lord Mayor pretended not to see.

The rain fell.

Under the trees it was dry. Several masters sat in their
cars: the remainder, together with the boys and their
parents, walked up and down to keep warm. It looked like a
German theatre audience on the *Bummel*.

I was walking gaily with the games master. As we came
to one of the turns in our promenade I glanced idly at the
cars. Somebody inside one of them waved to me. The
windscreen was steamed up, so I went closer. To my
astonishment I saw it was our senior science master,
Simms. He beckoned to me, and opened the door of his car.

Bolshaw had led me to believe he was at death's door.
Simms shook my hand with a light, firm grasp, and I found
myself looking into a pair of clear, healthy, blue eyes.

'I haven't risen from the dead,' he observed.

I was too embarrassed to reply.

'I expect I shall in due course,' he went on. He spoke
slowly. 'But I haven't yet passed through those preliminary
formalities that cause us so much concern.'

'I'm delighted,' I stammered.

I was very fond of Simms. I liked his face. He had a
broad head, bald with a fringe of grey hair, and narrow,
delicate jaw. His skin was pink, and his face showed his
passing shades of emotion. It was the face of a man who
had always gone his own way, and had thus arrived at a
state of lively self-satisfaction. He was now old and frail,

but it was probable that he had always looked frail. He was gentle and unaggressive – the opposite of Bolshaw. Yet had I been asked to say which of the two had done fewer things he did not want to do, I should have said Simms. The question would have been particularly relevant at this juncture, when the subject was Simms's resignation.

'Are you quite better?' I asked.

'My asthma still distresses me frequently.'

'I mean, well enough to come back to school?'

'Had you heard to the contrary?' He glanced at me. 'I'm very curious, my dear fellow,' he said, his hand on my arm. 'People come and give me advice, good and disinterested advice. And shortly afterwards I hear, to my astonishment, that I've taken it! Can you explain that to me?'

I shook my head.

'I'm very gratified that anyone should think I have the sense to take good and disinterested advice. One is. You would be, I'm sure.'

'When are you coming back?'

'Oh, quite soon, you know. This term. There's the matter of salary during the summer vacation to be considered.' He smiled slyly to himself.

I looked out of the window, amused.

The rain had stopped. I told him I must return to my telegraph-board.

'It has been nice to see you,' he said. 'I shall be seeing you again shortly. Next Monday.'

I stared at him. He was going to give up his job to nobody; and he had every intention of teasing Bolshaw and me for as long as he could spin out his time.

The weather was now colder. The headmaster and the Lord Mayor returned to their places of honour, but several of the other distinguished spectators and parents had quietly deserted. Before the headmaster sat down he called the boys to remove their overcoats from the prize table. They cheerfully obeyed, and after jostling and fighting they went away again, leaving the array of cups and cruets to shine sullenly in the grey light.

Fred joined me to watch one of the field events. His bare

arms and legs looked greyer than ever. He said:

'I saw your girl-friend, Joe.'

I was surprised, because Myrtle ought to have been at work.

'While you was talking to old Simms in 'is car. She just came in to shelter and went out again.'

'Are you sure?' I said.

'It's quite true,' put in Trevor. He laughed with nasal contempt as he said: 'She was with that awful man, Haxby.'

I said nothing, and the boys were diffidently silent. Fred was upset. ''Ave I said the wrong thing?'

I shrugged my shoulders.

Myrtle's action must have been deliberate. It could only mean the interlude was now over. More than anything else I felt irritation. If the interlude was over the whole thing had to end once and for all.

It had taken me a long time, far too long a time, to steel myself to do it. Now I was ready at last. It seemed a curious off-hand occasion on which to decide, but that is how it was.

My duties at the board came to an end. The only remaining event was the senior mile, and I decided to watch it from near the winning-post. It was one of the events in which Frank was hoping to shine, since he was in the running for victor ludorum.

While I was standing in the crowd of boys. I overheard a strange remark. 'Where's the victor ludorum's prize?' I turned round but I was too late to see who had spoken. I knew the answer, because I had labelled it myself: it was the case of a dozen silver teaspoons, right at the front of the table.

Frank won the race. There was cheering, and all the boys gathered round the Lord Mayor to hear him speak before giving the prizes.

The Lord Mayor spoke for a long time. He clearly had great stamina. His was the most Greek performance of all. I thought he would never stop.

At last the boys filed up to him for their prizes. He shook

hands vigorously. The boys blushed and grinned and walked away with cruets, toast-racks, jam-pots and so on. The safety-razor was very properly won by a bearded boy in the fifth form.

We came to the victor ludorum. The contest had been won by Frank. He came up, with a mackintosh thrown over his athletic rig, looking pale and handsome and unusually shy. The Lord Mayor gave Frank his warmest handshake and his most powerful glare: then he prepared to give Frank his prize. The victor ludorum's prize was not there.

A sudden hush fell on the crowd of boys.

'Where is it?' came the headmaster's nattering voice. 'Where is it?' I thought if there was one question not worth asking, that was it.

'Where is it? What is it? What was the prize, I say?'

'Some silver spoons,' came the voice of his secretary, from below the horizon.

'They're not here now!'

'It's no use blaming me.'

'I'm not blaming anybody! I only want to know where they are!' Pause. 'Who was responsible for the prizes?'

I thought of the prizes, my prizes.

'Mr Bolshaw,' said the secretary.

I looked round. There was no sign of Bolshaw: he had gone home.

'I thought it was Mr Lunn,' said the headmaster.

I trembled.

'No, Mr Bolshaw.'

Truth had prevailed. I could hardly believe it.

Meanwhile, the Lord Mayor was filling in time by giving Frank's hand more jolly shakes.

Murmurs ran through the crowd. 'They can't find the victor ludorum's prize. Someone's swiped it.'

'Be quiet there! Do be quiet!' cried the headmaster.

Undismayed, the Lord Mayor shook Frank's hand again. The headmaster whispered furiously into his ear. 'Send the boy away! Tell him we will give him his prize later!'

I wondered what would happen to Bolshaw.

The house-captains filed up for their shields, but the

crowd now paid the scantiest attention to the proceedings. Where were the teaspoons? Who was the lucky boy?

It was quite obvious what had happened. While the boys had been clustered round the table, struggling with their overcoats, one of them had smartly caught up the silver teaspoons. The games master and I could swear to the case's having found its way safely to the table. It was up to the headmaster to find out where it had gone next.

The headmaster did not find out, nor did any of the other masters. I can tell you now that nobody ever did find out. And was Bolshaw held responsible for it all? Was he asked to resign, for lacking sense of responsibility and discipline? Does justice prevail on this earth?

I went away from the field thinking about Bolshaw. I arrived home thinking about Myrtle.

The more I thought about Myrtle's appearance with Haxby, the more I felt venomous. My forbearance, my detachment, all those qualities to which I aspired, vanished. And I can only say that to the very depths of my soul I was fed-up with her.

CHAPTER III

SCENES OF DOMESTICITY

The newspapers were filled with international crises. They were beginning to have a mesmerizing effect. But I was not completely mesmerized: I had decided to see Myrtle as little as possible until the term ended; and then, whether I was going to America or not, to quit the town without leaving an address.

It takes two to make a parting, and it takes two to avoid a meeting if they live not much more than a mile apart. Never before had I been so intensely aware of playing out time. Sometimes I felt like a powerful man in control of his own destiny: sometimes I felt I was being hunted by Hitler and Myrtle in conjunction.

One evening I was sitting peacefully outside the french windows of my lodgings marking examination papers. At the bottom of the garden the landlady's niece and Mr Chinnock were working. It was one of what Myrtle and I had been used to call their 'off-nights', and they were spending it in weeding the vegetable plot.

Occasionally one or the other of us would stop to cough. This was because smoke was blowing over us from a bonfire of weeds in a neighbouring garden. It was always the same. There were so many gardens and the neighbours were such indefatigable incendiarists, that one could never hope to sit in one's garden for an hour or so without somebody lighting a bonfire. The breeze appeared to blow in a circular direction.

I was just completing my estimation of the mathematical powers of a junior form, when I heard the landlady showing someone into my room. I looked round, and saw Steve. He stepped out of the window.

'I'm sorry to bother you,' he said, and sat down on the step near my chair. He waited till I put down the last paper, and then pulled out of his pocket a poem that he had written.

'You see, Joe!' he said. 'When I can get away from Tom for a week-end I really do do some work.'

I read the poem. I have observed earlier that Steve's poems showed talent. This poem showed quite as much talent as usual and somewhat greater length. I congratulated him.

The trouble I find with a poem is that when you have read it, and congratulated the author, there is nothing else to say. It is not like a novel, where you can sit down to a really good purging burst of moral indignation at the flatness of his jokes, the shapelessness of his plot, and the immorality of his characters.

A silence fell upon Steve and me. 'Britons, never, never, ne-ever shall be slaves!' whistled Mr Chinnock.

'Tom isn't going to America,' said Steve.

'Why not? How do you know?'

Steve shrugged his shoulders. 'He says there's going to be a war.'

'Oh.'

'Don't you think there is?'

'What?'

'Going to be a war.'

'Possibly.' I paused, and said with shameful lack of conviction: 'I hope so.' The fact is that I did not want to give up the idea of going to America.

Steve glanced at me. 'By the way, you know Myrtle's going about saying that you intend to go to America if there *is* a war.'

'The devil!' I was very angry.

'That's what she's saying, anyway.'

'Who told you?'

'I heard it myself.'

Though my own conduct may not have been above reproach, I was infuriated by Myrtle's perfidy. I began to question Steve for more circumstantial evidence. He was speaking the truth, and he was in a position to know what Myrtle was saying to other people, since he was now going regularly to the parties she frequented with Haxby.

In my anger, I thought: 'That's one more thing against her!'

'Surely Tom's furious?' I said.

Steve said: 'I think he thought she was saying it to provoke you.'

'Well, it has!'

Steve laughed good-naturedly.

'What else has she been saying about me?'

'I don't think I ought to repeat this scandal, Joe,' he said with embarrassment.

'You can't put me off now, Steve.'

'She told Tom,' Steve began slowly, 'that she was never in love with you.'

'For what reason does she think she? . . .'

'I know, I know. She admits that you have a curious attractive power. You're now spoken of as if you were a sort of Svengali. It's ridiculous, of course. Anybody can see that you're not like Svengali.'

'Hell!'

'I think we ought to be a little quieter, Joe.' Steve motioned towards the landlady's niece and Mr Chinnock, who were easily within earshot.

With an effort I simmered down.

'Anything else?' I asked.

Steve did not reply.

'I bet Tom put that idea into her head.'

'If you're going to break it off, it's not a bad idea, is it, Joe?'

'That wasn't why he did it. He'll next prove that she's always been in love with him. And he with her.'

'Heavens!' said Steve, not having thought of this before.

'That's his plan, mark my words. It leads to a proposal of marriage.'

Steve looked distinctly crestfallen.

'Though what her plan is, I don't know,' I went on. 'No

doubt it will do her more harm than good.'

'I'm sorry,' said Steve.

I was regaining my detachment. There was much in what Steve observed about Myrtle saying she had never been in love with me. It was a face-saving device. It was the first sign of her beginning to protect herself. I suddenly thought: 'She's pulling out.'

Steve broke into my reflections.

'I suppose you know Trevor's safe.'

I felt as much shock that he knew about it as relief that a disaster had been avoided. I said: 'Oh!' in a sharp, off-hand tone.

We relapsed into silence again. Steve stepped indoors and brought a cushion to sit on.

It's very bad to sit on anything cold,' he said.

'Nonsense.'

Steve paused, and began to smile at me. 'I know what you haven't heard about. I've been learning First Aid.' He saw my look of disbelief. 'Honestly, I have Joe. If there's a war and I'm conscripted and I've got my certificates perhaps I'll be able to get into the Medical Corps.'

I had no idea whether he was speaking the truth, but I could see his aim was to soothe my feelings, so I let him go on.

'I've taken an exam in it,' he said. There was a glint in his eye. 'I doubt if I've passed.'

I said: 'Was it hard?'

'It wasn't hard,' said Steve, 'but it was terribly repulsive.'

Steve recounted his incompetent performance in the practical tests, and in spite of my woes I began to smile.

Steve played up.

'The theoretical was terrifying. They asked me what I'd do with a baby in a convulsion. Fancy asking *me*, Joe! I wouldn't know what to do with a baby if it was *not* in a convulsion.'

'What was the answer?'

'Put it in a bath!' Steve paused triumphantly. Neither of us heard my landlady show in somebody else. There was a bustling noise beside us, and there stood Tom. His face was like thunder.

'I have something to say to you. Would you mind coming indoors?'

Steve picked up his cushion and I my examination papers, and we trailed into my room. Tom closed the french windows behind us.

'It's as well to keep these matters private,' he said, with an air that was both polite and reproving.

I did not reply. I had no idea what Tom had come to say. Our laughter had disappeared, as if he had made us feel ashamed of it. Steve, on the grounds that nothing Tom would say was likely to make life easier for him, was already looking apprehensive.

I sat down. Steve sat down. Tom remained standing. By great effort he was keeping his features composed. I refused to open the conversation.

'I came to tell you that I've bought a new car.'

To be quite frank, the speech for me was something of an anticlimax, and also mildly funny. In my imagination Tom's new car had become mixed up with a steam yacht.

Steve had apparently not been previously informed of the manœuvre. He was not unnaturally surprised. Foolishly he said:

'What for, Tom?'

Tom turned his attention to him. 'Aren't you interested to know what kind it is?'

'Of course,' said Steve. 'But I wondered what you'd bought it for?'

'Don't you know?' Tom was looking at him fixedly. His tone of voice was level enough; but there was a look in his eye, a bursting, concentrated look.

'No,' said Steve, trying to look at me, but finding the hypnotic effect of Tom's gaze too powerful.

'Can't you guess?' Tom smiled at him.

There was silence; in which I thought of saying: 'Tom, for Pete's sake stop it!' and rejected the idea.

Steve looked down, shaking his head.

'I should have thought you would have realized,' Tom

aid, with ominous silkiness, 'it was to make our trip to
Paris more comfortable.'

Steve looked at him. Nothing was said.

I shifted in my chair. I was irritated that Tom had not
given me a chance to get out of the room if he intended to
make a scene. On the other hand I was faintly hypnotized,
myself.

'I said I couldn't go, Tom,' said Steve.

'Don't be silly, Steve. Of course you can.'

'I can't, Tom. You know my people want me to go away
with them.'

'They want you to come with me.'

'That isn't true.'

'Yes, it is.' Tom glared at him now. 'I have it in writing!'

'Look!' said Tom, pulling out an envelope from his
pocket. 'This letter's from your mother, saying she agrees to
your coming with me. Now we have it in black and white!'
He handed it to Steve. 'Read it!'

Steve refused to read it.

'All right,' said Tom, angrily. 'If you haven't the
manners to read it...'

'I'm *not* coming!' Steve interruped him.

'What's your excuse?'

'I don't need an excuse, Tom.'

Tom waved the letter in front of his face. 'What are you
going to say to this?' He waved it again, with a sweep of
greater amplitude. 'I've got it in writing!'

I thought he must be going slightly mad. The whole of
his face, though composed, now looked somehow inflamed.

'It's in black and white.' He deliberately lowered his
voice again.

Suddenly Steve leaned forward, snatched the letter from
his hand, and threw it in the fireplace. There was no fire.

Tom stared at it, and pursed his lips in a smile. Then he
glanced at me. I felt embarrassed.

Steve said: 'This is intolerable. Why do you make these
scenes, Tom?'

'Because I want you to go with me to France.'

'But I don't want to go.' Steve was looking miserable.

'I think you do really.'

'I've told you, I don't. I can't say more than that. I want to feel free.'

'I *want* you to feel free, Steve.'

'Then why don't you give me a chance to be it?'

'You can be perfectly free with me.' Tom moved nearer to him. 'You're perfectly free now.' He made a gesture 'There's the door. You're free to go out through it, this very moment.'

Steve did not move.

'At least go out and have a look at the car.'

'I don't want to see it. And I don't want to go in it!'

'Do you mean to say I've wasted my money?'

At the mention of money, I thought Steve looked startled.

'Are you going to let me waste my money, without even looking at it?' Tom's voice was becoming angry again.

I thought that as he must have bought the car on the hire-purchase system the waste was not permanent.

'Heaven knows!' Tom now burst out, 'I've spent enough already. And what have I got for it? I've spent pounds and pounds!'

'I didn't ask you to.'

'Pounds and pounds!' Tom shouted.

'I don't want the car.'

'Then at least, *see* it!'

'I'm not going to see it.'

'You're *going* to see it!' Tom had been getting nearer, and now he pounced on Steve.

There had been so much argument about the car that certainly I wanted to see it. Steve was determined not to. He resisted.

'Come and see it!' shouted Tom, and dragged him off his chair. He rolled towards the fireplace and upset the fire irons with a deafening clatter. Outside, in the hall, the landlady's dog began to bark.

'Pipe down!' I said.

They desisted. Steve picked himself up, and Tom stood glowering. Looking sulky and furious, Steve straightened his tie.

'I've had enough of this!' said Tom, in a powerful whisper.

'I'm sorry, Tom.'

'I've had enough of this! Are you going to come and see the car or aren't you?'

No reply from Steve.

'It's the last chance.'

No reply.

Tom was now oblivious of my presence. He thrust his face close to Steve's. Steve wilted.

'Are you going to come to France or not? I must have the answer now.'

No answer.

'If you don't answer now, I shall never give you another chance. I have my plans.'

Steve glanced at him.

'It may interest you to know that if you don't go' – Tom paused for dramatic effect – 'I shall take Myrtle!'

'Don't be ridiculous, Tom!' At last Steve spoke. He glanced at me for support.

Tom was furious. 'It's not ridiculous! Who told you it's ridiculous? Joe?' He glanced at me. 'You may think it's ridiculous, but Myrtle doesn't! I know Myrtle. You may not think I'm wonderful, but Myrtle does! She needs me. It's only my responsibility for you that's kept me from going to her. She needs me, and I need her! We need each other.' His voice, though kept low, had tremendous power. 'I want your answer now. Is it to end or isn't it? If you don't speak I shall go straight to Myrtle – she's waiting for me now – and ask her to marry me!' He choked. 'Is it to end or isn't it? I shall go straight to Myrtle!'

Steve did not speak.

Tom waited.

Steve still did not speak.

I saw nothing for it but for Tom to go.

Suddenly he let out an indistinguishable cry.

Steve and I looked at him in alarm.

Tom opened his mouth to speak again and failed. He had

to go.

Steve looked down at the carpet.

Tom picked up the letter from the hearth.

I thought: 'Come on, you've got to go!'

In a last dramatic move Tom tore up the letter and threw down the pieces. Then he turned. I made to open the door for him, but he pushed me out of the way. You may think it strange that I opened the door for him to go out and propose marriage to my mistress. The fact is that I was determined to see the car. I followed Tom across the hall and prevented him from slamming the door, so that I could peep out. I saw it as Tom drove away. And I concluded that Tom was not as mad as he seemed. In my opinion it was a car that would melt the heart of any boy.

I went back to Steve, who was sitting in his chair, shivering and almost of the verge of tears.

I said: 'You'd better have a drink, my lad.'

Steve waited helplessly while I mixed some gin and vermouth in a tumbler. He drank it.

I had nothing more to say, so I picked up another bundle of examination papers and resumed my marking.

After a while, when he had drained the glass, Steve stood up. I looked at him questioningly.

In a jaded voice he said: 'I suppose I'd better go after him.'

CHAPTER IV

ROUND THE CLOCK-TOWER

To relieve my feelings I wrote a letter to Robert. It will save writing anything fresh if I quote a piece of it. Here it is:

My sympathy for Tom is quite exhausted. And so is my patience. He said that Steve caused him a lot of pain, and I took it quite seriously. Sometimes the man was obviously in a state of abject misery and it would have taken a heart of stone not to be concerned for him. But his latest efforts are the limit. At one and the same time he's trying to get Steve to go away with him and proposing marriage to Myrtle! What he thinks he's doing, I cannot imagine. But it's me who's the biggest fool for being taken in by him. I thought he was heading for a tragedy. Instead of which it's quite clear it's nothing but a harlequinade. If clowns come in with red hot pokers and policemen with strings of sausages I shan't be surprised. Anything they can do has already been eclipsed by Tom's own clowning. As for his proposing marriage to Myrtle, it's laughable. What a proposal! Goodness knows how she'll take it. Faint with surprise – unless she simply concludes that he's gone off his head. It's time he went to America – only I doubt if he'll ever go. I really think he is a lunatic.

I wrote a good deal more in the same strain. After completing it I felt a certain satisfaction at having stated my position. To state one's position is a firm manly thing to do: it is right that it should give satisfaction.

There followed a few days of unexpected respite. I neither saw nor heard anything of Tom, Steve or Myrtle. I was very busy at school, because the end of the term was near. The days passed and I counted them as eagerly as my pupils counted them for not dissimilar reasons. They were days that separated me from freedom.

However I was doomed not to escape so easily. Myrtle began to ring me up again, wanting to see me. I tried to put her off.

'Surely you can spare me a few moments?' she said.

I felt bitterly cruel, but I kept to my resolve. Was I doing it for her sake? I do not know. But I do know that in the end it is harder to go on loving someone you do not see than someone you do.

When I refused to meet Myrtle I had not considered the possibility of our seeing each other by chance. Though the town was large, one was always running into people one knew. In the early days of my falling in love with Myrtle, when I did not know her well enough to ask her to meet me, I had spent many hours glancing into the windows of shops where I did not intend to buy anything. I used to have a superstition that if I circulated round the clock-tower long enough she would be sure to come.

I will not describe our clock-tower in detail, because I feel that if you were able to identify our town my novel would lose some of its universal air. Fortunately I can indicate its outstanding quality, since this does not distinguish it from the clock-towers in most other provincial towns. It was wondrously ugly.

Our clock-tower really did provoke wonder. Its ugliness set fire to the imagination, but that was only the beginning of wonderment. In the first place I always used to wonder why anybody had ever put it there. For displaying the time of day it was totally unnecessary: the surrounding shop-fronts were plastered with an assortment of clocks which offered the public the widest choice in times they could possibly have wished for. Could it be, I wondered as I stared at its majestic erectness, our contribution to the psychopathology of everyday life? And who had designed it? Was such a monument designed by an architect who specialized for life on clock-towers; or was it thrown off by some greater man in his hour of ease? Surely the latter! Small wonder, then, that the citizens of our town were proud of the clock-tower. It had its place in our hearts. 'It's ugly,' we thought, 'but it's home!'

Now my desire to avoid meeting Myrtle was not so frantic that I broke the routine of my movements round the town. If I happened to be circling the clock-tower, that was that. And one morning at lunch-time I happened to be circling it, on my way to lunch. It was not Myrtle I ran into; it was Steve.

Steve was walking alone, with his shoulders hunched and his face expressing misery. I caught him by the elbow, as it looked as if he were going to pass me without seeing me. He pushed the hair out of his eyes and tried to smile at me.

'I haven't seen you for a long time,' I said.

'No, Joe.' He looked down at the ground.

For some reason or other I noticed that he was taller than he had been six months ago.

'Have you been busy?'

'No. Just jogging along.' He glanced at me furtively. 'I couldn't face you after that scene Tom made in your house.'

I said: 'You shouldn't worry about that.' I paused. 'You're looking under the weather. Is Tom still playing hell?'

'I don't know.'

'What do you mean, Steve? You must know.'

'I don't, Joe. I haven't spoken to Tom since he left your house.'

I was astounded. I drew Steve out of the stream of men and women going to their lunch, so that I could go on talking to him. We leaned against some rails of steel tubing that had been erected to prevent people stepping off the pavement underneath buses.

'Where is he?' I asked.

'He's in Oxford today, but he was here before that.'

'And you didn't see him?' I continued incredulously.

'I've seen him in the office, of course.' He stopped. 'But he won't speak to me.'

'What a change for you!'

Steve did not smile. He looked extremely glum. 'It's a change for the worse.'

I had been tactless.

'He's been spending a lot of time with Myrtle, as far as I can gather. He won't spend any with me.'

I did not know what to say. I was trying to frame some appropriate remark when Steve burst out:

'It's really over!'

'Surely, it can't be.'

'You never took this business with Myrtle seriously enough!'

'I should think not. It's ridiculous.'

Steve shrugged his shoulders. He was completely downcast. He said:

'I feel absolutely lost without him.'

He must have noticed a look of alarm in my face. He moved away, saying: 'We can't go on talking about this, here.'

We moved a few yards further along, and then we stopped again, frequently being wedged against the railing by the passing crowds. Traffic swept by.

'Did you see his new car?' said Steve.

'Yes.'

'He's gone to Oxford in it.'

I thought this conversation was getting us nowhere. I said: 'I'd no idea you'd take it like this, Steve. I'm awfully sorry.'

'I'd no idea, either,' said Steve. 'It's come to me as a terrible shock.' For an instant I fancied I heard a dramatic note that rang false; and then it occurred to me that people often are dramatic when deeply moved. 'I suppose I shall get used to it in time,' Steve said, rather as if his mother and father had suddenly died. 'I was a fool!' he cried, and tears came into his eyes.

'This is beyond me,' I said.

'You don't understand, Joe!' Steve spoke with force: his voice was trembling. 'I feel terrible. I feel lost, Joe. There's no point in anything! . . . You can't imagine what it's like to feel that all your plans for the future have broken down.

You don't know what it's like, when you've had somebody who flatters your self-esteem all the while and makes you feel you're somebody – and then he stops, suddenly! I feel like a man in a ship that's sunk.' He was trembling with anguish. 'I feel,' he cried, 'like a banker who's lost his bank!'

At that moment a bus passed so close that I could not be expected to reply. A banker who had lost his bank – never had I imagined a remark could contain so much accuracy, penetration and truth.

Steve was waiting for me to say something.

'Poor old Steve,' I said. 'You'll find another.'

The following morning I received three letters. They were from Tom, Myrtle and Miss X.Y. I looked at the envelopes. I was sitting in my lodgings, just about to begin my breakfast. I was alone in the room.

'Dammit!' I said aloud. 'Art comes first, and I'm damned if I'll pretend it doesn't!'

And I opened Miss X.Y.'s letter first. It was short and to the point, and my spirits rose incredibly. She praised my book. I felt as if my hands were trembling. She suggested some revision and some cuts: instantly I saw how they could be done. 'I'm safe!' I cried. 'I'm safe!' I did not quite know what it meant, but I knew it was true. I was ready to begin work on the manuscript immediately: I could hardly wait. The world might be falling about my ears but something went on telling me – to be correct, I went on telling myself – I was safe.

In this mood I opened Myrtle's letter. It said:

I must see you. Please. M.

And then I opened Tom's letter. It began thus:

Dear Joe: I challenge what you say about me in the letter you have just written to Robert.

I was flabbergasted. I already knew that when Robert left his room Tom took the opportunity of reading his private letters, but this was the first time he had ever taken the opportunity of replying to them. I knew that Robert could never have shown him my letter. I remembered Tom's having read one of my postcards on a question of fact – namely, the date of his departure for America. He had replied with fact – namely, a date that subsequently turned out to be false. But this was quite different, and so was the nature of Tom's reply.

Tom's letter began with a challenge, moved on to a denunciation, passed through a reproach, and ended up with a rebuke. Was there any sign of his being ashamed of having read someone else's private correspondence? No. Was there any sign of his being aware of a weak moral position? No. Was there any sign of self-consciousness whatsoever? Not a vestige.

I glowered. 'I stand by every word of it!' I said aloud.

Had I known where he was I would have written to him on the spot. I threw down his letter, and picked up Myrtle's. My glowering died away. I realized that I must see her again. I went to the telephone.

Having made up my mind to see her I wanted to behave with some show of decency, but it was not easy. I wanted the meeting to be as short as possible. I pretended I was exceedingly busy; Myrtle said she was, too. After an awkward discussion we arranged to meet in the town immediately we came out of work that afternoon. Our routes home crossed at the clock-tower, and it was there that we fixed our rendezvous. I thought of Steve. I promised myself that after I met Myrtle at the clock-tower I would go nowhere near it for months.

It was an airless, golden evening. Early in the morning the clouds had drawn away from the sky, leaving a pale brilliant dome of pure blue, from which the sun shone all day upon the roofs and streets. I arrived at the clock-tower first. There was a big chemist's shop, and I leaned against the railings in front of it. From time to time I caught its characteristic smell, though there was no breeze. Trams halted and moved on at different points in the circle. Buses passed to and fro leaving a trail of petrol fumes. The sun went on shining. Myrtle was late.

I looked at the clocks. They all showed different times. Myrtle was late and I wanted to go away. Whatever the clocks said, I had to remain.

At last Myrtle came. It was quite a long time since I had seen her, and my first thought was that she was feverish. Her face looked heavily coloured, and her eyes seemed smaller. When closer I saw that she had been crying.

'Thank you for seeing me,' she said.

I could not answer. I meant to ask her where she would like to go, for us to talk in peace, but every thought left my head. She must have thought I intended us to go on talking at the clock-tower, for she said nothing about moving on, and so we simply remained.

Myrtle spoke in a distant voice, yet she was quite firm.

'I wanted to ask your advice,' she said. 'I expect you know Tom's asked me to marry him? Do you think I should?'

I could not speak, this time for entirely different reasons. 'It's laughable. What a proposal!' My words came back to mock me. Never had I made such a stupid mistake. 'Faint with surprise – or think he's gone off his head!' Nothing of the kind. I can laugh at myself now. I know now that no girl faints with surprise at any proposal of marriage, and never, never does she think the proposer has gone off his head. But when I turned to look at Myrtle, as we stood in the sunshine, the chemist's shop behind us and the clock-tower in front, she must have seen written on my face nothing less than mixed astonishment and chagrin.

'You look strange,' Myrtle said. 'Is there something the matter?'

'No,' I muttered. 'Just emotion, I suppose.'

'Unusual for you.'

I did not comment: she must have learnt it from Tom.

Myrtle was staring at me. In her eyes I saw the faintest shade of bitter detachment.

'I can't advise you,' I said.

Myrtle said: 'Why not?'

'I don't know. I can't.' I stumbled for words. 'I'm not in a position to. You must know why.'

At that instant Myrtle's gaze faltered, and her detachment vanished never to return. She looked down and clasped her hands together. I noticed the mole on her forearm, just where it came out of her sleeve.

'Then I suppose it was no good our meeting...'

Immediately, I drew back. I could see her expression beginning to change.

She said: 'What have you been doing? I haven't seen you for ages.'

I told her about my letter from Miss X.Y. Even as I spoke to her I could not help feeling my own interest quicken – and I saw hers fade. Her silence bore me down and my explanation petered out.

She went on clasping her fingers between each other. Suddenly she looked me full in the face for a moment.

'I suppose this is the end.'

The end. I looked at her. And I knew with certainty that she was there at last. I did not know the reason. I supposed that something I had said or done during the last few days must have been the last straw. I do not even now know what it was, and if I did I should not believe in it as she did. To most of us the movements of the soul are so mysterious that we seize upon events to make them explicable. Myrtle and I had come to the end because of movements of the soul. They had ebbed and flowed – we had swayed closer together and further apart. Events and actions. What were events and actions? Something I had said or done, or, if it came to that, more probably something Tom had said or done, must have seemed to her the last straw.

I said: 'Yes.'

Myrtle burst into tears.

I cannot well remember what we said after that. Some of her phrases echo still. 'After this last year I don't know how you can do it!' And, 'I only wish you were feeling half of what I'm feeling now.' But I will not go on. A love affair cannot end without heartbreak. And as I have already told so much, I think the time has come for me to draw a veil.

At last we parted. The trams were still halting and moving on. The buses were still passing to and fro. The clock-tower was bathed in golden light. There were sounds and smells, and many people going by. Myrtle lingered. Then suddenly among the traffic she saw a taxi. I did not notice her stop it. I only saw her get into it, and unexpectedly drive off.

I remained where I was. Now that I no longer needed to stay there I felt no compulsion to move away.

I do not know how long I remained there. The next thing I noticed was the glint of bright red hair in the sunshine, and a familiar vigorous swaying walk. Tom came to me.

'Ah, there you are!' he said. 'I heard that you were going to meet Myrtle ... I didn't expect to find you still here.'

I did not speak. ·

Then Tom said gently: 'Come and have some tea.'

Neither of us spoke as I let him steer me to the café. Outside the shop the smell of roasting coffee was stifling. We went upstairs, and sat down at our usual table. It was long after tea-time, and we were the only people in the room. The waitress brought our tea rapidly because she was waiting for it to be time to close.

Tom said: 'Is it all over?'

I nodded my head.

There was a pause.

Tom handled his tea-cup with a nervous gesture. 'She said she couldn't marry me, of course.'

'When?'

'Several days ago.'

It was my turn to pause. I drank some tea. I said:

'What are you going to do?'

Tom said easily: 'Oh, I've just come away from having a talk with Steve. While you were seeing Myrtle, actually. He's changed his mind, of course.' He smiled with self-satisfaction. 'He's coming to France with me next week. I think it wiser for us to go almost immediately.'

At the time I was in no state to comment, so I let it pass without comment now.

Tom went on talking, and, much as I deplore having to admit it, he restored my spirits a little. It was not the moment for bickering over his letter. He was in a pleasing, philosophical mood. His confidence had come back. He could see that he was restoring me, and could not resist the old temptation to try and impress. He was an affectionate and generous man, and he was devoting himself whole-heartedly to consolation; but he was as susceptible to human weakness as anyone else. He wanted to speak of Myrtle: he wanted to ease my heart and my conscience: and he could not resist giving me a lesson in psychological observation.

'I think the trouble arose from the grave mistake you, Joe, made about her,' he said.

'What?' I asked humourlessly.

Tom spoke with warm, enveloping authority. He moved his face a little closer to mine.

'Myrtle,' he said, in a low voice, 'didn't want marriage: she wanted passion.'

I looked at him. As an absurdity it was so colossal that it took on the air of a great truth. To it, as such, I bowed my head in silence.

CHAPTER V

PROVINCIAL LIFE-HISTORIES

That is the end of my story.

A few days later the school term ended, the holidays began, and I left the town for six weeks. When I returned the second World War had broken out.

The awkwardness about finishing a novel lies in blinking the fact that though the story is ended the characters are still alive. I have chosen to end my story at this incident, because it was the last I saw of Myrtle; because the war broke out and we were all dispersed. But we all went on living. It seems to me that if you have been sufficiently interested to read as far as this you can hardly help wondering what we did after the end of the story.

I can tell you what we did. I could call a roll, indicating the fate that befell each of us. If only print could speak, you would hear my voice ring out sonorously:

Myrtle: married,
Myrtle's dress-maker: married,
Tom: married,
Steve: married,
Robert: married,
Haxby: married,
The other Crow: married,
My landlady: married,
Frank: married,
Benny: married,
Fred: married,
Trevor: married – twice!

This is all very well. It will doubtless be of interest to the race, but not, I fear, to the individual reader. So I will stop playing and get down to business. I will push on with my story just a little way, and then sum up what happened to each of the main characters.

I completed the term at school without being asked to resign. I thought I was doing rather well. Bolshaw told me my retention was dependent on his patronage. I thought the headmaster had forgotten his threatening letter to me in his agitation over not being able to trace the teaspoons. Bolshaw ceased his practice of denigrating my character in the explosion of rage he experienced when he heard Simms was coming back.

The boys of the senior sixth form left, and in the fresh term I felt lost without them. However it was not very long before I was called up for military service, and I shook the dust of the school off my shoes for ever.

Shortly after leaving for ever I had to go back for some books, and I heard that Simms had died suddenly.

'Of course it was a happy release,' Bolshaw said, in what I thought was a very ambiguous tone. He blew through his whiskers and stared at me. Certainly it had been a happy release for Bolshaw. 'I'm glad to say the headmaster has listened to reason over the reorganization. He asked me to take over both jobs. I'm now senior science master *and* senior physics master. It will mean I shall have less time for teaching.' He gave me a grandiose smile, in which his moustache drew back from his tusks.

I left without calling on the headmaster, and I never saw him again.

My landlady must have had enough of schoolmasters. In my place she took an insurance agent twenty years older than me. Her choice could hardly have been wiser, because he married her and was kind to her dog. On the other hand, her niece has still had nothing like enough of Mr Chinnock, who calls on her at two-thirty every Sunday, like clockwork.

The friends of mine who were killed in the war are not

any of those who appear in this story. Trevor, Benny, Frank and Fred all escaped.

Trevor dabbled in what he called art until he was called up, when he got into the Intelligence Corps. He remained a sergeant till the end of the war, and then he married the big girl over whom we had had all the fuss. Tom was furious when he heard about it, and proposed that Trevor should start paying back our money. After marrying her, he divorced her and married another big girl.

Frank had a year at Oxford doing science and then he became a radio officer in the Navy. He had a creditable career, he looked very handsome in uniform, and he married a thoroughly nice girl. Somehow he feels he has missed something.

Fred got a job in the corporation electricity department, did his military service, and returned to it. If you happen to be near the clock-tower and go into the electricity department's showroom, the stocky man with brilliantined hair and a good-natured soppy voice, who is trying to interest you in an immersion heater, is Fred. He has begotten a large family.

Benny worked his way into the Royal Army Medical Corps. After congratulating himself on his apparent safety, he found to his consternation that he could not be commissioned without being a doctor. Towards the end of the war the regulations were changed and he became a 2nd Lieutenant. On the basis of this medical career, he set up in a room above one of the shops in the market-place as a radiologist. He now has three rooms, an assistant, a nurse, a lot of ponderable equipment and the minimum qualifications. He has offered to X-ray me at any time free of charge.

So much for the boys.

And now we come to Steve. It will be no surprise to you that Steve did not free himself from his patron. They continued to enjoy scenes of violent emotion both with and without motor cars. Steve's French accent was improved by a holiday in France, and Tom did not go to America.

On the other hand, in the following year, the war removed Tom from the town, and his devoted interest in his protégé seemed inexplicably to wane. Steve found his freedom returning at an embarrassing pace; and soon there was literally nothing to stop him becoming as ordinary as he pleased. When he was called up Steve finally showed his independence: he volunteered to become a pilot in the Royal Air Force.

Steve actually reached the stage of flying an aeroplane – he flew it with skill, but he was unable to land it. With all his gifts, Steve had been born without the knack of bringing an aeroplane down intact. Everybody recognized it; some of us, including Steve, with relief. The Air Force tried to make him a navigator, but Steve's arithmetic let him down. They tried to make him a wireless operator and he mysteriously developed sporadic bouts of deafness. Steve was unglamorously kept to the ground. However, one thing Steve had mastered from life with his patron was the art of bearing up. Indeed he must have had a talent for it. His gesture had failed, but he was more than content from merely having made it. He bore up remarkably well. He soon began to look round.

What Steve saw was the daughter of the junior partner in his old firm of accountants. She was an attractive, strong-minded girl, and she had fallen in love with Steve. Steve wanted to be married: he wanted to be a father. And in the end he accommodated himself to the idea of becoming an accountant. This, too, cost him some suffering, but his fortitude saved him. He was just the sort of man the firm wanted back; a young Air Force officer, clever, charming, well-bred, conventional and right-minded. He married the girl.

And there in the town Steve remains. He is unostentatiously successful as an accountant. He and his wife live in style. He is very proud of his children. As the years pass he deplores other people's divagations with decreasing self-consciousness. Steve has become respectable.

There is something peculiarly edifying about Steve's life-history. Steve is now respected by others. I should like to

call him a pillar of society. Yes, I will call Steve a pillar of
society: it is fitting.

I said that Tom did not go to America. That is not true.
He did not go to America as a prospective political refugee
in August 1939. None of us went. Tom delayed and
delayed, and Robert exerted no pressure to make him leave.
'There's going to be a war,' Tom said, first of all because he
did not want to go, and then because there was going to be
a war.

Before he was due to be called up Tom was offered a job
in the Ministry of Aircraft Production. He took it, and
before long he had become successful in it. He went to work
in Headquarters, in London, and was unexpectedly promoted by Lord Beaverbrook. It was reported that he was
promoted because the Minister left his brief-case in the lift
and Tom chased after him with it. I do not think the report
is true.

With the changes of regime in his ministry Tom moved
up and down the scale; till finally he quarrelled with one of
his superiors and was sent on a mission to Washington. So
he went to the U.S.A. after all.

Now you ought to know Tom well enough to answer in
one go the simple question: 'What did Tom do in America?'

Tom became an American.

In America Tom found a limitless field for his bustling
bombinations, spiritual, emotional and geographical. Sug-
gestibly he began to speak with an American accent.
Rashly he proposed marriage to an American girl, who
accepted and made him marry her. He was offered an
attractive job if he would take out first papers. The war
ended, he stayed on, and there he is.

Some time ago I was in America, and I stayed with Tom
and his family. I found his appearance had changed a little:
his red hair is still as thick and curly as ever, but his
physique is showing signs of portliness. He has not become
as portly as he would have become in England, but the
signs are there. Otherwise he had not changed.

On my second evening he sent his wife to bed early,

brought out a bottle of whisky, and began to talk about old times.

He asked about Steve, who no longer writes to him, and Myrtle, who no longer writes to either of us. Talking of Myrtle threw him into his pleasing philosophical mood. In the intervening years he had learnt more of the secrets of the heart, so he informed me. The thought of Myrtle stirred him.

'Ah, Myrtle,' he said, pursing his lips and smiling.

'Ah, Myrtle,' I said, myself, and drank some whisky.

'You made a grave mistake over her, Joe.'

'What?'

'Myrtle,' he said, in a low, authoritative voice, 'didn't want passion. She wanted marriage.'

I might have been listening to him in the café.

It all came back to me. The low tone of voice was exactly the same: only the words were exactly the opposite.

Tom smiled with self-satisfaction. You see that he had not changed at all.

At last, Myrtle. Myrtle married Haxby.

During the months I lived in the town after the summer holidays, I saw her only twice by chance in the street. We did not stop to speak to each other. I supposed that she must be hearing scraps of information about me as I was about her. Her bohemian parties were still in full swing, attended by Trevor and Steve. Her rejection of Tom's proposal of marriage appeared to cause neither of them any embarrassment. I think Myrtle liked him the more for it. Tom went to her parties and told me the news about her.

The first subject of gossip was my resemblance to Svengali. This wilted as a love-match with Haxby came into view. I did not pretend to try and keep up with it. At this point I left the town for good, and they had been married for some time before I heard.

Myrtle became a success in the advertising business. She remained a success. When you see the advertisements for a well-known brand of nylon stockings, sleek, attractive advertisements that at first glance look perfectly innocent and at second perhaps not, you are looking at the work of Myrtle – and she is being paid a lot of money for it.

Myrtle is happy. She looks sad and her voice sounds melancholy. Only Tom's insight could pierce to the depths of her heart: I would say she was happy. She still looks meek, and she still smiles slyly. When hard-natured business men offer her contracts she gives a fluttering downward glance, as much as to say she knows they are only doing it to be nice to her. And often they, poor creatures, grin foolishly in return.

Myself. I knew, as soon as I started telling the life-histories of the others, that I should be left with the embarrassing prospect of telling my own. It is one thing to give away what belongs to somebody else, quite another to part with what belongs to oneself. I think of the string of delights and disasters that have come my way since 1939. And then I think of all the novels I can make out of them – ah, novels, novels, Art, Art, pounds sterling!

My own life-history. The past years suddenly spring up, delightful and disastrous, warm, painful and farcical. I reach for a clean new note-book. I pick up my pen.